THE
BONDS
OF
SISTERHOOD

WILLIAM DANCE

ISBN
978-1-957378-96-1 (Paperback)
978-1-957378-95-4 (eBook)

TABLE OF CONTENTS

BOOK DESCRIPTION

Tammy, Cashmere and Stephanie set sail on the trip of their dreams. No work, no drama, no nothing, but fun in the sun. They have been planning this trip for two years, now it's finally here. The perfect vacation for these ladies, or is it? Before they actually set sail, there are some things that they will go through that will make you wonder if they will even make it to see the ship set sail.

The struggles that one has in their life may alter their perfect intentions slightly. We may be driven by living life beyond our means. We may not want to take the journey to achieve our goals the right way.

The quest for love may have been given up on far too soon. After having one torrid relationship after another, some would turn their attention elsewhere. Set their goals in another direction. Concentrate on refining other points of their life, all along realizing that the one important thing to them is missing.

Turmoil may step in the way for some, but determination can lead to success. When life throws its many curveballs at you. You can either lie down and take it or you can recover and persevere over that hurdle.

Come on in and explore the journeys that these ladies will take you on. Come one come all ... see what The Bonds of Sisterhood is all about!

One

Tammy, a prominent lawyer in the Richmond, Virginia area has been practicing law for ten years now. She started out as a little girl growing up in Petersburg, Virginia. The youngest of two children. At an early age Tammy got a taste of the judicial system when her older brother Edmund was sentenced to life in prison because of a mistaken identity. Edmund was out with some friends, cruising down Wythe Street, when they saw a woman lying bloodied on the sidewalk. Edmund shouted "stop, we need to help her". He walked up to her, noting that her blond hair was bloody. There was a cut on the left side of her face as if she was attacked with a knife. Edmund bent down to check on her and accidentally touched the knife that was lying by her hand. At the same time that he realized what had just happened, a policeman was walking up behind him. The policeman asked Edmund what he was doing. Edmund began to explain that he was trying to help the lady. The policeman noticed the knife, asked Edmund to step aside, while he picked up the knife and placed it in an evidence bag. The policeman then turned to Edmund and asked him to put his hands behind his head. Edmund was in disbelief. "Surely there must be some mistake. Surely you do not think I had anything to do with this." Edmund stated. The policeman shouted to Edmund, ``Put your hands behind your back, right now!" Edmund did as he was told; as the policeman read him his rights, he put the handcuffs on him and took him away in the squad car. Edmund thought that everything would pan out as soon as the truth was out. Once he got to the station on East Tabb St., he was given his one phone call. He called home and Tammy answered the phone. He immediately said "Put mom on the phone!" When his mom got on the phone, Edmund began to tell her what happened. His mother burst out in tears, Tammy saw the horrifying look on her mother's face. She started to cry because she knew her brother was in trouble. Tammy's mother hung up the phone, grabbed her car keys and told Tammy to get in the car. They drove as fast as they could to get to the police station. Once they arrived, they spoke with Officer Jamison at the front desk. Officer Jamison told them that they would have to be seated; it would take some time before they would let them see Edmund because he was being interrogated.

Edmund was terrified as the officers kept interrogating him. The more he denied having anything to do with this assault, the more they continued to try and make him admit to it. The officers were adamant that he was the culprit. He knew that he was in a bad situation. He also knew that his prints were now on the knife. There was blood on his sleeve as well. It didn't look good at all for him and he knew it. He needed help! The police were very serious about pinning this murder on him.

Out of nowhere he heard a loud voice, which sounded like it was getting closer. He began to recognize the voice. He knew the voice; it was the voice of his mother. She was screaming his name as she walked down the hall, looking for him. He knew that she was about to lose it and would probably end up in jail herself. Edmund asked the officers to let him speak with his mother to calm her down. The officers hesitated, and then Edmund said "I will tell you everything, if you let me talk to her." The officers looked at each other and decided to grant him his wish. They then unlocked the door and opened it. The three of them walked out and met Edmund's mother along with two other officers that were about to handcuff her. Edmund went straight to his mother asking her what she was doing. She indicated that she was looking for him, that she wanted to make sure he was okay. She looked at her son and saw the blood on his hands and his sleeves. He started to cry because he knew that when he went back into the interrogation room that he would never see his mother again, as a free man anyway! He told his mom that he was innocent! He said "Don't worry, everything will be okay." The officers started to pull his mother away, making her walk down the hall. She looked back at her son, shouting "I will get you out baby, I will get you out!" Unfortunately, Edmund knew that she would not be able to change things. He kept thinking to himself, why did I get out of the car. He watched his mom walk around the corner, and then they made him go back into the interrogation room. The officers told him, "If you don't tell us what we want to hear, we will lock your mother up for obstructing justice." Edmund knew that they were serious. He didn't want to see his mother go to jail. He thought about it and did what any son would do, he uttered those words... "I AM GUILTY!" They ushered him out of the interrogation room, down the hall to the receiving room, where he would then be processed to a holding cell. This was the beginning of the end for Edmund.

One of the officers called Officer Jamison to tell him that Edmund had pleaded guilty and that they were starting the inmate process. After hanging up the phone, Officer Jamison called Edmund's mother to the desk. When she and Tammy approached the desk, he told them that Edmund had plead guilty and that he was beginning the inmate process. He also told them that they would not be able to see him at this time.

Tammy burst into tears. She knew that her brother was innocent. He would never do anything to hurt anyone. She couldn't understand why they were not letting him go free. Something was wrong and she knew it. Her mother asked Officer Jamison when they would be able to see him. Officer Jamison said "The best thing to do for him now is to get him a lawyer. If you don't get him a lawyer, you will never see him again!" Tammy knew that her parents couldn't afford to obtain a lawyer. They were very poor. Her father had been in a near fatal car accident a couple of years back. He was paralyzed and bed-ridden for the rest of his life. Her mother worked as a janitor at her school, A.P. Hill Elementary, during the day. At night, she took care of her father and the family. Money was more than tight; they barely had enough money to buy anything extra, much less afford a lawyer.

FAST FORWARD TO THE PRESENT

Tammy is probably one of the most mundane ladies you will ever meet. Standing at 5'5 and physically fit with very nice features. Her hair is short with locks. Her eyes are hazel, stunning to look at. Her physical form is very attractive to the male sector. The only constant occurrence in her life is her rigid work-out routine. She is not really into the party scene (unless her girls make her go out). After work she goes by and checks on her elderly mother, who is now ailing with multiple sclerosis. After that, it's back home for a night of Jeopardy and a glass of Moscato. At the end of the night, she normally lies in bed with a good book, until drifting off to sleep. She's currently reading a poetry book entitled "Words From Me To You!"

Tammy hasn't been on a date since her last true love, Aaron, broke her heart five years ago. Aaron decided that they needed time apart, which really meant that Aaron wanted to date other women. Tammy decided at that time that love wasn't her top priority. She focused on loving herself, her mother and work. To Tammy, life was complete, she had it all. Well, almost, she has wanted to take a luxurious all-inclusive cruise with her girls. The Bermuda cruise is all that she can think of. It is only a couple of months away!

Two

Cashmere grew up in Matoaca, Virginia. She and her sister were raised by a single father. She was a tomboy growing up. Skinny and goofy, she loved playing with the guys. They would play dodgeball, basketball, even football. She was no stranger to playing rough because she didn't really hang with the girls in her neighborhood. By the time she entered Matoaca Middle school on Holloway Ave., she was standing at 5'9. She gained interests in the school basketball team. After trying out, she quickly learned that all those days of playing basketball with the neighborhood boys had paid off. She was one of the best on the team and quickly gained recognition for being a baller.

Once she became popular for handling that rock, life made a drastic change for Cashmere. She found out exactly what it was like to be popular. All of a sudden, everybody wanted to hang with her. She got invited to all the parties. All the guys were vying for her attention, especially Damion, the most popular jock in the school. Damion was the quarterback of the Warrior's football team.

Once Cashmere started hanging out with Damion, she began to notice that even more people were trying to get her attention. She also began to notice that some of the wrong people were trying to get her attention. The problem was that they had Damion's attention already. Of course Damion was trying to talk Cashmere into going along for the ride. One thing about Cashmere is ... she does not succumb to peer pressure. She follows no one, but GOD and family! Needless to say, Cashmere and Damion did not last long!

FAST FORWARD TO THE PRESENT

Another beautiful day in Richmond Virginia, Cashmere is hard at work in her office listening to some great music. She has been working this same humdrum job as the administrative assistant to Herbert Peterson, the owner of Psychedelic Clocks, a thriving East coast business entering its tenth year.

Cashmere got the job, because Herbert is her uncle. She has been there ever since she graduated from Cornell, 8 years ago. Her days normally start out anything but normal. She starts out with a morning jog at 5:30, and then she works out for an hour. She then comes in and eats her morning grapefruit, then showers and dresses for work. Upon arriving at work, she is tasked with maintaining Herbert's calendar, which is always in disarray. When the calendar is not in disarray, Uncle Herbert maintains the disarray. The only brightness to her day is her picture of Bermuda, the island of her dreams, and of course hanging with her girls, Tammy and Stephanie!

Cashmere is probably one of the most outgoing people you will ever meet. She is drop dead gorgeous. Even on a bad day, she still radiates beauty. She's 5'10, green eyes, caramel coated skin and long flowing hair. She works out several times a week to maintain her stunning figure.

She has never had an issue with attracting the opposite sex or the same sex for that matter. Everywhere that Cashmere goes, heads turn in her direction. She is definitely used to being the center of attention, through no fault of her own.

Three

Stephanie was born in Philadelphia. Her parents Stephen and Tiffanie moved the family to Petersburg, Virginia, when she was still a baby. Her parents wanted to get out of Philly, they had family that lived in Virginia. They had been to Petersburg many times before. They knew the exact area where they wanted to live. They bought a nice four bedroom house in Cool Springs. Stephanie grew up enjoying all of the great things in life. She was fortunate to have two very loving parents. They both were professional people who taught Stephanie the value of a dollar as well as a great work ethic. They groomed her for success. From an early age, Stephanie was expected to do well. She was immersed in the finer things in life. She spent her school years from 2nd to 12th grade at the same school. The School of the Skilled, located on Old Wagner Rd., in Petersburg provided the sort of education that Stephanie's parents desired for her. They were very happy with the initial consultation, so much so, that they didn't have to visit any other schools. There were a vast amount of children that were from all walks of life attending this academy. The ratio of teachers to students was 8:1, which Stephanie's parents knew would give her the personal attention she needed. Stephanie was a quick study anyway, so they knew that she would excel at The School of the Skilled. After enrollment, the school had a gala event to welcome the students both past and present to the upcoming school year. There were political figures, military people, sports figures as well as actors and actresses attending this affair. Of all the notable guests at the event, the one that stood out the most to Stephanie was Char, the beautiful model from Port Harcourt, Nigeria. Char lived in Nigeria until she was five, then her family moved to Ettrick, Virginia. That was the best thing that ever happened to Char. It was there that she met Stephanie's father, a lawyer whose clients were some of the world's most famous celebrities. Stephanie's father was so amazed by Char's beauty that he immediately called M.T. Brooks, agent to some of the hottest models that ever graced the runway. He told M.T. "I have the perfect person for you to represent!" M.T. responded "You know what to do, forward me the pic and information." Luckily, Char's parents had photos and a bio on hand. Stephen immediately faxed the information over to M.T's office. M.T. called Stephen immediately and asked "When can we meet with her?" Stephen told M.T. that Char and her parents were in his office as we speak. Stephen asked M.T. "Can you come now?" M.T. replied "I would love to come now, but I have a meeting in twenty minutes." Stephen asked "When will you be free?" M.T. replied, "You can come in about an hour, bring them to my office." Stephen told Char and her parents the news. They agreed to meet with him in an hour. Char was beyond excited; she thanked Stephen over and over. Char said "I have to call Stephanie and tell her the news!" Char's mother reached in her purse and got her cell phone, pressed * five, which was the speed dial number for Tiffanie. "Hello." Tiffanie said. Char immediately said "Hello, may I please speak to Stephanie?" "Yes, you may. Stephanie ..." "This is Stephanie." "You'll never guess what your father did for me." "What? What did my father do for you?" "He set up a meeting with his friend M.T. for me!" "Are you serious?" Stephanie replied. "Yes, this is the greatest day of my life!" replied Char.

FAST FORWARD TO THE PRESENT

As Stephanie reflected on those days, she couldn't help but to smile. It was many years later, her and Char were still the best of friends. There was not a more meaningful relationship for Stephanie, other than her parents. Char was like a sister to her. Her and Char shared everything! Stephanie told Char that Cashmere, Tammy and her were thinking about going on a cruise. Char immediately said "I know the perfect cruise line for you and your girls!" I sailed on it last May, when we went to Aruba. It's called The Diamond Line. You are going to love it, I guarantee it." Char said. "Thanks Char, what would I do without you?" Stephanie said. "Call your girls and get a time frame and I will take care of everything for the three of you! Stephanie couldn't believe that her girl was being so generous." "Wow Char, you are going to take care of everything for us?" "Of course, you are my girls!" Char told Stephanie that if it wasn't for her, she would not be successful. Stephanie said "It was your beauty that got you this far"

Four

Tammy was still shocked, after getting the great news that Char was springing for the cruise. She couldn't help but to wonder why Char would be so generous. She had hung out with Char several times, but their relationship was nowhere near the relationship that Stephanie had with Char. Rather than look a gift horse in the mouth, she decided to go with it. After getting off the phone Tammy decided to go down to the corner cafe and get something to eat. It was Thursday night and she didn't feel like cooking. She also wanted something quick so that she could get back and watch her favorite show at 8:00. She put on a grey sweater, which went perfectly well with her black top and grey slacks. She refreshed her make-up and perfume to make sure that she was more than presentable. Got her keys, opened the door and stepped out. It was a beautiful evening as she strolled down the street. When she got to Layla's Cafe , she went inside, walked straight up to the counter and spoke to the gentlemen behind it. "Good evening, lovely lady, how may I help you?" Now Tammy had been to Layla's many times, but she had never seen this fine looking specimen before. She smiled and was at a loss for words.

Tammy was standing there taking in all of his masculinity, noting his very muscular arms, shiny bald head, hazel eyes and the whitest teeth ever. "Miss", he said. "Yes, I am sorry I will have a Caesar salad and some sweet tea, please." "Will there be anything else, the young man asked?" "Yes, I'll have your phone number as well, please." Smiling, the young man said "Will that be to go?" "Sorry, I am not normally this forward, but I do like to appreciate a handsome man when I see one." Tammy stated. Rico couldn't help but smile at her. She gave a sweet smile back to him. He was flattered that she was obviously flirting with him. He certainly made sure that she had everything that she ordered, including his number. "Please make sure that you don't take too long to use that number. I would hate to have to have to wait for an opportunity to see you again." Rico said with another smile. His pearly white teeth were gleaming at her. She took her order, started to walk away, then stopped mid stride, turned to him and said "Please believe you won't have to wait too long. Just long enough!" Then she turned and exited the cafe. Before she exited, she left a great impression on Rico. An impression that he would not soon forget. For he knew that he had just made the acquaintance of someone that would be unforgettable to him. He watched her leave the cafe and instantly wished that she was still in his presence. Her fragranced lingered in the air, reminding him of their encounter. She was more beautiful than any woman he had seen before. And to think, she had set her sights on him.

Tammy walked home thinking about what she had just done. That was a bold move for her. A move that she hadn't made in years. She didn't know what came over her. He just struck her in such a way that she couldn't let the opportunity pass her by. She had to express her interest and see if he would reciprocate. Reciprocate he did. Which made her very happy. She would wait a day or two before contacting him. She needed to give him a chance to think about her and to wonder if or when she would call. Although she was just as anxious to contact him, she would have to wait as well. This would also give her time to think about him. Her mind would wonder, just as his would.

Her thoughts were interrupted by a call from Char.

Tammy ... What's going on girl?

Char ... Just checking on you to see how things are going.

Tammy ... Things are going well. Things are going very well, indeed.

Char ... Oh, and why is that?

Tammy ... I met someone last night. I'm not sure where it is going, but I certainly hope it goes somewhere.

Char ... Well, don't leave out the juicy details. Tell me about him.

Tammy ... Well, his name is Rico. He works down the street at the cafe. I asked him for his number.

Char ... You asked him for his number? What came over you? That is not like you.

Tammy ... Yeah, I did. I am not sure. I just knew that I wanted to get to know him.

Char ... Very nice for you. Have you told the rest of the girls yet?

Tammy ... No, not yet. You are the first to know.

Char ... Okay, I won't say anything. Oh, are y'all still planning on going on the cruise to Bermuda?

Tammy ... Yeah, I thought you were going too.

Char ... I was going to go, but I can't now. I have a photo shoot in Italy during that time. Since I can't be there, I wanted to spring for everybody's tickets. That way, y'all can use your money to actually enjoy the vacation.

Tammy ... Spring for our tickets. I don't know about that.

Char ... Girl, be quiet and let me take care of it.

Tammy ... Well, I guess so. Okay, sounds good. Thanks.

Char ... Cool. I'll call Stephanie and let her know.

Tammy ... Okay cool, Thanks again girl. My bank account appreciates it as well!

Char ... No problem. Consider it a gift. Alright, I have to go. I'll talk to you soon.

Tammy ... Alright Char. Bye.

Five

Stephanie called Cashmere as well, giving her the great news about the cruise. Cashmere was very shocked and thankful. She told Stephanie that she just couldn't let Char pay for her cruise. "Why?" Stephanie asked. "Because, I would feel like I owed her for the rest of my life." Cashmere just felt like that was not a good thing to have over her head. "I understand." Stephanie said. After getting off the phone with Stephanie, Cashmere decided to just chill, have a glass of Moscato and take a bubble bath. Her day was hectic and she just wanted to relax. She went to the bathroom and turned on the faucet to fill the tub. She grabbed her jasmine scented bubble bath, poured some in the tub.

Then she reached for her jasmine candles, she lit them and then went to the kitchen. Once in the kitchen, she grabbed a wine glass from the cabinet.

Poured her a nice tall glass of Moscato, went into the bathroom and turned on some R&B. Easing herself in the tub, she took a sip of her Moscato. The water was just like she liked it. It felt good against her naked body. It had been some time since anything had felt this good against her skin. At this moment, life was great for Cashmere. She moved her legs up so that her knees were sticking out of the tub. She moved some of the bubbles over her body, paying close attention to her breasts. Cashmere's breasts were her favorite part of her body. They were ample in size. She knew that her 38 DD's definitely caught the eyes of men and women alike. Hell, Cashmere liked looking at them too! The scent of the candles, mixed with the softness of the water, along with the smooth sounds of R&B filling the air, made Cashmere think about making herself feel better. After all, it had been a while since she felt the way she wanted to feel.

She began to rub her breasts, paying close attention to her nice size brown nipples. Just the feel of her wet fingers gilding across her nipples aroused her. She began to cup her breast, squeezing them and pushing them together. Her breasts were very soft to the touch. Things were going great for her tonight.

She began to move her hands down her stomach, traveling downward until she got between her legs. BOOM, BOOM, BOOM... there was a loud sound coming from the front of her house. BOOM, BOOM, BOOM, she heard it again. This time Cashmere felt aggravated. "Who in the hell could that be?" She got out of the tub, blew the candles out and turned off the music. BOOM, BOOM, BOOM!!! She toweled herself dry, put on her robe and started walking to the door. BOOM, BOOM, BOOM!!! "Who the hell is knocking on my damn door?" she said. Cashmere peeked through the peep hole to see her sister Ingrid. She opened the door, "What?" After looking at Ingrid, she noticed that she didn't look well. Her hair was all over her head. Her clothes were torn as if she had been in a fight. "What the hell happened Ingrid?" "I can't believe it. I can't believe what just happened to me!" "What the hell happened Ingrid? Tell me already." "I was chillin' over at my girl Denver's crib with her and her man Nigel, there was a knock at the door. Nigel got up to answer it, when he opened it there was some crazy chick out there screaming at the top of her lungs."

"Wait, I can explain", Nigel said. "Apparently there was more than one girlfriend for Nigel. She storms in the crib cussing and fussing at Nigel for being at my girl's crib. She begins to punch Nigel. Denver gets up and tries to stop her. She punches Denver in the stomach. Denver kicks the girl and Nigel puts Denver in the head lock. Hell naw, you know I wasn't having that. I got up and kicked Nigel between his legs. Down he went! The chick turns on me and starts hitting me. She pushed me down, screaming "You don't hit my man!" Denver ran over to pull her off me and Nigel jumped on her again. I was able to get up and I started whipping that chick's ass. I mean I went old school on her. I tried to break her damn face!" "Are you okay?" Cashmere asked. "Do you need anything?" Ingrid looked a lot worse than she felt. "I am fine, thanks for being concerned." "How is Denver?"

"Physically, she is fine. Emotionally, she is a wreck!" "I can't believe this happened. It is a good thing you were there or your girl would have had her hands full. So, what did Denver say to Nigel and the girl?" "She cursed them both out and told them to get the hell out of her crib before she called the police! The whole scene was truly unbelievable. I couldn't believe that all this happened. Girl, what are you doing in your robe at 5:00 in the afternoon?" "Umm, I was relaxing." "I am hungry sis; do you have anything to eat?" "Damn girl, every time you come over here, you are hungry.

How come you don't eat before you come over?" "Because, I am never hungry until I get here!" "Well, pretend that you aren't here, that way you won't be hungry!" "Damn girl, you are stingy with your food." "Yeah, and you are very free with *MY* food!" Come on Cashmere, feed your little sister. Isn't that what big sisters are for?" "Okay, damn! There is some fruit in there." "Is that all you have?" "Nope, but that's all you are welcome to eat." "Are you serious Cashmere?" "Ingrid, you know you are greedy. You can have something to eat, but don't eat all my damn food! I'm going to put some clothes on." Ingrid went in the kitchen, opened the refrigerator and pulled out some wheat bread, cheddar cheese, bologna and mayo. She made two sandwiches, and grabbed the bag of puffed Cheetos off the top of the refrigerator. She saw a bottle of Moscato on the counter; she grabbed a wine glass and helped herself. After finishing the meal she went into the living room and turned on the television. Cashmere came out of the bedroom in some burgundy shorts that showed her long luscious legs. She had on a black halter top that accented her gorgeous breasts that she loved so much. "Damn girl, are you expecting company or something? Why are you dressed in those clothes?" "I am comfortable in these, if you don't like it, there's the door girl!"

Six

September 13th is the departure date to Bermuda. The ticket says the ship sails at 9:00 a.m. from Cape Hatteras, North Carolina. "Thank you so much Char, I can't believe you did this! You have to let me pay you back for this." "Girl, don't even trip. I am happy to do this for you! I wish your girl Cashmere would let me hook her up too. I bet Tammy is really happy though. Has Cashmere gotten her ticket yet?" "Yes, she got it a couple hours ago. We decided to drive to North Carolina a couple days before and get the party started there. I am so excited; this is going to be the best vacation ever. I wish you were coming Char!" "I wish I could go to, but I am supposed to be in Italy for a photo shoot from September 1st through September 10th" "Girl, call in sick." "Yeah, okay!

I am actually excited about going to Italy. It is supposed to be beautiful this time of year. It should be in the 70's all week." Stephanie went out to the backyard to light the grill. She felt like grilling some salmon with bacon wrapped asparagus. She had some Red Stripes chilling in the refrigerator.

"Char what are you doing tonight?" "I am just chilling right now?" "You should come over, I feel like grilling a little." "Okay, I will pick up some Barbera and some pizza Bianca." "I have had Barbera before, what is pizza Bianca?" "Pizza Bianca is Italian bread. It is really, really good!" "Sounds tasty, hurry up. I am about to put the fish on in a little bit." Char got in her burgundy Bentley Continental SuperSport ISR that she just got last month, drove to her favorite wine shop, in the Fan to pick up the Barbera. The great thing about this wine shop is that it wasn't far from Stephanie's place. Char loved going there to get her wines; they even sold the finest cheeses. She decided to pick up some gorgonzola to go with the wine and bread. She knew that this evening would be very nice. She knew that Stephanie could cook her butt off, so she had to bring something special to the table tonight. She felt like just enjoying her friends company as much as possible before immersing herself in preparation for her Italy trip. When she got to Stephanie's house in Shockoe Bottom, she pulled in the driveway, got out and went to the door. She knew that the door would be unlocked, so she walked right on in. "Stephanie, where you at?" "Out back, make yourself at home Char." "You know I always do girl." Char went into the kitchen; put the wine on the counter. She sprinkled a little olive oil on the bread, sliced some cheese and placed it on the bread. After wrapping the bread in some aluminum foil, she went out to the back to put the bread on the grill. Stephanie was dressed in a light blue shirt and her black capris. "What's up girl?" said Char. "Just trying to have a great meal and enjoy the company of my bestie!" "Who are you wearing?" "Just a couple of items, I picked up the other day." "I can always count on you to keep me up on what's good. Who are you playing?" "That's a new singer out of England; she is nice with her stuff.

You should check her out too." "I always learn something new when we hang. That's why I love you girl. You keep me up on things." "So Char, sit down and tell me what's going on with you." "Girl, I have been so busy, I don't know if I am coming or going these days. I wake up at 4:30, work out for an hour. Take a shower, head to a photo shoot or fashion show. My schedule is hectic, but I wouldn't trade it for the world!" "I am glad you are happy and enjoying your career. I have seen you grow so much since you started modeling. I truly am very happy for you. Okay, so what's up with your love life girl? I know there is some young man trying to get in those panties." "To be honest Stephanie, I wish I had time for a love life. I meet people everywhere I go, but I'm never around long enough to really get to know them. I guess I will just grow to be a lonely old woman. What about you? Is there anyone special?" "I'm still rolling solo dolo. I just haven't found the right man for me. I am sure he is out there, but he just hasn't approached me yet."

Seven

There was a knock at Stephanie's door. "Who is it?" "Girl, it's me. Sorry for just popping up." "You know you are always welcomed here Tammy. Come on in, girl. Char is out back." "Cool, hey Char, how are you?" "I am well, thanks Tammy. How are you? "Girl, I am fabulous. I think I might have met someone." "Now, you know you have to tell us all about it. Let me get you a glass of Moscato first." "Okay, tell us everything!" Char said. "Good for you girl, you are going to have to bring him around so we can meet him. You know we have to check him out. Make sure he is right for you." "Girl, let me get to know him first, let me see what he is talking about first" "What did you do tonight?" "Char came over and we were about to have some dinner, Italian wine and Italian bread." "Sounds good. Oh Char, thank you so much for taking care of the tickets for us? That is so cool of you. I still can't believe that she sprung for all of us. Cashmere was tripping when she didn't take you up on that. Oh well, she can be proud if she wants to, I'm good with accepting it." "Char is going to Italy when we will be on vacation." "Italy, now that is nice!" "I am happy for you." "So, how is the restaurant coming along? I bet you are excited to have your own restaurant. I know you have wanted to do that for some time now." "Actually, it is coming along nicely. The building is almost completed. I have ordered all of my kitchen equipment, furniture, artwork and everything else that I need. It should all be delivered in October. I anticipate opening the doors in late December." "Are you going to have a huge grand opening?" "Yes, I am in the process of planning that now. Don't worry you and all my girls will be there! I'll be running ads on 106.5 and a couple other stations. I still have to work those out though" "Sounds like you are getting things together. Good, I can't wait to see your place! Have you decided on a name yet?" "Yes, I decided on "Rains". "Rains, that's very interesting, how did you come up with that?" "Well, initially I was going with "Essence", but I wanted a name that really stuck out and would make people curious. And "Rains" kind of popped out at me, because it was raining when I was trying to come up with a name. I know it sounds corny, but it might just work." "I hope so girl, either way, I know the food will be great. It always is. Richmond needs what you have to offer." "Thanks girl, I appreciate the love. I really do." "Alright, Stephanie, is that meal ready? I bought some Caesar salad from Layla's."

Eight

Cashmere looked over at Ingrid; all she could hear was her snoring loud like a marching band. She couldn't even enjoy the movie anymore. "Ingrid! Ingrid!" "What?" "Girl wake up you are snoring and drooling all over everything. You might want to get that on your lip." "Okay, my bad girl, can I stay here tonight? It's late and I don't want to drive to Petersburg tonight" "Yes Ingrid, you can stay tonight. This is a stretch, but maybe we should go shopping tomorrow before you go back to Petersburg? " "Are you feeling okay Cashmere? You never invite me to go anywhere." "I know Ingrid and I feel bad. I want to be a better sister to you. I do love you. You get on my damn nerves, but I love you!" "Wow Cashmere, this is weird. I don't know what to say." "Girl, you better accept my love before I change my damn mind." "Okay, it might be fun to hang out with my big sis. I'm in." "Cool, can you stay up long enough to finish this movie?" "That depends." "Depends on what?" "Depends on if you have anything to drink in this place. Girl, I want to get my drink on." "I think I have some wine in there." "Wine, I'm trying to get down with the Henny tonight." "There's some of that in there too. While you're at it, bring me a glass with two rocks girl." "Now that's what I'm talking bout. Let's do this girl. Ooh you got a big bottle of Henny. It is on tonight. I am about to do the damn thing. You don't know how I roll with the Hen, that is my drank. I hope you are ready Cashmere. I am about to put it down tonight." "Alright, bring the bottle in here then, let's see what you are made of. Please believe, I can do the damn thing too." "Well, let's crack it then. You want ice, I take mine straight up. I don't play around with the Hen girl." "Girl, less talking, more pouring. Put something in the glasses so we can do the damn thing." "Yeah Cashmere this is what I'm talking about. I have wanted to drink with my big sis for a minute now." "Really, I never knew you wanted to party with me." "Yeah, here you go girl, cheers! This is some good stuff right here. I am going to enjoy this night. I'm about to get my drink on with my big sis." "Be careful Ingrid, you're supposed to sip this, not guzzle it." "Girl, you do you and let me do me. I got this. You need to catch up." "Okay, I will take your advice and do me." Cashmere enjoyed sipping on her Henny, while Ingrid guzzled another glass. "Do you want to watch another movie, Ingrid? Ingrid?" She looked over at Ingrid and saw her sleeping again. This time she was snoring louder than before. She was out for the count. All Cashmere could do was laugh after all that madness she talked about. She put a blanket over her and let her sleep it off. She turned off the television and lights then went to the bathroom, lit the candles, added some more bubble bath and hot water to the tub and hit play so the music could fill the air. She took off her clothes and got back in the tub to finish what she had started before Ingrid had interrupted her. Her breasts filled her hands and felt better than anything she had ever touched before. She continued to squeeze them. She truly enjoyed touching her breasts. She let her left hand slide down south to enhance the pleasure. She rubbed her pleasure spot and began to enjoy the sensation. She continued to rub until she was on the verge of climaxing. She did it just a few more times. "Damn, that's it. That's what I need, right there. Oh damn, this feels great. Shit!" Afterwards, she laid her head back on the tub and just basked in the moment. She took a sip of her Henny, it went down nice and smooth. She just laid there in the tub and enjoyed the warmth of the water, the scent from the candles and music flowing in the background. Nothing could be better right now. She took another sip of the Hen, feeling really relaxed she laid her head back on the tub. She started to doze off in the tub. She awoke to the glass of Hen hitting the floor. "Damn, now I have to clean this up." She got out of the tub and toweled herself off, put her robe on and went into the kitchen to get the broom and dustpan. Returning to the bathroom she began to clean up the broken glass. She walked back in the living room to check on Ingrid, who was still passed out on the couch with a drool hanging out her mouth. "Damn that girl is a nasty sleeper." She went into the bedroom and laid down on the bed, grabbed the poetry book "Words From Me To You" to read until she fell asleep. The next morning Cashmere awoke to the smell of eggs and bacon coming from her kitchen. She got up, went into the kitchen to see Ingrid making breakfast. "Good morning big sis. How are you this morning?" "Good morning Ingrid, I am well. More importantly, how are you this morning? How did you sleep?" "I'm good, thanks." "You know you talked a bunch of shit last night. You had two glasses of Hen and your ass passed out. After all that shit talking, you passed the hell out. "Wow... I was tired." "Yeah okay, is that what they are calling it these days? Your ass passed out on me! Way to go light weight." "Whatever Cashmere, you want some breakfast or not?" "Don't trip lightweight this is my crib, so most definitely I am getting breakfast. Are you still down to go to the mall or are you too hung over to hang? " "I'm still down, let's eat, then we can roll over to Chesterfield Town Center." "Cool, I need to get some gear for my trip to Bermuda. And I know you are a fashionista, so I need to know what's hot." "I got you, I know a couple of designers that you should check out. I love their stuff. They have a real sense of what women want, plus their stuff is hot.

Nine

Char called Tammy and Cashmere from Stephanie's, "Ladies we should go out for brunch today. Who's down to go to Layla's Cafe over in Innsbrook?" "That sounds cool with me." Tammy replied. "We can do that. I have something to take care of real quick though." Cashmere replied. "Cool, Stephanie and I are down too. Let's meet up about 1:00 P.M." "Okay, see y'all there." Cashmere replied. Char hung up the phone and told Stephanie that everybody was meeting up over at Layla's cafe about 1:00. "Sounds good, I love Layla's Cafe. The food is always so delicious." "There are some nice looking brother's that hang out there too." "Why yes there are Char, yes there are!" "I have a meeting at 11:00 with M.T., and then I can meet you guys there." Alright cool Char, see you then." Char grabbed her keys and headed out the door. She got in her Bentley and headed to her meeting with M.T. at his office on West Hundred Road in Chester. M.T.'s office was not too far from Stephanie's place. It took her about 20 minutes to get there.

Stephanie took the time to go over the specifics for her restaurant. She wanted to make sure that she had everything ordered that she needed for the grand opening. She also had to make a few phone calls, one to the health department to set up the inspection before the opening. She also had to call the Better Business Bureau to register her restaurant. Then, she made a call to the florists because she wanted fresh flowers for the opening night. The restaurant opening had to be nothing short of perfection. She was calling in a bunch of favors from some of her celebrity friends to make an appearance at the opening. Of course Char was included in the list of celebrities to attend.

After handling her business, Stephanie decided to take a nice hot shower, and then get ready to go to Layla's Cafe. Stephanie put on her clothes, grabbed her keys to her BMW SUV and left for Layla's. She always enjoyed the ride to Layla's; the scenery was very pretty along the way. There were rows of trees that lined the streets, the buildings were historical. There were brownstones along the streets as well. She made the trip to Layla's at least once a week.

That was her and her girl's meeting place. By the time she pulled up, she saw Tammy and Cashmere walking in the cafe. She parked her car beside Cashmere's Honda Accord, got out and went into the cafe to join her girls. She saw Tammy and Cashmere sitting at a table, looking at menus. There was a waiter at the table, which she hadn't seen before. She pulled her chair out and sat down. Greeted her girls and asked if she could have a menu. "Good afternoon, I am Rico and I will be your waiter this afternoon. Our specials today are salmon croquette with a raspberry reduction or buttermilk fried chicken and waffles with sweet potato fries." "Both of those sound very good. I will have the buttermilk fried chicken with a glass of raspberry tea." Cashmere stated. "I will have the salmon croquette." stated Stephanie. "What do you suggest Mr. Rico?" "I would suggest the salmon croquette, it is heavenly." "Well, I will have that then." Tammy said. Tammy couldn't help but flash a smile at Rico. She had thought about him ever since they met. It was nice to see him again. "Umm, what was that all about?" Cashmere asked. "Girl that is Rico, I met him the other night when I was in here. He is a nice young man." Tammy stated. "Yes, he does seem nice." Cashmere stated. "So, this is the young man that you told me about Tammy?" "Yes, Stephanie, that is Mr. Rico." "Well I must say Mr. Rico is quite nice, quite nice indeed." "Have you been out on a date with him yet?" Stephanie asked. "Not yet, it's only been a couple of days since we met." "Girl, what's the scoop on him?" Cashmere asked. Well, he wants to own his own restaurant someday." Oh really? That is very coincidental, I just happen to be opening up my own restaurant. Let me know if he has any questions or needs any advice. I would be glad to help Tammy. " said Stephanie. "Hey ladies', how are you today?" said Char. "We're fine." the girls stated. "Sorry, I am late. My meeting ran a little long with M.T." "It's all good girl, we just ordered a few minutes ago." Cashmere stated. "Hello, I see we have someone new joining us today. Wait a minute

I know you! You are...oh my gosh...You are Char the model, aren't you?" said Rico. "Yes and who might you be?" said Char. "I'm sorry I should have introduced myself first. I am Rico, your waiter." "Well, it's very nice to meet you Rico." "It's nice to meet you as well.

Would you like to see a menu?" "No, I already know what I want. I'll have the tilapia with mushroom risotto, please." "Very well, thank you for your order." Rico said. "My, he is simply divine." stated Char. "Guess who's got dibs on him?" "That would be me, thank you very much." Tammy stated. "Details girl, details!" "Well, there's not much to tell, I met him a couple of days ago when I came in for dinner. He seems really nice though." "Well, keep us posted." Stephanie said. "So what's up for tonight y'all? I feel like getting out." Cashmere stated. "Have you heard about that new club in The Fan? I think it's called "The Crib". They say it's supposed to be off the hook." Stephanie stated. "We should check it out, y'all down?" "Your meals ladies... The Crib is a nice spot. If you are looking to have a great time and get your dance on, I definitely recommend it." Rico said. "You've been there?" Tammy said. "Yes, my cousin owns the joint, so I go there often." "Would you like to go with us tonight?" Tammy asked. "Well, I would love to, but I wouldn't want to interrupt your girl's night out." "It's all good Rico, you should come, that way we can get free drinks, since your cousin owns the club, right?" Cashmere said. "Cashmere, no you didn't girl." Char said. "Sorry Char, some of us aren't rich like you. I have to ball on a budget. You feel me?" Cashmere said. "It's all good ladies; I'll see what I can do about those drinks. I'll also see if I can get you in for free too. How's that?" said Rico. "If you can work that out, it would be very nice of you." Tammy said. "Okay ladies, enjoy your meals." "Thank you!" the girls said. "Tammy, he is really nice. You better hurry up and get with him before someone steals him from you." Stephanie said. "Okay, so let's talk about the trip. We were talking about going down to Cape Hatteras a couple of days before the ship sails? How are we getting there and where are we staying?" Cashmere said. "Well, I was thinking we could rent a car, drive down, use it until we set sail and turn it in the morning before we leave. What do y'all think?" Stephanie said. Sounds good to me, and then we can rent the car again when we get back from the cruise." Tammy said. "Okay, so that is settled, now where are we going to stay?" Stephanie said. Tammy pulled out her phone and looked up hotels in Cape Hatteras,

North Carolina. She found three motels right by the cruise line. There was the Cape Hatteras Motel, Lighthouse View Motel and Cape Pines Motel. "Motels, girl where are the hotels? You mean I am going to have to carry my own bags? Hell naw!" said Cashmere. "It doesn't matter to me where we stay as long as I am with my girls. This is going to be a vacation to remember!" said Stephanie. "Okay, I will call and make the reservations; I'll put it on my card." Tammy said. "Okay, if you are going to do that, then I will rent the car." Stephanie said. Stephanie and Tammy looked at Cashmere. "What the hell are y'all looking at me for?" Cashmere said. "We were wondering what you were going to handle?" Stephanie said. "I have to pay for my trip. You girls are cruising for free. In case you didn't know. It is $900.00 dollars to take this cruise." Cashmere said. "You had the same offer the other girls had Cashmere. You chose to pay for your own ticket. That's on you!" Char said. "Damn, y'all are trying to break a sister. I will see what I can do." Cashmere said. "Okay, the reservation for the Lighthouse View Motel has been made. We are all sharing a room for two days. We're arriving on the 30th of August. Check in is at noon." Tammy said. "Great, I am on the phone with Thrifty Rentals now, they have a mid-size Chevy Malibu available for the trip down. They can't guarantee that we can get the same car for the return trip though." Stephanie said. "Why not? You might want to ask to speak with a manager about that." Char said. "Are you sure you can't guarantee us the same car for the return trip?" Stephanie asked the rental car agent. "Let me see what I can do ma'am. Hold please." the agent said. "And how is everything ladies? Are you enjoying your meals? Can I get you anything else?" Rico said. "Everything is lovely, thank you very much Rico." Char said. "May I please have a slice of carrot cake?" Tammy asked. "Of course you can, would you like some ice cream to go with that?" Rico said. "Sure that would be great Rico, thanks." Tammy said. "Hello, ma'am... I spoke with my manager and we will definitely be able to accommodate your return trip in the same car." the agent said. "Thank you very much. I really appreciate that." Stephanie said. "We are good to go on the rental ladies." Stephanie said. "What time do you want to leave? It is 183 miles from Richmond to Cape Hatteras. So, that's about 2-3 hours on the road." Stephanie said. "How about we leave at 8:30 in the morning? That should put us there around noon, just in time for check in." Tammy said. "That sounds good to me. Oh I will cover the drinks when we go out. Will that work?" Cashmere said. "Sure Cashmere that will work." Tammy said. "Cool, are we meeting at Stephanie's or are you picking us all up Stephanie's?" Cashmere said. "I think we should have a sleepover at my house the night before, get up and roll out. I'll pick up the car the night before, that way we don't have to pick it up the morning of." Stephanie said. "Sounds like a plan then." Tammy said. "Your carrot cake and ice cream Ms. Tammy." Rico said. "Thank you Rico."

"Enjoy." Rico said. "Sorry to cut this short ladies, but I have to go by the job, then meet up with Ingrid." Cashmere said. "Okay, before you go, let's meet at Tammy's tonight before we go to the club." Stephanie said. "How about around 7:00 or so?" Tammy said. "Cool, see y'all then." Cashmere said. Stephanie and Char got up to leave as well. "Bye ladies, see you tonight." Tammy said. "Did you enjoy your lunch Ms. Tammy?" Rico said. "Yes, I did. Thank you very much." Tammy said. "Were you serious about getting us in to The Crib tonight?" "Yes, no doubt. It would be my pleasure. I will call my cousin in a little bit and hook everything up." "Are you going as well?" "Would you like for me to come Ms. Tammy?" "You can't answer a question with a question." "It appears that I can Ms. Tammy." "Okay Rico, yes. I would like for you to come. It will give me a chance to get to know you a little better." "Nice, I will be there." Tammy paid her bill and left Layla's Cafe.

Ten

Stephanie drove by the restaurant to check on everything. The sign had been delivered and looked very nice. She also saw that the outer menu board was hung. She had to create the menu for the opening night and place it in there. She unlocked the door, walked in and saw that the kitchen equipment had been delivered. Unfortunately, it was still in the boxes. She wondered why the equipment hadn't been installed yet. She pulled out her phone and called Matthius, who was in charge of the construction for her restaurant. "Hello." Matthius said. "Hello Matthius, it's Stephanie from Rains." Oh, Stephanie, hi.

How are you?" "I am concerned Matthius." "About what?" "Well, I am at the restaurant and I see that the kitchen equipment was delivered, but it hasn't been installed yet. Can you please tell me why?" "Well, the equipment arrived right at quitting time. We just had enough time to get it in the building." "Matthius, you do realize that we only have a week left before the inspector will be here?" "Yes ma'am, I am aware of that. It will be tight but we can do it. I will have my men start on it, first thing in the morning." "Okay, please make sure that this is taken care of. I don't want any setbacks. This has to be perfect Matthius." "No problem ma'am, I will make sure that everything is taken care of. Please don't worry! By the way, a package came for you. I left it on your desk." "Thanks Matthius, I will see you tomorrow morning." Stephanie hung up the phone and placed it back in her purse. She went into the kitchen to check on the lay out for the equipment. Everything looked great on paper; hopefully it all would go in without any issues. She walked over to her office, went in and saw the package on the desk. She looked for a return address, but didn't see one. She thought that was odd. She opened the package and pulled out its contents. There was a note. The note read "I know something you don't know!" signed Guess Who? There was nothing else in the package, nothing else on the note. She was puzzled as to what the note meant and wondered who it was from. She put the note back in the package; put the package in her purse to take with her. She took one more look around the kitchen to make sure everything was ready for the crew. After walking out and locking the door to Rains, she went to her car. There was a note on her windshield. She opened it and it read "Guess Who?" She looked up the street, then down the street. No one was in sight. She got in her car and drove off. She couldn't help but wonder about the package and now the note on the window. This made her feel uneasy, she didn't know what was going on, who would possibly be sending me these notes. Obviously, it was someone who knew her schedule and whereabouts. Someone had followed her to the restaurant. They could possibly be following her right now. The more Stephanie thought about it, the more worried she got. She tried to think of anybody that she knew that would possibly do something like this. She couldn't think of anyone, no matter how much she racked her brain. No one came to mind. One thing is for sure, she was going to find out who was doing this and why? She pressed the phone button on her steering wheel, and then she said "Dial Tammy" "Hey girl." Tammy said. "Tammy, you are not going to believe this. I think I have a stalker." "What?

What are you talking about?" "Somebody is following me. Someone sent me a package to the restaurant. When I opened it, there was a note in it that said "I know something you don't know!" Then I went to my car and saw a note that read "Guess who? So someone is following me. I don't know why, but someone is definitely following me!" "Have you called the police yet?" "No, it just happened, I called you first." "Well, you may want to involve the police before this gets worse. That way they can start an investigation." "Suppose it's just some prank kid playing a practical joke?" "Suppose it's not a prank kid playing a joke, but someone that actually wants to do you some harm? You can't procrastinate on this Stephanie. I have a friend in the police department that owes me a favor. Just say the word and I will give him a call." "Okay, let me think about it. I will let you know in the morning. Right now, I have to get over to the Better Business Bureau." "Okay girl, don't forget. Just let me know. I will see you later at my place." "Later girl, see you tonight." When Stephanie was done at BBB, she went home, poured a glass of wine. Sat down on the couch, picked up the remote to the stereo and started listening to 106.5. They were playing some good music as always, then she heard it. She heard the radio ad for her restaurant. She couldn't believe it. This was exciting! Her phone beeped, she had a text message from Cashmere:

Cashmere: I just heard the radio ad for Rains. I am so excited for you girl. We have to celebrate!

Stephanie: Yeah, I heard it too. I can't believe it. I really can't believe it. It is really going to happen. This restaurant is going to be great for Richmond, and great for me.

Cashmere: See you later tonight!

Stephanie: Yeah, see you tonight!

Stephanie continued to enjoy her glass of wine. She was excited about seeing her girls tonight. She needed to let off a little steam, let her hair down. Today was very trying and she desperately needed to relax. Tonight was about her and her girls. Nothing would mess that up. Nothing at all! Stephanie got up, went to her bedroom to pull out her clothes for tonight. She wanted to look stunning, because she knew that all her girls would be stunning as well. She pulled out her new dress, her new shoes that matched perfectly. To accent she decided on her diamond earrings and diamond tennis bracelet. This was going to be a great night...The Crib was in for a surprise tonight. She looked in the mirror to make sure that she looked okay. She decided that she looked fine.

She grabbed her keys and was out the door. The closer she got to Tammy's the more excited she got. For some reason she had a great feeling about tonight.

Maybe she will meet someone special tonight. Maybe tonight would be a night to remember.

Eleven

Tammy was getting ready because her girls would be there shortly. She made sure that she was on her "A" game tonight. Rico would be there and she knew she had to make him want her more than anything in the world. Her hair was stunning, her dress was beautiful, and her shoes went perfectly with her dress. She sprayed on her favorite perfume. She went to the kitchen to pour some glasses of Moscato for her and her girls. Ding dong, the doorbell rang. She opened the door. "Hey girl!" Stephanie said. "Come on in, have some Moscato?" "Yes, thank you. Am I the first one to arrive?" "Yes, the others should be on their way. You look beautiful Stephanie!" "Thank you Tammy, you look beautiful too." "Thanks Stephanie!" "So, is Rico going to meet us there or is he coming here to ride with us? "Oh, Rico is meeting us there. Why do you ask?" "I just wanted to know how we were going to work this out. I mean we really didn't work it out at lunch today." "Yeah that's right. We didn't." Ding dong...Tammy goes to the door to see who's there. "Hey ladies, how are you?" "We're fine, how are you?" Cashmere and Char said. "Come on in and have some Moscato. Stephanie is here already." "Yeah, we saw her car out front." Char said. "Here you are ladies." "Thanks girl. I could use this right about now." Cashmere said. "So what's the plan for tonight?" Char said. "I figured we'd leave about 9:30 or so. I don't want to get there too early." Tammy said. "I feel you, when I walk in; I want all eyes on me! Cashmere said. "Girl save some for us now." Stephanie said. "Tammy, what about you? What's on your agenda for tonight? Are you going to make your move on Rico?" Char said. "We'll see what happens." Tammy said. "Girl you trippin', you better handle your business. That man is fine. If you don't one of those ho's in the club might snatch him up." Cashmere said. "He's not my man." Tammy said. "Okay, you keep talking that ish. Don't come crying to me when someone else gets your man. You know he is interested and I know damn well you are interested in his fine ass! Don't trip." Cashmere said. "Okay girl, I am interested. I just don't want to seem desperate or anything." Tammy said. "Yeah, but you don't want to seem uninterested either." Stephanie and Char said. "That's true." Cashmere said. "Would anybody like another round?" Tammy asked. "Yeah girl. I am ready." Stephanie said. "Okay, I'll be right back." Tammy went to the kitchen to refill the glasses. Stephanie, Char and Cashmere waited in the living room for her to return. Tammy's phone began to ring. "Tammy, your phone is ringing." Char said. "Okay, let it go to voice mail, I'll return the call." Tammy said. Char looked at the phone and saw that it was Rico. She told Stephanie and Cashmere. "Should we answer it?" Cashmere said. "She'll be pissed, if we do." Stephanie said. "Oh well. Hello!" Cashmere answered the phone. "Hello, may I speak to Tammy, please?" Rico said. "Sure, give me one minute. I have to go get her. May I ask whose calling" Cashmere said. "Tell her it's Rico." Cashmere took the phone to Tammy." "Tammy, you have a phone call." Tammy shot a look at Cashmere that said "I hate you" Tammy took the phone. "Hello." Tammy said. "Hello Tammy, this is Rico." Rico said. "Hi Rico, how are you this evening?" "I am well, thank you. I was wondering what time you were going to the club?" "Well, we were thinking about leaving at 9:30." "What time are you planning on being there?" "I will get there about 10:00. I hope that's not too late." "That's perfect; we should be pulling up right around that time." "Cool, I will wait for you outside the club. My cousin R.J. said that he will hook you and your girls up." "We really appreciate you taking care of us Rico." "Not a problem Ms. Tammy. Not a problem at all! I hope that I can do more for you in the future." "Oh really now?" "Yes really." "I just may hold you to that Rico." "Please believe, I hope you do. I will see you tonight Ms. Tammy." "Yes, you will." "Good night Ms. Tammy." "Good night Rico." "Well, what did he say?" Cashmere said. "He is interested girl. He really is." Tammy said. Tammy and Cashmere went back to the living room with Char and Stephanie. "Well, how did that go?" Stephanie asked Tammy. "It went very nicely. We will see what happens tonight" Tammy said. They all raised their glasses in happiness for Tammy. "We should probably get ready to go after we finish these." Char said. "Who's driving?" Cashmere said. "We can take the Bentley, if you want?" Char said. "Yes, let's take the Bentley. I haven't ridden in it yet." Cashmere said. "Girl, it is nice!" Stephanie said. "Okay, let's go." Tammy said. The ladies grabbed their purses and headed for the door.

Twelve

The girls got in the car and headed out. "This is a really nice car Char. I have never been in a Bentley before. How much did it cost you girl?" Cashmere said. "Thanks Cashmere. I really like it. Please believe it cost a lot." Char said. "Cashmere, you know better than to ask how much it cost." Tammy said. "Look, I don't make the money that y'all make. I just wanted to know. I don't see what the big deal is." Cashmere said. "Of course you don't Cashmere. You are so damn ghetto!" Stephanie said. "Wow, that's messed up Stephanie. I can't believe you called me ghetto." Cashmere said. "Don't act like you're not ghetto girl. It's all good. We love your ghetto ass just the way you are." Tammy said. "Okay new subject. It's time for you to leave me the hell alone." Cashmere said. "Okay, okay Cashmere we will leave you alone. I am ready to party. I hope The Crib is the place to be tonight." Char said. "I hear you girl, I haven't been out in so long. I forgot what it's like to go to a club." Tammy said. "Why not Tammy?" Stephanie said. "All I do is work girl. I can't seem to get any time for myself." Tammy said. "I hear you girl. I feel the same way. It seems like all I do is work on getting my restaurant opened." Stephanie said. "All work and no play...that's not the case tonight ladies. We are going to get it in tonight" Cashmere said. "I know that's right girl!" Tammy said. Char pulled into the parking lot of The Crib, drove right up to the front of the club. Hello, welcome to The Crib. Would you like to valet?" The valet attendant said. "Yes, please. Park it in a spot by itself please. Don't let anything happen to it, please." Char said. "No problem Char. We'll take care of you. You are Char the model, right." the valet said. "Yes, I am Char the model." "I knew it. Welcome again. My name is Teddy." "Thanks Teddy, it's nice to meet you." "It's nice to meet you as well Char." Teddy said." "So, the deal is, we go together we leave together. Okay?" Stephanie said. All the girls agreed that if they went together, they were leaving together. That was the plan.

The girls got out of the car, Tammy immediately looked for Rico. All of a sudden she saw a burgundy Benz pulling up to the front of the building. Teddy walked over to the car "What up Rico, how are you my brother?" "I'm cool Teddy Ted, what's good my brother?" "Things are well, thanks." "How's it looking tonight?" "Rico, the place is packed. These four beautiful ladies just rolled up in a Bentley. Damn they are fine as hell!" "Oh yeah, where are they now?" "Right over there my man, right over there." "Nice, I may just have to go over there and see what's crackin'." "Handle your business dawg." "Alright, watch this!" Rico started walking towards the ladies; he couldn't help but smile, especially when he saw Tammy. They all were looking great, but Tammy was eye catching. "Good evening ladies, how are you this evening?" "Wow Rico, you clean up really nice!" Stephanie said. "Thank you Stephanie, you all look really nice as well." "Thank you very much Mr. Rico." Tammy said. "Well, shall we go in?" Rico said. "Let's go." Cashmere said. Rico lead the girls up to the door.

Tammy was checking Rico out and she liked what she saw. "Hey Johnson, the four ladies are with me. Do me a favor and ask R.J. to come out to our table, please." Rico told the doorman. "Cool, come on through ladies. Have a great time!" Rico stepped aside and let the ladies walk in before him. They stopped and took a look around the club. "Ladies, I took the liberty of having one of the VIP tables set up for you. I hope you don't mind." Rico said. "Now that's what I'm talking about Rico. Handle your business man." Cashmere said. "Great, right this way ladies." Rico lead the ladies up to the VIP table which overlooked the club. When they got there, the table was lined with 42 Below, 7 Leguas Tequila Anejo, Moscato, Chardonnay, chocolate covered strawberries, a cheese and shrimp platter. There were even name cards placed around the table. Tammy has a single rose in her spot. "Wow Rico, you did all this for us?" Cashmere said. "Rico, this is really nice. You didn't have to do all this." Tammy said. "Have a seat ladies, if there is anything else that you need, don't hesitate to ask. I will make sure that you are taken care of." Rico said. "Wait Rico, are you leaving us?" Tammy said. "Well, I wasn't sure if you wanted to do your own thing or not." "Rico, please sit down and join us." Stephanie said. Rico pulled up a chair and sat between Tammy and Stephanie. "I would love to hang out with you lovely ladies, especially you Ms. Tammy." Rico looked at Tammy with wanting eyes. Tammy looked back at Rico and smiled. "You are too sweet Rico. Thank you." "You make it easy. Thank you very much and you're welcome." Rico told Tammy. "So, who are these lovely ladies Rico?" R.J. said. "What's up R.J., from left to right, we have Stephanie, Char, Cashmere and last but definitely not least, we have Tammy. Ladies, this is my cousin R.J., the owner of the club." "Hello ladies, I am glad you could make it. I hope you are enjoying yourselves. By the way, my cousin Rico is being way too modest. I own the club with him." R.J. said. "Is that right?" Stephanie said. "Yes, that is true." Rico said. Rico shot R.J. a look as if to say "You've said enough." "Well ladies, I will leave you in good hands. Have a great night!" R.J. said. "So, who would like something to drink?" Rico said. "I would Rico. I would like some Moscato please." Stephanie said. "Moscato coming right up. Would anyone else like some Moscato?" Rico said. "Yes, I would like some Moscato please Rico." Char said. Rico poured two glasses of Moscato, he gave one to Stephanie and the other to Char. "What would you like Cashmere?" Rico asked. "Rico, I would like some Chardonnay and some shrimp please." "Okay." Rico poured the Chardonnay and then put some shrimp on a plate for her. "Tammy, what would you like?" Rico asked. "Well Rico, I would like to dance with you." Tammy said. Rico offered his hand to Tammy. She graciously accepted and walked to the dance floor with Rico. She looked over her shoulder and smiled at her girls.

When they got to the dance floor her song came on. "I love this song." Tammy said. "Let me see what you're working with then." Rico said. Rico and Tammy were doing their thing on the dance floor. Then her song faded out and a slow song faded in. Rico looked at Tammy, held out his hand. Again Tammy took his hand stepping closer to him. Rico eased his arms around her waist.

They began to sway to the sexy groove. "Ms. Tammy, I must say, you smell very good. You look marvelous as well!" Rico said. "Thank you very much Rico. You smell wonderful yourself. You look very handsome too." Tammy said. "Not to be too forward, but you feel great in my arms." "Is that so? Well, it's finally nice to be in your arms." "I could get use to this." Rico said. "So could I Rico, so could I." Tammy laid her head on Rico's shoulder, feeling the groove move her seductively. "This is nice." Rico said. "Yes, it is." Tammy said. The deejay took the mic "You know what time it is now at The Crib? It's time to bring back those old school dances. Yeah, anyone who can bring back the oldest old school dance and rock it the best, will win a free drink." the deejay said. Tammy saw her girls coming out to the dance floor. She saw this as an opportunity to keep Rico to herself. "Would you like to go back to the table Rico? I am a little thirsty, how about you?" Tammy said. Rico saw the girls coming to the dance floor. "Yes. I am a little thirsty, let's go." Rico reached out for Tammy's hand and guided her back to the table. They passed the girls on the way. "You go girl." Cashmere said. The girls went out on the dance floor. "Okay, here's the lowdown. Line up in two lines. Girls on the left. Guys on the right. I am going to call out a dance, you have 30 seconds to do the damn thing. If you feel a tap on the shoulder, you're done. Step off the floor and watch.

Cool! Alright, the cabbage patch...let's go." The girls were standing beside one another doing their best rendition of the cabbage patch.

Tammy was sipping on some Moscato; Rico poured himself some 42 Below. "So Tammy, you have some moves young lady. I may have to get you back on the floor again before the night is over." "Rico, that would be really nice. I love to dance. I don't get to do it as much as I would like." "Why is that?" "Well, I don't really go out a lot." "We may have to do something about that Ms. Tammy." "Sounds like something I can work with, Rico."

"Now I know y'all are feeling that groove. Time to change it up though. Gimme me some of that running man." the deejay said. "Girl this club is lit!" Char said. "Hell yeah! We are going to have to hit this spot more often, especially if Rico is going to hook us up like this." Cashmere said.

"It was really nice of you to treat us like royalty tonight. I think you may be spoiling us though." Tammy said. "It would be my pleasure to spoil you Tammy. Give me a chance to get to know you. Hopefully, I can make you feel that way more often." Rico said. "I think we can definitely do that Mr. Rico."

"Yeah we getting down to the real party people now. It's time to stop playing around and find us a winner. Here it is y'all...the Rubik's cube. Get it!" said the deejay. "The Rubik's cube, now he is reaching way back." Char said. "Get it girl, you can do it Stephanie." Cashmere said. Right at that moment Char felt a tap on the shoulder. "It's cool; I have to go to the ladies room anyway. Good luck ladies." Char said. Char made her way off the dance floor. She saw R.J., asked him to point her in the direction of the bathroom. "Here, I'll take you there."

R.J. said. "Thank you, but you don't have to do that." Char said "It's not a problem. You're a guest of the club. We treat our VIPs right." "Okay, that's nice to know." R.J. showed Char to the bathroom. "By the way, please tell me you're not Char the model." "Well, actually I am." "Very nice, you are probably use to this treatment then?" "Well, yes and no. I do get VIP a lot but it is not as sincere as tonight. Most people want something from me. Tonight it's not about me, it's about my girls. So, I like this better." "That is very humbling. You seem very down to earth. I like that." "I am very down to earth. I haven't forgotten where I came from and I certainly don't take any of my blessings for granted." "I have to admit, I expected you to be stuck up. I am glad you're not. I hope I didn't offend you." "No, it's all good. I have heard that before. I just try to treat people the way I was raised to treat people." "That's very nice to know. Let me know if you need anything else." "Thank you R.J." "You're very welcome." R.J. walked back up to the bar to check on things.

"Okay, it's on now, down to the last two dancers. Who will it be? We are about to find out! The next dance is the robot. Let's go, " the deejay said. Stephanie and Cashmere were handling their business, then Stephanie received a tap on the shoulder. "Yeah, we have a winner y'all. Come on up here and get your ticket for your free drink. Give it up for her y'all. What's your name sweetheart?" "Cashmere." "Give it up for Cashmere!" "Thank you." Cashmere took the ticket and went to the bar to get her drink. "May I help you?" the bartender said. "Yes, I just won a free drink." "What would you like?" "I'll have a long island ice tea, please." "Nice, I'll hook it up for you too!" "Now that's what I'm talking about boo. Give me the hook up."

Stephanie saw Char coming out of the bathroom, they both walked up to the bar with Cashmere. After Cashmere got her drink, the three of them walked back to the VIP table. Tammy and Rico were deep in conversation. They didn't really notice the ladies had returned until Cashmere said "Hello..." ""Hey ladies, are you having a good time?" Rico said. "Yeah Rico, this place is off the hook.

Thanks again for hooking us up." Cashmere said. "It's all good. It is definitely my pleasure ladies." Rico said. At that moment, Rico placed his hand on Tammy's thigh. He was hoping that she wouldn't move it. She definitely didn't move it; in fact she smiled at him. Tammy thought, this is it, he is about to make his move. She was right; Rico leaned over and asked her "Would you like to go somewhere a little quieter to get to know each other?" "Where did you have in mind Rico?" "Well, I was thinking we could go to my place." "I'm not sure if I am ready for all that Rico. I don't really want to leave my girls either." "Okay, I understand. How about we go to my office?" "Okay, maybe for a little while." "Cool, let's go." They got up and Rico led Tammy to the office at the back of the club. "Here we are. Have a seat. Would you like something to drink?" "I would like some more Moscato, please." Rico walked over to the bar in the office and got some Moscato for Tammy. "So Rico, why didn't you tell us that you were part owner?" "I really don't talk too much about it." "Why not Rico?" "To be honest, I want to make sure that people like me for who I am, not for what I have. So, I keep it low key." "I totally understand. I can appreciate that." "Your lips look divine." Rico told Tammy. "They taste divine too. You should try them again." Tammy didn't have to tell Rico twice. He leaned in and gave her a kiss that was far better than the first one. Tammy felt his lips touch her lips; she felt his tongue against hers as well. She pulled him closer to feel his body pressed against hers. Rico moved in closer. He let his hands slide down to her sweet juicy backside. Enjoying what he was feeling, he squeezed her cheeks. Tammy was enjoying his touch too. She rubbed her hands up and down his back. Chemistry was flowing between them. Desire was building.

Tammy felt things that she hadn't felt in a while. She was beginning to feel strongly for Rico. As soon as their lips parted, R.J. opened the door. "My bad, I didn't mean to interrupt, but I need to do the books." R.J. said. "It's all good man, we were just leaving anyway." Rico said. He looked at Tammy, she took his hand and they left the office. "Sorry about that Tammy. I don't know why he needed to do the books right now." "No worries Rico, I enjoyed the time we had. I look forward to more." "Good to know Ms. Tammy." When they got back to the VIP table, Char was ready to call it a night. "I'm sorry ladies; I have to get up early tomorrow. I really need to get home and get some sleep." Char said.

Thirteen

Cashmere woke up the next morning, feeling the pain from the night before. "Oh damn, I did way too much last night." She could barely force herself out of bed. "Coffee ... I need coffee!" The room was spinning, she could barely walk straight. Her head was throbbing. Although she had a great night with her girls, she was paying the price now. She couldn't get to the coffee fast enough. Her vision was blurry from all the alcohol that she had consumed. There was a knock at the door. Of all the things she didn't need now, it was guest. She walked slowly to the door; each step seemed to take an eternity. It seemed to take a lifetime to get to the door. As if she walked for miles and miles. Finally reaching the door, she asked "Who is it?" "Girl, open the door, its Stephanie and Tammy." Cashmere opened the door, her girls walked in. They both looked and felt as bad as she did. "Y'all want some coffee?" Cashmere poured coffee for the three of them. The girls sat down and talked about the night before. They reminisced on a wonderful night. Tammy began to talk about Rico and how nice he seemed. "Girl, that man is fine and the best part is he is all about you." Cashmere said. "I did have a good time with him." said Tammy. "So when are you seeing him again?" Stephanie said. "I don't know, he hasn't called and asked me out yet." Tammy said. "You know you don't have to wait on him to call. You can call and ask him out too." Cashmere said. "If I ask him out, how will I know if he is truly interested?" Tammy said. "Girl, he showed you he was interested last night. Didn't you see all that he did for you/us?" Cashmere said. "Maybe she should wait to see how interested he is. The man should be the aggressor. " Stephanie said. "Girl, you sound like you're straight out of the Stone Age. Times have changed and you need to change with them." Cashmere said. "Whatever! I believe a man should initiate interest, and then I will reciprocate." Stephanie said. "I see...and who are you dating these days?" Cashmere asked. "Well, right now I'm single. You know that." Stephanie answered. "Exactly, now you know why." Cashmere said with a smirk. "You didn't have to go there Cashmere. That was rude." Tammy said. "You have to wear your big girl panties if you are going to roll with me. I give it to you straight, no chaser baby." Cashmere said. Tammy's phone chirped. She picked it up and saw a text from Rico.

Rico... Hello, I just wanted to thank you for coming out and allowing me to have a wonderful night with you.

"Well, what did he say?" Cashmere asked. "He thanked me for allowing him to have a wonderful night." "Are you going to respond?" Stephanie asked. "Of course I am going to respond. I'm just not sure what to say right now." "Just tell him you had a wonderful night too and go from there." Cashmere said.

Tammy...You're welcome. I had a wonderful night as well.

Tammy's phone chirped again.

Rico...You clean up very well.

Tammy...Thank you. So do you.

Rico...I would love to see you again.

Tammy...That would be nice. What do you have in mind?

Rico...Well, there is a jazz festival today at Maymont Park. I was hoping we could check that out.

"He wants to go to the jazz festival at Maymont Park today. Should I go?" "Umm, hell yeah!" Cashmere said. "Stephanie, what do you think?" asked Tammy. "I think if you like him, you should go and get to know him. At the very least you will hear some good music."

Tammy... That sounds like it would be fun.

Rico...So, is that a yes?

Tammy...Yes.

Rico...Great, I can pick you up at 2:00. Is that good for you?

Tammy...Yes, 2:00 is fine.

Tammy was excited now. She thought about the intimacy that they shared the night before. His kiss was more than nice; she felt a true connection with him. She knew she would have another opportunity to be intimate with him.

"I'm sorry girls; I have to cut this visit short." "Girl, it's all good. Have a good time. Call me tomorrow with the details." Cashmere said. "Stephanie, are you going with me or are you staying with Cashmere?" "Girl, hang out. I'll take you to the crib later." Cashmere said. "Sounds good to me." Stephanie said. "Okay ladies, have a great day. I will talk to you later." Tammy said. She grabbed her things and headed to the door with Cashmere. "Handle your business Tammy. Make Rico yours!" Cashmere said. They hugged and Tammy left. Cashmere went back to hang out with Stephanie. "So, how is the restaurant coming along?" Cashmere asked as she sipped on her coffee. "It is coming along. The kitchen equipment is in. We are in the final stages now. I am ordering food next week to prepare for the grand opening." "Girl that's great. I am so happy for you. I can't wait until opening night. I am going to get my eat on!" "Speaking of eating... what do you have in the fridge? I feel like cooking." "By all means, do your thing. Don't let me stop you." "Okay, cool. Let's go see what you have." "Cool, I'm down to eat." They walked to the kitchen. Cashmere pulled out a bottle of Moscato. "We might as well enjoy ourselves." She said. "That sounds good to me." Stephanie said as she looked in the refrigerator. She saw crab meat, mini sweet peppers, mushrooms, green onions, shredded mozzarella cheese, rice, bacon and parsley. She decided to do some bacon wrapped stuffed peppers. Stephanie began chopping the ingredients for the stuffed peppers.

Cashmere decided to play some music. She put on some jazz, poured some Moscato for both of them. It had been a long time since anybody had cooked for her. She knew that Stephanie's bell peppers were going to be great. She couldn't wait to try them. Stephanie was chopping away, enjoying the wine and music. She felt good because she was doing what she loved. Cooking was the one thing that took her to places beyond her imagination. She knew that cooking was her passage to enjoying her life. Cooking made her feel alive! She began to mix the ingredients in the pan. Added some seasonings and stirred everything together. Cashmere poured some more wine and they clinked glasses. The food smelled good, the wine tasted great, the music was on point. Stephanie put some of the ingredients on a spoon and asked Cashmere to taste it. Placing the spoon in Cashmere's mouth, she asked "How is it?" "This is really good girl. I can't wait to taste some more." "Thank you, I'm glad you like it." Cashmere had a little crab on her lip. Stephanie wiped it away with her finger. Cashmere grabbed her finger and placed it in her mouth to eat the crab. Stephanie just looked at Cashmere, she wasn't sure what to say or do.

Stephanie leaned in and kissed Cashmere. Cashmere placed her hands on Stephanie's waist and pulled her closer. Stephanie placed her arms around Cashmere's neck. When the kiss was over, they both looked at one another in disbelief. "Oh damn, that was hot!" Stephanie said. "Yes, it was."

Fourteen

Rico and Tammy pulled up to Maymont Park, parked the car. The place was packed. It seemed like everyone from Richmond, Chesterfield County and Petersburg were there. Rico popped the trunk, grabbed a blanket and a basket. They walked to find a spot as close as they could to the stage. Rico laid the blanket out, helped Tammy to sit, and then he opened the basket. He presented her with one long stem rose. "I give you this single rose to symbolize the most wonderful night that I have ever had. I hope there will be many more to come." Tammy took the rose; she couldn't hold back the smile that was worn all over her face. Rico pulled out some cheese and wine from the basket. He poured the wine for Tammy, placed some cheese on a paper plate for her. Reached into the basket and pulled out some crackers and prosciutto. He placed the prosciutto and crackers on her plate as well. Tammy could not stop smiling. This date was turning out to be something wonderful! She was glad she had accepted. Rico seemed to be very sweet. He seemed to have thought of everything. He was doing and saying all the right things.

Tammy was in her heaven right now. She glanced over at Rico and smiled at him. She noticed him looking, checking her out. "You are simply beautiful!" Rico told Tammy. "You are quite fine yourself." Tammy told Rico. Rico leaned in and gave her a kiss that told her just how much he liked her. His lips pressed softly against hers, parting her lips with his tongue. He eased his tongue inside her mouth. His kiss was passionate enough to get her juices flowing. They both were so in to the kiss that they forgot that they were in the park with plenty of other people around. Rico thought to himself, this is going to be the night that I know her intimately. The concert started with some smooth soulful sounding jazz. Rico fed cheese and crackers to Tammy. She enjoyed the attention she was getting from him. The wine was flowing nicely; soon Tammy was starting to feel very good. One of her favorite groups Up to the Bottom came on stage singing her favorite song; Rico pulled Tammy close to him, kissed her neck and nibbled on her ear. "I love this group. The lead singers voice is just so smooth." Tammy said. "That is very good to know." Rico said. The singer continued to woo the audience with his love laced lyrics. Tammy kissed Rico with more passion than ever before. She placed her hand on his chest and Rico eased his hand up her leg. Her legs were so soft, Rico's anticipation of having Tammy only grew with every ounce of softness that he felt. Tammy let her hand slide down from his chest to his muscular legs, and then she went for it. She placed her hand between his legs and felt his manhood swell. She knew that this would turn in to much more as the night progressed. It had been some time since Tammy had wanted to give herself to a man. Tonight was going to be the night that she gave herself to Rico. Another one of her favorite groups walked out on the stage accompanied by jazz saxophonist River Run. The night was turning out to be something very special. The music was great. The food was wonderful and the company was very desirable. A gentleman walked up to them, and said hi. Rico looked up and said "What's up man, how are you?" The gentleman said "Could you please come with me?" Tammy looked at Rico, then looked at the gentleman, she wasn't sure what was going on. Rico said "Sure, no problem. Let me get our stuff." "Don't worry about your stuff, we will take care of it for you." The gentleman motioned for two men to come over. They began to pick up Rico and Tammy's things, while they followed the man to a trailer behind the concert area. When Tammy walked in, she couldn't believe who she saw sitting at the table. It was none other than her favorite group Up to the Bottom. "Oh my goodness, it's Up to the Bottom!" Tammy said. "Hello Tammy, how are you?" Jeffrey, the lead singer of Up to the Bottom said. "I am well, thanks. How? What is going on?" Tammy said. "Well, Jeffrey is a good friend of the family. I knew that they were performing tonight and I thought it would be nice for you to meet him." Rico said. "This is truly turning out to be a great night. I can't believe I am standing in the same room with my favorite group. Tammy said. "Rico, tell me how you met this lovely lady?"

Jeffrey said. "I was truly in the right direction at the right time. We met at Layla's Cafe." "I've heard of Layla's Cafe, but I have never been there. I may have to stop by there sometime." Jeffrey said. "I am sure Layla would love that. She has some of the best food in Virginia." Tammy said. Rico grabbed Tammy's hand and they said their goodbye's to Jeffrey. Tammy could not believe that she had just met Jeffrey from Up to the Bottom. She talked about it the whole way back to the car. She had a smile on her face that radiated throughout her whole body. Rico had impressed her yet again. This evening couldn't possibly be any better. The best part is that the night is still young. "Are you having a good time?" Rico asked. "I have never had a better time than I am having tonight!

Thank you so much!" "Great, I wanted to make sure this night was memorable for you. There's more to come." "I can't wait!" Rico drove to The Crib; they were having a VIP party for some of Richmond's most affluent citizens. The club was closed to the public. Everybody who was anybody was there tonight. Tammy couldn't believe that she was in the same room with some of these people. Rico continued to amaze her. They mingled with some of the attendees. Tammy met so many of Richmond's socialites; she took the opportunity to network, as so many others were doing. Rico brought over some champagne for them to enjoy while they were socializing with Richmond's finest. Tammy noticed Char walking over to them. She was happy to have someone there that she was friends with. She also knew that Char would attract a lot of attention, so she would meet more people. "Hey girl, how are you doing?" Char asked. "I am fine, how are you girl?" Tammy replied. "I am well, thanks. I have been working so much lately. I couldn't wait to get some fun time in." Char stated. "You are looking lovely as always Char." Rico commented. "Thank you very much Rico. It is good to see you again. You look very handsome as well." Char replied. Char noticed someone that looked familiar at the affair. He was very handsome. She couldn't really place where she had met him, but knew that he looked very familiar Wherever she knew him from, he had her attention, that's for sure. She would make sure that she spoke with him before the night was over. Of all the men in the place tonight, this one had her attention and didn't even know it. He didn't know that she knew he existed, but he would find out soon enough! "Tammy, do you recognize that fine brother over there?" Char asked. "He does look familiar; I can't remember where I've seen him before." Tammy said. "Damn, he sure looks good. I may have to go over there and talk to him. Wait...where did he go?" "Girl, he disappeared. He may be leaving already." Tammy said. "I sure hope not, I would like to meet him." Char said. Char and Tammy were looking all around for the brother. They didn't see him anywhere. Char was beginning to lose hope. Tammy wasn't able to locate him either. From out of nowhere she heard someone call her name... "Char." She turned around and there he was, standing directly in front of her. "Hello Char, it is truly nice to see you again." "It is very nice to see you as well. Please forgive me, I do recognize you, but for the life of me, I can't remember your name." "It's Teddy, we met here, last night." By the smile on Char's face, Teddy could tell that she was happy to see him again. Rico grabbed Tammy's hand and led her away, so that Char and Teddy could get to know each other better. Rico wanted to introduce Tammy to some other people before they left for the night. They grabbed some more champagne from the waiter and walked around the room, socializing with others.

Fifteen

"I know something you don't know!" signed Guess who...was posted on the door of Rain when Stephanie arrived moments before the inspector was due to arrive. She quickly pulled down the note, placed it in her purse to deal with later. Stephanie pulled out her keys to unlock her restaurant, hoping that she would have some time to prepare before the inspector showed up. She walked through the restaurant, looking for anything that didn't look right. She went in the kitchen to make sure that everything was perfect. She inspected all the reefers to ensure that they were at the correct temperatures to hold her food. Everything looked great; she was ready for her inspection. Stephanie heard a knock on the front door. She walked toward the door and saw the inspector outside. She smiled and quickly unlocked the door, so that the inspector could enter. "Good morning, please come in." "Good morning, I am Brie from the Virginia Department of Health. How are you today?" Brie showed Stephanie her credentials, as she entered the restaurant. "I am very well, thank you. Well, actually I am a little nervous." "Please don't be nervous, I am sure everything will be fine. If it isn't, I will give you all the information you need to make the necessary corrections." "Great, would you like something to drink before we start?" "Yes, I would love a glass of water, thank you Stephanie." Stephanie went to get a glass of water for Brie. While Stephanie was gone, Brie took a look around the restaurant. She was impressed by the decor of the restaurant. It had a very elegant feel to it. Rains would definitely be a place to celebrate a special night. It was very upscale. Stephanie returned with the water and Brie began her inspection. "Stephanie, feel free to handle business as usual, I will ask if I need anything." Stephanie went into her office to go over some paperwork and make some last minute checks before her grand opening, which was scheduled for the following weekend. She couldn't help but think about the note that she had in her purse. She pulled the note out of her purse and read it again. Who could possibly be behind this? Why would anyone want to do this to her? Stephanie was beginning to feel a little worried about these notes. She text Tammy:

Stephanie: Hey girl, are you busy?

Tammy: Just looking over some briefs. How are you?

Stephanie: A little worried.

Tammy: Worried?

Stephanie: I received another note today. This one was taped to the entrance of the restaurant.

Tammy: Can you think of anybody that would want to stalk you?

Stephanie: Why would anyone want to stalk me? I haven't an enemy in the world.

Tammy: Apparently you do. You may want to think about it, seriously. If I were you, I would take this more seriously!

Stephanie: What should I do?

Tammy: First, you should contact the police. Then you should purchase some mace. You may want to take some self-defense classes. And above all, please make sure that you are always aware of your surroundings.

There was a knock on her office door. The inspector was ready to talk to her. Stephanie, put up one finger, to let her know that she would be out in a moment. She sent Tammy a final text.

Stephanie: Okay, I have to go; the health inspector is ready to talk to me.

Tammy: Okay, call me if you need me! Be safe!

Stephanie put her phone away, got herself together and went to see what the inspector had to say. She took a deep breath, opened the door and walked over to Brie. "I am hoping you have good news for me." "Well Stephanie, here are the results of my inspection. After looking over everything, I did notice that there was one issue. I didn't see my invitation for your grand opening." Stephanie looked at Brie quizzically. "Are you saying what I think you are saying?" "I am saying that your restaurant "Rains" passed with flying colors!" Stephanie could not believe her ears...she was so excited; she started jumping up and down, clapping her hands. "Hell yeah, thanks so much. You have no idea how much this means to me. I have wanted to have my own restaurant ever since I was a little girl" "Well, you already have your restaurant. Now you have a clean bill of health for your restaurant. I wish you the best of luck!" "Please have a glass of wine with me to celebrate." "Well, you are my last inspection for the day. Sure, that would be fine." "What kind of wine would you like?" "Well, to be honest, I would rather have a mojito. Would that be too much trouble?" "Not at all, I will make two of them. I love mojitos." "So do I. Thank you very much!" Stephanie could not stop smiling, she felt like a huge weight was lifted off of her shoulders. Life was good for her right now. It seemed the sky was the limit. All her dreams were coming to fruition. All except the creepy notes that she had been receiving. She put that out of her mind for right now. She wanted to bask in this moment! To enjoy all the hard work that she had endured to get to this point. She was determined not to let anything ruin this moment. Rains would be her focus from here on out. She and Brie finished their mojitos. The inspector left her card and wished Stephanie a great grand opening, then headed out the door. Stephanie locked the door behind her, then went back to the bar and made another mojito with a shot of Jack Tennessee Honey to help her celebrate her good news. She was very happy, happier than she had been in days. This would put her closer to the grand opening. She went to her office to confirm the food orders from the various vendors, now that she had passed the inspection. The food was the very last piece that she needed delivered before the grand opening. Everything else was set. The security company would be here an hour before the opening. She was going to use a couple of her staff members to valet the cars. She had invited the press and received confirmations that they would be in the house. She had also received

RSVP'S from the entire list of special guests that were invited. Above all, her girls were all set to be in the house as well. This was going to be a night to remember. All of Central Virginia would be in the house. It was going to be her night, as long as there weren't any hiccups, she would be happy. She was hoping that the place would be standing room only. She imagined a line around the corner. Then she wondered who would accompany her to this special event. She currently isn't dating anyone. Although she and Cashmere did share an intimate moment, it was just that...an intimate moment. Stephanie had never kissed a girl before, she hadn't even thought about it. It was just one of those things that just sort of happened. She and Cashmere really didn't discuss it. They just let it happen and left it at that. Neither of them spoke about it, they certainly weren't going to tell Char and Tammy about it either. Stephanie had finished up for the night. She gathered her things and headed out the door to get ready to go. On her way home, she got a call from Char. Stephanie hit the call button on her steering wheel to answer the call.

Sixteen

"Hey girl, what are you up to?" she said to Char. "Girl, Tammy and Cashmere are here. We are having some drinks. You should come join us. Where are you?" "I am just passing CareMed on Hull Street. I'll be there shortly. I could use some girl time." "Cool, see you in a minute." She couldn't help but think about her grand opening. Her excitement was building, she found it hard to focus on anything else, even the creepy notes that she had been receiving. She did think about one of Tammy's last text messages though...specifically the one where she said "always make sure you know your surroundings." For some reason, that kept playing in her head. She started checking her mirrors, looking for anything that looked suspicious. She began to get nervous, all of a sudden, Char's place seemed like it was on the other side of the world. The road seemed to never end. She had driven that drive many times before, but now it seemed like she was driving cross country. She looked in her rear view mirror and noticed a car following closely behind her. She put her blinker on and got into the left lane. The car pulled up alongside Stephanie, she tried not to look over. She kept her head pointed straight ahead. The car slowed down and got behind Stephanie again. She immediately called Tammy. "Hello, girl where are you at?" "I am on my way. Tammy, I think I am being followed." "What, being followed. Hurry up and get here. Don't stop before you get here.

If you can get the license plate number, write it down." "Okay, please stay on the phone with me until I get there. I am really scared!" "Okay, I won't get off the phone. I will talk to you until you get here. Tell me when you get here and we will come out and get you." "No, don't come out and get me, something may happen to y'all." "Stephanie, we're not going to let someone follow you and not help you." Char and Cashmere overheard Tammy talking and asked "What the hell is going on?" Tammy told them that Stephanie thinks she is being followed. Followed… oh hell no. We don't play that shit. Where is she?" Cashmere said. "I am turning on your street now; I don't see the car anymore though." "Pull in the driveway, the front door is open." Stephanie pulled in the driveway, looked around before she unlocked the car door. She saw a man walking up the street with a hoodie and some sweats on. He had earphones in his ears as if he was listening to music. She waited for a minute to watch him pass, and then she got out the car, clicked the alarm and ran as fast as she could to the front door. Right when she grabbed for the door knob, the door opened in a hurry. Char was standing in the foyer "Are you okay?" she asked. "Yeah, I am fine, just a little scared." "What the hell is going on? Who is following you?" Char asked. "I don't know. I have been receiving these strange notes. One was on my car. Another was on the front door of the restaurant."

"What does the note say?" Cashmere said. "They say "I know something you don't know." "That's a strange note to leave someone. I mean, if you are a stalker or something like that." Char said. Char grabbed a wine glass for Stephanie, poured her some Moscato. Stephanie turned the glass up and finished the wine practically in one sip. "Damn girl, you really are spooked." Cashmere said. "Do you have anything stronger?" Stephanie asked Char. "Sure, what would you like?" "Girl, I want some Jack Tennessee Honey. That will calm my nerves" "Okay, Jack it is. I will be right back." "Umm, bring the bottle, please." "Damn girl, okay." "So, let me ask you this, have you called the police yet?" Tammy questioned. "No, I have not. If it happens again, I will call them." "Girl, what are you waiting for? Do you want to be attacked or worse, killed?" Tammy asked. "Of course not, I'm not really sure that this isn't some prank being played on me." "Who do you know that would do something like this?" Cashmere asked. "Nobody, but that doesn't mean that it's not a prank." "Are you telling us everything? You seem like you know a lot more than what you are saying." Tammy said. "Girl please believe if I knew anything else I would definitely tell you. Do you think I want to be in this situation?" "I'm starting to wonder. If it was me, I would have called the police." Tammy said. Char came back with a couple more bottles of Moscato and a big ole bottle of Honey Jack for Stephanie. "Don't worry girl, we are here for you."

Cashmere said. "That's very good to know." Stephanie replied. "You don't seem to be taking this very seriously." Tammy said. "Just because I haven't called the police yet, doesn't mean that I am not taking this seriously." Stephanie replied to Tammy. "Okay, I'm not going to argue with you. Just be careful girl. We are all worried about you!" Tammy said. "I know you all are worried, I am worried too." "Do you promise to call the police the next time?" Tammy asked. "Yes Tammy, I promise." Just then Tammy's phone vibrated. There was a text from Rico.

Rico: Hey...are you busy?

Tammy: Just hanging with my girls. What are you up to?

Rico: I was just thinking about you.

Tammy: Awe...so sweet. What were you thinking?

Rico: I was thinking that I would love to kiss you right now!

Tammy: That would be very nice. I would love to feel your lips on me.

Rico: How about later tonight?

Tammy: I look forward to it. I will text you when I leave here.

"Did you just get a booty text?" Cashmere asked. "Come on now, he just wanted to know what I was up to?" "Yeah okay...Rico is going to tap that ass tonight." Cashmere said. "Girl, you are bad...so bad!" Tammy said. "Char, so what happened with Mr. Teddy the other night?" Tammy asked trying to change the subject. "Teddy and I talked. We talked a lot! He is a really nice guy!" "And?" Tammy said. "And, that's it. He's really nice." Char eased a huge smile on her face, which let them know that she was very interested in getting to know Teddy a lot better. "So, how is the restaurant plans coming along?" Cashmere asked Stephanie. "They are coming along nicely. I passed my inspection today; I also ordered the food for the grand opening and finalized some last minute items. Are y'all still coming?" "Hell yeah, I wouldn't miss it for the world girl! I am so excited for you!" Cashmere answered. "Great, I will make sure there is a special table for y'all. How many shall I plan for?" Stephanie looked at Tammy and Char for answers. "I will invite Rico, hopefully he will be able to come." Tammy said. "We'll see what happens with Teddy, I'll let you know soon." Char said. "Char you better work that charm and get that brother on your arm for that night." Cashmere said. "Umm excuse me, you do know that I am a supermodel, I can have any man that I want!" Char said boldly. "Great, since you want Teddy, get his ass to the grand opening then." Cashmere told Char. "I got this ladies, I'll have him there! Don't worry." Char said. Char grabbed her phone and typed in Teddy's name, she pressed the little phone button and the phone started dialing Teddy's number. Teddy answered the phone "Hello!"

"Hello Teddy, this is Char. How are you this evening?" "I am well, thank you. How are you Char?" "I am well, thank you Teddy." "I really enjoyed talking to you the other night." "I enjoyed talking to you too Char. I hope I get another chance to see you again." "It's funny that you mentioned seeing me again. That's why I was calling." "Oh really, what did you have in mind?" "Well, my friend Stephanie is having a grand opening for her restaurant "Rains" next week. I was wondering if you would like to accompany me to the grand opening." "Char, I would love to accompany you to this grand opening. I have heard great things about "Rains". This restaurant is going to be one of the greatest things to hit Richmond." "Sounds good, you can pick me up at 7:00. I will give you my address later tonight when I see you." "Okay, wait a minute, we're seeing each other tonight?" "Yes, Teddy, I would love to see you tonight." "How is 8:00 for you?" "I can do 8:00 that's fine. What do you want to do tonight?" "I was thinking about having you over for some dinner and a movie." "I am definitely down with that!" "Okay, I will text you the address, see you at 8:00." Char hung up the phone and text Teddy the address. "Damn girl, you handled that. I like the way you got him to come over tonight." Tammy said. "The brother didn't know what hit him." Cashmere said. "So, what are you going to cook for him?" Stephanie asked? "Girl, I don't have a clue. I was hoping you had some ideas." "You need something quick, nothing too elaborate or he will be expecting you to be able to cook great dishes all the time." "So true, we can't have that. You know I can't cook." "I got it; you can make some spaghetti with garlic bread. Have some red wine with it and it will be all good." "Nice, I can do spaghetti and garlic bread." "Well I guess we all better leave so Char can get ready for Teddy." Tammy said.

Seventeen

Tammy got in her car and all she could think about was seeing Rico. She had gotten quite fond of him and sooner or later, she was going to show him just how fond of him she was! She turned on the radio, one of her favorite songs was playing. There was nothing like listening to her favorite slow song to get her thoughts flowing. This group was one of her favorite groups. It truly broke her heart when they broke up. She had heard rumors that they were supposed to get back together...she was still waiting! If things go right tonight, just maybe she would put on some of their stuff for Rico and go from there! It had been a long time since Tammy had anticipated such intimacy with a man. She was sure that Rico was worth her love. She intended to shower him with her essence. This was going to be a night that neither of them would forget. She thought about Rico's massive arms being wrapped around her. Suddenly, a smile creased her lips. She knew that soon he would be with her. Not only would he be with her, but tonight was going to be their night! It was going down tonight! Her ringtone started playing. She instantly knew that Rico was calling.

Tammy: Hello.

Rico: How are you?

Tammy: I am fine. I was just thinking about you.

Rico: Oh really? What were you thinking?

Tammy: I was thinking that I can't wait to see you!

Rico: That's great because I can't wait to see you either.

Tammy: That makes me happy!

Rico: Great, I was thinking about bringing over some wine. How does that sound?

Tammy: That sounds great, thanks.

Rico: I am leaving my place in about 15 minutes. Are you almost home?

Tammy: I should be home by the time you leave.

Rico: Sounds good. I will see you soon.

Tammy: Okay, bye Rico.

Rico: Bye baby.

There will be wine, music and Rico, all in the same place. That could be a dangerous combination. Tammy was going to have to prepare for this. She was determined to make this night a great one. She was playing for keeps with Rico. He had no clue what was in store for him. It seemed like Rico might have some surprises of his own. She pulled into the driveway, got out and went in the house. She pulled out candles, wine glasses and jumped in the shower to freshen up. She wanted to look her best! She wanted him to want her more than anything he had ever wanted in this life. He was all that she could think about tonight. Her hopes were that he felt the same way. She lit the candles, turned on some music and awaited his arrival. Her excitement was building. She anticipated him showing up at any minute. She went to the bathroom to make sure that she looked beautiful. After making sure that she was alluring, the doorbell rang. Oh, yeah it is on now Mr. Rico was at the door. She opened the door and couldn't hold back her smile. Rico was standing there looking as hot as ever. He had on a blue blazer with a black shirt and some blue jeans that fit him nicely. She couldn't wait to get him in the house. "Hey baby. How are you?" she said. "I am fine. You look great baby." "Come on in, have a seat." "I bought a couple of bottles of wine. I bought a Moscato and a Cabernet Sauvignon to enjoy." "Thank you, I love Moscato." "I love Cabernet Sauvignon." "Let me get the glasses." While Tammy went to get the glasses, Rico was checking out the candles in the dimly lit room, while listening to some nice rhythm & blues flowing through the air. She returns with the wine, looks at Rico with inviting eyes. They relaxed on the couch, clinked their wine glasses together and took a sip. "Rico, I do have a question. Why do you work at Layla's Cafe and you're part owner of a club?" I know it seems strange, but I really wanted to see the restaurant side of things. I also wanted to learn from someone that is in business because they really care about what they do and the people that they serve, rather than to just make money. I already know how to make money." "That's a different approach. I get it though." "I don't believe that we've talked about your profession yet." "Well, I'm a professional, can we leave it at that?" "It would be nice to know what you do for a living. Are you in the C.I.A.? Please tell me you're not a drug dealer." "No, I am not in the C.I.A. and I am certainly not a drug dealer." "Then, why all the secrecy?" "To be honest, it isn't a secret. It's just that once people find out what I do, they tend to shy away." "Try me. I just might be different." "Rico, I really like you. I don't want this to be a big deal." "It won't be a big deal. I tell you what; you can tell me when you feel more comfortable." "Okay, I will do just that. Thanks for being so understanding." "I really like you Tammy. I want to know everything there is to know about you." "As do I Rico. In time we will know so much about each other." "I like everything that I know so far." "I am looking forward to showing you more to like." "Is that so?" "Yes, that is so Mr. Rico." "I haven't felt this way about anybody in a very long time. You excite me in ways that I haven't been excited in what seems like forever!" "Tammy, I can relate. You excite me as well. I wanted to share something with you." "What is it? Please do." "It is something that you inspired me to write. Every time I thought about you since we met, I wrote a line or two down. I completed it last night and I want to share it with you." "I can't wait to hear it." Rico pulls the piece out and begins to read it to Tammy:

2 Tempting 2 Resist

There you are looking very enticing
Got me so hot...got me blazing
You are truly beautiful
Simply amazing

Just to press my lips against yours
Anytime with you would never be a bore
One taste could never be enough
A great desire to enjoy your stuff
Sweet and sexy...the way you stir your musk
Self-control intact...that you can trust
Love the way everything goes together
Built for the duration...no matter what the weather
Just the thought of playing in your playground
Has me wanting to travel southbound
Do it so that you can't help but make a sound
Grabbing the sheets...head thrashing all around
Feeling good to you...because
I'm putting it down
Taking you farther than you've ever been before
Feeling your climax begin to soar
Unable to control your passion
Trying your best to maintain a calm fashion
Experiencing far too much satisfaction
You can't control your thoughts
Because my efforts are a distraction
Enjoying every minute of this action
Surprised...you thought I would be slacking
I can tell that I got you by the way your body's reacting
It's unbelievable, inconceivable and unthinkable
That I would have your body uncontrollable
Enjoying this bliss
Because you are 2 tempting 2 resist

"I love it Rico!" She leans in and gives him a kiss. She starts to pull away, but he pulls her closer to enjoy more of her soft sensuous lips. Placing her hand alongside his face, she moves in closer. When their lips part, they both stare in each other's eyes in amazement, knowing that there would be more to follow. "I look forward to experiencing everything you wrote." "Tammy, you have no idea just how bad I want to do those things to you!" Tammy picks up the stereo remote and plays some music she thinks it's time to turn things up a little. "Jodeci, very nice, that is my group." Rico pulls Tammy closer, gazing in her eyes, he gently kisses her neck. She leans her head away, to give him full access. Her scent flowing from her neck entices Rico to no end. He eases his hand on her thigh, gently gliding his hand upwards toward her sweetness. The movement of his hand and the kisses from his lips sets her body on fire. Her fibers come alive with the anticipation of Rico's desires. He lowers his head just a little to kiss the front of her neck. She tilts her head back. Sliding his hand higher up her dress, caressing her thigh, he has awakened her inner sweetness. Tammy's thighs are so soft to Rico's touch. He begins to squeeze a little, letting out a soft moan. Candles are flickering, music flowing, Tammy is feeling very comfortable and Rico is starting to feel his manhood rise. His anticipation is building. He wants Tammy more and more. Wanting to feel her body pressed against his, he slides his hand between her thighs and grazes against her sweetness. Tammy's body flinches just a little from the touch. She spreads her legs just a little to let Rico know that he is welcomed to her sweetness. "Your scent is driving me wild baby." Rico tells her. He lowers his head between her girls. Kissing and licking her breasts, she arches her back so he can get the full benefit of her girls. His fingers sliding in and out of her sweetness, his lips providing kisses to her girls, she is trying to maintain.

Everything that she is feeling at this point just about has her over the edge. Her sweetness is fully alive and teetering on the brink of satisfaction. She can't let him know that he has her almost there. She won't let him know that he has her almost there. Trying to concentrate, she unzips her dress, giving Rico more access to the girls. Her dress falls revealing her beautiful breasts that are nestled in her burgundy lace bra, which matches her burgundy dress that is now only covering half her body. Rico unhooks her bra; she pulls it off, dropping it to the floor. He begins to pay closer attention to the girls. Licking and sucking them, one at a time. He's paying close attention to her protruding nipples. Tammy can barely hold it any longer. She lets out a sweet moan followed by the words "Oh my goodness, that's it Rico. That's it, don't stop!" Rico stood up, extended his hand and Tammy accepted it, when she stood up her dress fell to the floor. Rico picked her up and took her to the bedroom.

Placing her on the bed, he laid down beside her. They began to kiss again.

Tammy enjoyed feeling Rico's lips against hers. He looked at her and said "You mean the world to me and I am glad you are in my life!" She looked at Rico, put her hand on his face and pressed her lips against his again. This kiss had much more passion, much more feeling in it than any other kiss they had shared.

This kiss meant so much more to her. She hoped he felt the same way. Rico reciprocated by kissing her as passionately as he could. She could feel his tongue tickling hers. He held her closer than he had held anyone before.

Easing down to her neck, he placed soft kisses along each side. He slid down a little further and kissed her breast ever so gently. Tammy began to feel excitement. Her sweetness had awakened again. Traveling downward, he placed kisses along her stomach. Her legs began to move as she anticipated what was to come next. Easing down further, Rico placed several kisses on her sweetness. His kisses seemed to last forever, which Tammy enjoyed. Her sweetness was more than awake now, it was thriving. She was on the cusp of singing her sweet song for him. He continued to kiss more and more, without fail; Tammy's sweetness started singing her beautiful melody for Rico to enjoy. Tammy couldn't help but to smile, for it had been a long time since someone made her song sang like that. "Rico, I want to share all of me with you." she spoke as easily as she could. Rico continued to place kisses on her sweetness. She pulled him up to look in his eyes and said "Baby, please make love to me."

He eased himself into her. She took him deeply inside of her with all her worth. He slid in and out, feeling all her greatness with every stroke. He took great care to kiss her breasts again. She put her hand on the back of his head to move him closer, so that he could have more of her breasts in his mouth.

Kissing her lips and holding her tightly until they both exchanged their greatness. It was everything that she had anticipated. Afterwards, they held each other close and slept until the wee hours of the morning, when they made love again!

Eighteen

Cashmere decided to finally make good on going shopping with her sister. She had so much going on that she hadn't had time to go with her. She called Ingrid and asked her to meet her at the mall about one. When they met at the mall, they went straight to the food court for some lunch and to catch up. Ingrid told her that she met and older guy that seemed very interesting. "Tell me about him girl. First, how much older is he?" "Well, he is about your age." "Okay, give me more details please." "Well, he is a middle school basketball coach. Girl, he is so nice. He takes me to nice places and buys me things." How long have you known him?" "It's been about two weeks, I guess." "Where did you meet him?" "We actually met at the mall. Remember when you and I were supposed to go? When you couldn't make it, I went anyway. We met at the music store." "Well, just be careful girl. I hope you know what you are doing." "Why do you say that?" "Cause he is five years older than you. I know you are 21 and grown, but you still need to be careful out there." "Okay, are you done with the big sister speech?" "Whatever girl, let's go get some clothes." They got up, threw their trash away and went to The Rack to see what was in there for them. Looking through some clothes, Ingrid found some things that she liked. Cashmere found a coat and some shoes that she just had to have. They walked up to the counter to pay and Ingrid looked at Cashmere. "What?" "I don't have any more money, you got me right?" "How are you going to go shopping without any money?" "Girl, you invited me, so it should be on you." "Yeah, okay. You might want to go and put those back." "I will pay you back, come on Cashmere." "Girl, you are always trying to work somebody. Okay, you better pay me back too!" "I will, don't worry." Ingrid's phone vibrated. She had a text from her new man.

D: Hey, how are you, baby?

Ingrid: I am well, thanks and you?

D: I am great now. What are you doing?

Ingrid: Shopping with my sister. You?

D: Bout to go shoot some ball with one of my boys. What's up for later?

Ingrid: I don't have any plans. Do you want to hang out?

D: Most definitely. I will call you later. I'll come get you.

Ingrid: Okay, talk to you later.

"So, I take it that was him?" "Yes, it sure was." Ingrid couldn't stop smiling. Her face told of her excitement about talking to him. "Okay, you haven't told me his name yet." "You're right. Sorry. His name is "D"." ""D" is not a name. It is an initial. What is his real name?" "He just goes by "D"." "Are you telling me that you don't know his real name?" "No, I don't know his real name." "That doesn't seem strange to you?" "I will know it in time, stop tripping." "Oh, I'm not the one tripping, you are!" Cashmere started walking towards the parking lot. "Are you leaving?" "Yeah, you don't have any more money, so it's time to go." "Wow ... so much for us hanging out." "Let me know when you get some money and we will do it again." "You are a trip. We don't have to shop. Let's just hang out." "What's up Ingrid? What's on your mind?" "Nothing, I just want to hang out with my big sister, that's all." Okay, sure. We can hang out." "Okay, cool. So what's going on with you?" "Nothing really, I'm just trying to get ready for this trip with my girls." "That's right, y'all are going to Bermuda. Not to be nosey, but how can you afford that trip?" "Well, I have put some money away for a rainy day. I got this, don't worry." "Okay, well I hope you have a great time." "I am sure we will!" "So how are your friends doing anyway?" "They are fine.

Tammy met a guy that she is crazy about. Char is still doing the modeling thing. Stephanie is getting ready to open her restaurant." Wait ... Tammy met a guy? How did that happen? She's never interested in men, not since that one guy." "I know right! Rico is a really nice guy though. We all like him. I know he will be good to her!" "I hope so. She definitely needs someone to be good to her, after all she went through." "Yeah, I know. I thought she had given up on men and was going to switch teams for a minute." "Funny, so did I. I am glad she found someone though. You should see her face when she is talking about him. She can't stop smiling." "That's good for her girl! Now, what about you?

When are you going to meet someone?" "I guess when it is the right time. Someone will come my way, I'm not really thinking about all that right now though." "Okay, I guess. What are you thinking about then?" "I'm thinking about my financial future. That's why I have been saving for a rainy day." "I hear that. I should be doing the same thing." "Girl, you have to get a job first." "I've been looking. I just haven't found anything exciting yet." "You know you can always come and work at the store with me and Uncle Herbert." "Oh hell no, you can have that all to yourself! I want something a lot more exciting than that" "Like what?" "Well, I was thinking about something that deals with travel or entertainment or maybe both. That would be exciting." "Well, you could be a talent agent or something like that." "That's a thought. How would I get into something like that?" "I would start with the internet. That should point you in the right place. Maybe, they have a school or something for it." "Would you do it with me?" "You need help researching on the internet?" "No, I don't need help. I want you to do it with me!" "Okay, Ingrid. I will do it with you. Are you sure you are okay?" "Yes. I am fine. Why do you keep asking me that?" "You just seem different that's all." "Well, I'm good. You can stop worrying now." "Ingrid, you know if you need to talk, I am here for you." "I know sis. Don't worry I am good ... seriously. Can we change the subject?" "Okay, I have a hair appointment in a little bit. Did you want to roll with me or are you doing something else?" "Where are you getting your hair done?" Girl, you know I get my hair done at Ruby's Styling's. You should make an appointment too. Ruby can hook your hair up." "Girl, I may roll with you, maybe she can take me today." "Clearly, you have never been to Ruby before. She is appointment only. I had to make this appointment a month out. That's how busy she is." "Well, I'll still roll with you."

Nineteen

It was a beautiful morning when Stephanie opened her eyes. The sun was shining through her window. She had hung out with her girl Char the night before. They enjoyed wine, conversation and great food. She picked up her phone to check her appointments for the day. She knew that there was a full day ahead of her. She would start her day with meeting Matthius at the restaurant for a quick walkthrough. Then she had to meet with the BBB to finalize her rating. After that she needed to order some last minute things for opening night. Things were moving along quite nicely for her, with the exception of the notes she had been receiving. She still didn't quite know what to make of it. She knew that she had to be very careful. She began to wonder if this person was going to cause her any harm or if they were going to show up again. Pushing those thoughts out of her mind, she got ready to start her day. She grabbed a granola bar and a protein shake on her way out. She opened the sun roof letting the sunlight shine in as she rode towards the restaurant to meet Matthius. Even though she had a lot on her mind, she couldn't help but smile because for the most part, she was truly happy with the way things were going for her. She was on the verge of making her dreams come true. There was just one hiccup that she needed to solve, but didn't really know how to do that. How would she get rid of this stalker person that has involved themselves in her life? The question is why have they involved themselves in her life? She couldn't focus any more attention on this subject right now, she had other things to consider that were more important. After parking and going into the restaurant, she noticed Matthius pulling up. She grabbed a cup of coffee and looked over some papers while she was waiting for him to come in.

Finally, she hears him open the door. "Good morning Stephanie, how are you this morning?" "I am well, thanks Matthius and you?" "I am well also, thanks." "So, what do you think of everything so far?" "Everything looks fine. What else needs to be taken care of before the opening?" "Well, we still need to get the fire extinguishers inspected; there are some outlets that we need to test to make sure that they have power. We also need to get some more light bulbs for the reefers and the kitchen. In the dining area, there is a small hole that needs to be patched and painted." "How long do you think all of that will take?" "Well, one of my guys is going to start on the small hole as soon as he gets here. The fire extinguishers should be taken care of tomorrow. I can go to the store and get the light bulbs today. So, I would say everything should be completed in the next couple of days, at the latest." "Great, that's what I want to hear. I don't need any surprises popping up." "I totally understand. We will do our best to make sure everything is perfect for the opening." "Okay, let me know if you need me, I am going to be in my office for a little bit, and then I have a meeting to attend." "Will do, I think we will be fine though. My men are here now. I'll get them going. Let me know if you need anything. My crew will be here all day." "Actually, I have a couple of paintings that need to be hung. They are in my office." "Okay, just let me know where you want them hung and I will get it done for you." "One, I want them to go behind the Maitre d's station. The other should be hung in the VIP section behind the couch." "Okay, I will hang them myself in a few minutes." "Thanks Matthius, I appreciate it." "You're very welcome Stephanie." She went into her office and closed the door. After going through some papers, she noticed that her office phone was blinking. She had a message. Listening to the message, she instantly got frustrated. The BBB had called to reschedule her appointment to next week. Of course, that wouldn't work for her because she needed this taken care of this week. She picked up the phone and called them back, hoping to be able to get through to someone that could help her. For some reason, all she could do was leave a message. She called back, hoping to get through. Again, all she could do was leave another message. Suddenly, Matthius was knocking on her office door. "Come in. Come in Matthius!" "Stephanie have you heard? Have you heard what just happened?" "What happened?" "I can't believe it, there is a bomb threat at the bank up the street from us. Someone has threatened to blow up the building and everybody in it, if their demands are not met. The police have blocked off the street, they are not letting anyone in or out, until this is over." "What do you mean they are not letting anyone in or out? I have places to go." "Sorry Stephanie, but you are going to have to take care of that stuff after this is over." "You're kidding right?" "I wish I was kidding, they just brought the S.W.A.T. team in a few minutes ago. Turn on the news and see for yourself." "Great, this is just great. What else can go wrong today?" Her phone began to ring. It was her mother calling. "Hello mom. How are you?" "Stephanie are you watching the news?" "No, but I heard about the bank?" Stephanie, your father is in that bank. He went to put something in the safety deposit box." "Please tell me he is okay." "Turn on the news Stephanie and you will see for yourself. She turned on her office television and saw her father among the other customers in the bank via the live feed provided by the bank robbers. He was sitting on the floor with his hands tied behind his back. "Oh my God mom, what are we going to do?" "Stephanie, we can't do anything right now. The police have to take care of this. All we can do is keep waiting and pray that he makes it out of this safely." "Have you talked to him mom?" "Baby, I spoke to him right before he walked in the bank." "This is unbelievable. I can't believe this is happening right now. Why did he have to be in the bank today?" "I know, baby. I am worried too. I just want to hear his voice again." "Mom, I think we should both try and think as positively as we can. Daddy is a very smart man. He will find a way to get out of this." "You're right baby! We should think positive thoughts!" There is a buzzing sound coming from her desk. She looks down and sees that Char is calling. "Hello!" "Stephanie, oh my GOD, I just saw the news. I can't believe your father is in the bank while this is happening. Girl, I am here for you. Let me know if you need anything. Where are you?" "Char, I am freaking out! I don't know what to do. I can't even think straight right now. I am at the restaurant. Damn Char, can I call you back? I am talking to my mom right now." "Yeah, sure. You know what, I am on my way to the restaurant to be with you." No, they have closed off the street. You can't get here." "Okay, well call me later." "Okay, I have to go Char." "Okay girl." Stephanie ended the call and put the phone back on the desk. Although her mom was still on the office phone, they weren't really talking. They seemed to just take comfort in being connected to one another right now. They knew that they needed each other to get through this ordeal. Nothing like this had ever happened to their family before. The news kept updating on the bank hostage situation. So far everybody was still okay. She could see that her dad was unharmed. It was still just a waiting game. She had hoped that the police would resolve this as quickly as possible. Of course these things take time. Then she heard an update that stated the bank robbers saying "If our demands aren't met in the next hour, we will start executing one hostage every fifteen minutes until there aren't any more!" Things just got really bad, is all Stephanie could think. "Stephanie, did you hear what they just reported on the news?" her mother screamed. "Yes mom, I heard it. Oh my God, I don't need this in my life right now. I can't believe this is happening?" "Baby, things will work out. I promise. It just has to work out for us." "Mom, what if it doesn't? What if daddy doesn't make it out of there?" "Stephanie, don't talk like that. Your father is going to be fine!" "How can you be so sure?" "Baby, I can be so sure, because I have to be! I am not ready to be without him yet! I can't be without him yet" "Neither can I mom. Neither can I!"

Twenty

The next morning when they awoke, Tammy was in Rico's arms. She felt safe and secure with him. She felt so good in his arms that he didn't want to let her go. Rico knew that she was everything he had been longing for. She was more than worth the wait! All he could think was that he had to make her his. "Baby, may I fix us some breakfast?" he asked. "Sure, make yourself at home Rico!" "Baby, I think I did that last night … and this morning." "Oh, you definitely did that baby. You were amazing baby!" "Only because it was you baby! You made me feel free and I wanted you to enjoy yourself." There was a buzzing sound coming from her nightstand. It was Char calling.

Tammy: Hello

Char: Tammy, have you heard?

Tammy: Heard what?

Char: The bank up the street from Stephanie's restaurant is being robbed.

Tammy: Okay, what does that have to do with me?

Char: It has to do with you because Stephanie's father is being held hostage in the bank.

Tammy: WTH … you can't be serious.

Char: I wish I wasn't. Check out the news!

Tammy: Okay, I am going to turn it on right now!

Tammy clicked the remote to turn the television on. She saw the news coverage of the hostages in the bank.

Tammy: I am watching it now. How is Stephanie?

Char: How do you think she is doing? She is going crazy. Suppose something happens to her father.

Tammy: OMG, I have to get in touch with her. How is her mother doing? Have you talked to Tiffanie?

Char: No, I haven't. When I called Stephanie she was on the phone with her.

"Is everything okay baby?" Rico said. "No, Stephanie's father is being held hostage at the bank up the street from her restaurant."

Char: Umm, is that Mr. Rico?

Tammy: Girl, mind your business.

Char: Yeah, okay. Call me later. We need to see how we can help Stephanie.

Tammy: Alright, thanks for letting me know. I will talk to you later. Bye.

Char: Bye.

"I guess breakfast is going to have to wait." "Yeah baby, I need to check on my girl." "Is there anything I can do to help?" "Baby, I don't know if there is anything any of us can do, except wait this out. I just need to hear Stephanie's voice to make sure she is okay." "Okay, I will get out of your way, so you can check on her." "No baby, please don't go. I want you to be here with me. I don't think I can do this by myself." "I'm here for you Tammy. We need to eat, so I will start breakfast while you get in touch with your girl. Let her know that if she needs anything, *we* are here for her." "Baby, thank you for saying that. I will definitely let her know that *we* are here for her." Tammy got out of the bed, went to the bathroom to collect herself. She felt tears start to flow down her face. This ordeal was far too much for her to deal with in front of Rico.

Stephanie's father had been there for her when her father passed away many years ago. He was like a father to her as well. She couldn't bear the thought of losing another father figure. The truth is Stephanie's father had put her through law school. Everything that she had accomplished, she owed to him. She knew she had to collect herself before Rico started to wonder if she was okay. There was a knock on the bathroom door. "Baby, are you okay?" "I'm fine baby, thanks. I'm just finishing up." She tried to hold back the tears, but they kept coming. Rico opened the door. She tried to wipe the tears before he noticed. Walking up to her, he noticed that she had been crying. "Baby, how can I make this better for you?" "Rico, Stephanie's father means a lot to me. He is like a father figure to me. It's because of him that I am the person I am today." "What do you mean?" "Well, when my father died, he stepped in and helped out our family. He made sure that I went to college. I wouldn't be as successful as I am without him." "What is it that you are successful at? I still don't have a clue as to what you do for a living." "I know, I haven't told you yet because I don't want you to run away." "Baby, why would I run away? Just tell me, I won't run. I promise!" "Rico, I am a lawyer for one of the most prestigious law firms in Richmond. Okay, so now that you know … feel free to walk away, if that's what you need to do." "You're a lawyer? Why would I walk away from you because of that? Baby, I was thinking you were involved in something illegal. A lawyer, I can deal with. Cool with me." Is there anything else that I need to know?" Once again, Rico had put a huge smile on her face. All the worry that she had put into telling him was for not. Rico didn't have a problem with her being a lawyer like so many other men she had dealt with before him. That's when she realized that Rico was definitely different from any other man. That's when she knew that he was the man for her! "Come on baby, you need to check on your girl. Let's make sure she is alright."

Twenty One

Ruby's Styling's is packed as usual. Everybody in Virginia must be in here getting their hair done today. "Hello, come on in." stated Ruby. "Hey Ruby, I brought my sister Ingrid with me. She needs her hair done something awful." "Hey Ingrid, welcome to Ruby's Styling's. I am Ruby. I am not sure if we can work you in, we are very busy today, we will try though." "Hello Ruby, I have heard you do great things here." "Thank you so much. We do what we can." "She's being modest Ingrid. Ruby is the best at what she does, that's why I come here. Look around, that's why they all come here! She always hooks a sister up!" "Good to know, I would like to make an appointment, just in case you can't get me in today." "That's fine; please see Grace at the appointment desk to make your appointment. We can always cross it off if we can fit you in today." Ingrid walks over and introduces herself to Grace to schedule her appointment. "Cashmere, please have a seat in the chair, I am ready for you now." Ruby says. "Thanks Ruby." Cashmere gets a magazine and notices that the television is on in the beauty shop. Glancing back and forth between the magazine and the television, she notices breaking news that there is a hostage situation occurring down the street from Stephanie's restaurant. The news reporter is reporting that one hostage; a young woman has been killed. The robbers are demanding a helicopter on the roof in less than an hour. They also want the S.W.A.T. team to leave the area. They will continue to kill hostages every fifteen minutes until their demands are met. Then she sees him, she sees Stephanie's father in the bank with his hands tied behind his back. "Oh damn, she screams out!" "What's wrong, Ingrid asks?" "Stephanie's father is being held hostage in the bank. It's right there on the T.V." "Girl, call Stephanie to see if she is okay." "You're right. I'll call her now." Cashmere pulls out her phone and dials Stephanie's number. "Hello," Stephanie answers. "I just heard, are you alright?" "I am a nervous wreck. This is a night mare. I just want to see my father." "I know. How is your mother?" "She is hysterical, especially since they have killed one of the hostages already." "Yeah, I heard about that. Then I saw your father. I am glad he is okay." "Thanks. I don't know what I would do if he didn't make it out of this." "Girl, don't think like that. Your father is going to be fine. You'll see. He will make it out of this. Let me know if you need me." "Okay girl, thanks for calling." "You're welcome. Bye" "Bye Cashmere." "Well, how is she?" Ingrid asks. "She is very worried. She sounds like she's trying to hold it together for her mom." "I can understand that. I know I would be a mess if I had to go through something like that." "As would I. I can't imagine going through something like that. I hope her dad makes it out of this alive." "Either way she is going to need her girls to help her through this." "Yeah, we will definitely be there for her." Cashmere sat back and let Ruby start to work her magic. All she could think was how scared Stephanie and her family must be. Her father is a great man; he doesn't deserve any of this. He wouldn't hurt a soul. All he ever did was help people. Clearly, he was in the wrong place at the wrong time. She tried not to think the worse, but it couldn't be helped. She knew that his life was in the hands of some unsavory characters. At any moment one of the hostages could be killed. This whole situation was way too crazy to be happening to anybody. The news started reporting that the hostages were threatening to kill another hostage in five minutes. All you could hear was everyone in the salon screaming "No, don't kill anybody else!" Watching this unfold was just as hard for the people watching the news as it was for the people that were actually being held hostage. The police picked up the phone to talk with the bank robbers. "Hello, this is Detective Cruz. Whom am I speaking with?" "Detective Cruz, you can call me "B"." "B", do you have a real name that I can use?" "That's real enough for your purposes!" "B, I think we need to establish some form of trust, that way we can move forward." "Trust me Detective Cruz; we are going to move forward, one way or another! It's up to you how we play our next move." "I think it would be nice if you showed a sign of good faith and let a couple of the hostages go. That way the department would feel that you are trying to work this situation out. How does that sound "B?" "How does that sound? How does that sound? Did you really just ask me that craziness? It sounds like you want me to kill somebody else right now! That's how it sounds to me." "No, we don't want you to do anything like that. We want to help you out of this situation." "If you want to help me, then get me a damn helicopter and get the S.W.A.T. team out of here now!" "What about this, what about sending out one of the hostages and let us send the paramedics in to get the young lady that you shot?" "Why would I do that Detective Cruz?" "Well, because it would really make it a better situation for you and the rest of the people in the bank. Don't you want to give them some hope of getting out of this alive? Don't you want to get out of this alive? I can help you do just that. You have to trust me though and let somebody go." "Man you do a lot of talking. Give me a minute I will have to think this over." "Okay, but do I have your word that you won't kill anybody else?" "I can't give you my word on that, but I will tell you this, I don't want to kill anybody else." "Okay "B", I will call you back in five minutes to see what you have decided. Is that okay?" "Give me ten minutes and I will call you back Detective!" "That's fine. I will be waiting for your decision." After hanging up the phone "B" went over to one of his cohorts and began to discuss Detective Cruz's request with her. "What do you think we should do Sheila?" "Man, I am not sure; so far things haven't gone as planned. If we don't do something soon, we won't make it out of here." "I know. We need to get this money to the helicopter and fly away. The only thing that is keeping them from coming in here are the hostages. If we start letting them go, they will kill us for sure." "Right, but if we don't at least meet them halfway, they may just kill us anyway. At least this way, we have some room to negotiate." "So, we should let one of them go, then?" "I think so. Maybe we should let the old man go." "No, old man money bags stays. He looks like he might be important."

Twenty Two

Stephanie is pacing back and forth in her office. She has already had three cups of coffee, which may have been a mistake since the caffeine has her all worked up. Unfortunately, she can't get anything accomplished because she is so worried about her dad. She's been on and off the phone with her mother while they try and wait this whole thing out. All this is still so unbelievable. Just to think yesterday, their world was a great place to be. Today, they fear the worse! To take her mind off of the news she walked out to see how Matthius was doing with the work that needed to be done. She saw Matthius talking to some of the crew members about the outlets and lights. As soon as he was finished, he walked over and said "Stephanie, I am so sorry you and your family have to go through something like this. If you need anything I am here for you. We all are here for you, right guys?" All of the guys shouted "Of course we are." "Thank you all so much, I really appreciate it. I need to get this off my mind for a minute. How is the work coming along Matthius?" "Oh, we are moving along nicely. I expect to be finished with what you asked tomorrow. All of the other work is right on schedule as well. I don't anticipate any problems or hiccups before the grand opening." "Good, thanks." "I do have a question though. Given the current situation, are you sure we are still going to have the grand opening this weekend?" "I have thought about that as well. I am hopeful to still have it. I know my father will be fine. I know he will make it out of this alive." "Great, we will continue to strive for that then." Walking away, she wonders if her father will still be alive this weekend. She wants to appear strong but the truth is, she is as freaked out as she can be. This whole thing is too mind boggling to deal with right now. Unfortunately, she doesn't have a choice but to deal with it, since it is breaking news and plastered all over the television. Her thoughts took her back to when she was a little girl and her father taught her how to ride a bike. To when she scored her first goal in soccer. When she went to her prom. She even thought about when she went off to college. At each instance her father was right there urging her on. He would tell her "You see what you can do when you put your mind to it." It was because of that type of support that she decided to open her own restaurant. Her most favorite thought was that her parents would be at the grand opening to see just how much she had accomplished. Now her thoughts took her to a scary place. She wasn't sure if her parents would be there to see her greatest moment thus far. Anger started to build inside her. The more she thought about it, the more fire she felt burning inside her. How could someone be so hateful towards people? How could you threaten to take someone's life? Much worse, how could you just take another's life to get what you want? Those thoughts took her beyond where she wanted to be ... she put her hands on her face and just lost it. Tears flowed heavily. She cried a much needed cry. She needed to get all of it out.

There was no need to hold onto any of it. Letting it out was overdue right now. She just sat there and let the tears flow until there were not any left inside of her. When she was done, she forced herself to do something to take her mind off of it. She still needed to finalize the menu for the grand opening as well as the upcoming week. She read over her menus to ensure that everything was in order. She placed marks by items that she considered changing. The grand openings menu has to be spectacular to say the least. She had spent many nights thinking about the perfect dishes that would set the tone for her place. She also knew that she needed something to make the people beg for more of her cuisine. Everything was riding on the choices she made for her menu. After checking over the menus one more time, she got up and went to check her inventory to make sure that she had all that was needed. She checked the reefers, the pantry, the food bins, and the beverages. She made sure that everything was in the correct place and ready to go. Then she remembered that there were two more positions that she needed to fill before next week.

That would be hard to do since they still weren't letting anyone in and out of the area for a two block radius. She decided to deal with that after the hostage situation was over. Hopefully that will be very soon. She needed it to be very soon. As much as she knew that she had to accomplish many things before the weekend, it was far too hard for her to focus. The time seemed to just drag on ever since the news report aired that there was a hostage situation at the bank. Everybody's life seemed so unimportant right about now. All anybody could do was pray that Stephan would make it out of this unscathed, especially Stephanie and her mom.

Twenty Three

"Urgent news break! Urgent news break!" screams the television in Tammy's crib. "The hostages have been released. I repeat … the hostages have been released. All the hostages have been let go by the bank robbers. The S.W.A.T. team, dressed as paramedics, have captured the assailants. Stay tuned for a full report." reported the news anchor. Tammy was overjoyed from the news. Both she and Rico hugged one another tightly. Rico liked the way she felt in his arms. He didn't want to let go and she didn't pull away from him either. Tammy was enjoying feeling him pressed against her. She totally lost track of what they were hugging for. Then her phone started ringing. She looked down to the table where her phone was to see who was calling. It was Char, she decided to let it go to voicemail and continue enjoying Rico for the time being. Besides he was smelling way too nice to let go of right now. Rico certainly didn't object.

Matter of fact, he used that time to plant a kiss on her soft lips. She reciprocated, enjoying the taste of his lips against hers. He picked her up with his massive arms and started carrying her to the bedroom. Laying her down gently on the bed, she looked up at him and said "I love the way you kiss me Rico!" "And how do I kiss you baby?" "You kiss me as if it is the last time you are ever going to see me. Your kisses are filled with passion!" "You bring that out in me. I can't get enough of you!" Tammy's phone began ringing again. She let it go to voicemail again, unfortunately for her and Rico, it started ringing again. She got up to go see who needed her attention so urgently. When she listened to her voice mails, she heard one from Char, one from Stephanie and the other was from Cashmere. They all were talking about the hostage situation. She decided to call

Stephanie back first. She needed to make sure that Stephanie and her mom were doing okay. Plus she had to find out what her father had to say. She poured a couple of glasses of Moscato for Rico and her to enjoy while she talked to Stephanie on the phone. Stephanie had excitement in her voice. Tammy just listened to her, letting her get everything out that she had pent up inside her. She went on for ten minutes before she finally asked Tammy if she was busy tonight. Stephanie wanted to get the girls together and go over to her parent's house to celebrate his return. "Are you sure you want all of us around tonight? I would think your father would want some alone time with his family. He might want to rest as well Stephanie. He has been through a lot today." "We all have been through a lot today. Plus, you know my father loves all of you. Y'all are like family to him. Besides, I have already talked to him about it. He is expecting us about seven or so." "Have you talked to the rest of the girls?" "I still have to call Cashmere, but Char is in." "Okay, well let me know what Cashmere says. I'm not sure if I am going to make it though. I will try." "Okay, you will have to deal with my father on that one, if you don't come." "I know ... I know." After ending the call Tammy told Rico about being invited over to her parent's house tonight. He told her that they obviously think of her as family and want to include her in their celebration. She understood that but felt that it was just too soon to celebrate with everyone. She thought that they needed time to adjust and get over what happened. They hadn't had a chance to really deal with their emotions just yet. This was way too new to just be able to get over. She knew they needed time to share their feelings without everybody else hanging around. Her phone dinged, she had received a text message from Stephanie.

Stephanie: Cashmere is in. She will be there at seven. Are you?

Tammy: Okay. I am not sure yet."

Stephanie: Well, I hope to see you there.

Tammy: Okay.

Stephanie: Bye.

Tammy: Bye.

"Sounds like you might have to show your face on this one. They really want you there with them." said Rico. "I know. I guess I am just overthinking it. I guess I will go for a little bit." "Good, I know they will be happy that you showed." "Anything to support my girl and her family." "Well, I am going to get out of your hair and let you do your thing. Maybe we can get together tomorrow." "Tomorrow? What about tonight?" "I wasn't sure if you would be up for company after dealing with them." "I am sure that I will be up for spending time with you." "Okay, well call me when you are about ready to leave and maybe you can come by my crib." "Your crib? Oh nice. I would love to see where you live." "Then you shall see tonight baby."

Twenty Four

It was just after seven and everybody had shown up at Stephanie's parent's house. After all the hugs were given, Stephen thanked everyone for taking the time away from their busy day to come and celebrate with them. He began to talk about everything that went on from the time he entered the bank until they let everybody go home from the police station. His descriptions of the events were very hard to listen to because everyone knew that he could have been killed at any moment. Tiffanie couldn't take her eyes off of him. She knew that she was lucky to be hearing his voice right now. Everybody paid close attention to everything that he said. Not one person spoke as he looked around the room at the shocked faces surrounding him. He told them that he was standing a few feet away from the young lady when they shot her. That young lady had just graduated from college. She was in the bank depositing her first check from her new job. The robbers made them draw straws to see which of them would lose their life. It was the most horrible ordeal he had ever been through. Just to think that his life would be determined by a simple piece of straw. In that moment his life was as insignificant as a small piece of straw. "That got me thinking about family and how precious life is. That's why I wanted you all here tonight, so that I could be around the people that mean the most to me. I just wanted to be surrounded by family." There wasn't a dry eye in the room, even Stephen had tears strolling down his face. "You girls have always been like family to us. We hope that you feel as much a part of this family as we feel you are." Tiffanie said. There were plenty of emotions floating around the room. The girls had always felt like a part of the family, but tonight Stephen and Tiffanie acknowledge just how much they were. The mood in the room was heavy. Hearts were enlightened tonight. There was a moment of silence that seemed to just appear out of nowhere. They all were looking around the room at one another taking everything in. Tiffanie took that time to get up and go to the kitchen, when she returned she had a tray of wine glasses. After passing the glasses around the room, she raised her glass and said "To family today and to family forever!" Glasses clinked and they all enjoyed their wine. Stephanie and Stephen hugged one another again. Her eyes began to water all over. She was glad to have her father back. For a moment she thought that it was all over. By the grace of GOD, he was back at home safe and sound.

Hopefully life will be back to normal very soon. Deep down Stephen knew that he would never be the same. He knew that he would be worried every time he went to the bank or anywhere else for that matter. His sense of security had been taken away from him today. How many times would he walk out that door and wonder if he would return to his lovely wife. How many nightmares would he have after seeing that young girl lose her life? Nope, his life would never be the same. It had been severely altered without his permission. Someone had taken it upon themselves to rob him of his right to a comfortable and normal life. He began to wonder what he did in his life to deserve this. All he ever tried to do was live his life as a God fearing man. He would go out of his way to help anyone that needed it. How could this be his fate? It just didn't add up. This was not supposed to happen to him. Was this some type of punishment? If so, what was it punishment for? Everyone could see that Stephen was deep in thought. Tiffanie knew that he was worried, she tried to bring him back to the rest of them by saying "Baby, would you help me in the kitchen for a minute?" He followed her to the kitchen. She placed her hands on each side of his face, looked in his eyes and said "Baby, I love you with everything in me. I know you are worried, but please know that our lives are held in God's hands. As long as your faith remains strong, we will be fine" He looked her straight in her eyes and said "You always know exactly what to say to me baby! Thank you so much for being there for me." Then he pulled his wife close to him and gave her a much needed kiss. After the kiss they just hugged one another for a few more seconds. Tiffanie needed the kiss and the hug just as much as he did. She knew that she had almost lost her man. She also knew that he was returned to her by the grace of God.

In her mind, things might not be the same, but she would cherish every single day that she had to spend with him for the rest of her life. He was her one and only true love. They had been through everything together. There was no way that she would lose him before it was his time. "Baby, I feel like we have a second chance. Let's make the most of it from now on." "What do you mean make the most of it?

What do you have in mind?" he asked. "Well, I just mean lets live life to the fullest. We've always talked about traveling. Maybe it's time we take some trips." "You may have a point there gorgeous. Where would you like to go?" "Baby, let's figure it out together. I have some ideas and I am sure you have some places that you would like to see." "Sounds good to me baby. We can start later tonight, after everybody leaves." They hugged and kissed again. "Really mom and dad ... get a room." "We have several rooms young lady." Stephen replied. "Well, we have guests. Y'all should not be doing that stuff with all these people around." "Child please. We are all adults in this house. How do you think you got here? You better ask somebody!" Tiffanie said. Stephanie just looked at them, shook her head and said "That's the problem, y'all think you are grown." Then she laughed and went back to join the others before they could say anything in response. Her parents soon followed with another tray of wine and some cheeses for everyone to enjoy. It would appear that the mood was lightening. Stephen had managed to crack somewhat of a smile. Stephanie was smiling. Everybody was happy that things turned out for the better. The road was bumpy for a minute, but now things would be back to normal, as much as they could anyway. They all could get back to their lives again.

Twenty Five

Ring, Ring, Ring. "Hello" "What's up girl what are you doing?" "Bout to go out with "D", what are you doing?" "I have to go into the office for a little bit. I was just calling to see how you were doing. We haven't really talked since we were at Ruby's." "I am okay. Is Stephanie and her family okay? I saw the news." "Yeah, they are cool. I think they are still a little shaken up about it though." "Please give them my best. I just can't believe that any of that even happened." "What's going on at work?" "I just have some things I need to get done before the morning." "Oh okay, well call me tomorrow. "D" just pulled up. I'm about to be out." "Alright girl, be careful out there with this "D" person." "Oh don't worry; nothing will happen that I don't want to happen." After hanging up the phone, Cashmere got out of the car and went into the store to take care of some things before they opened in the morning. She turned on the computer to check her file that she had created some time ago. This particular file would access the company's bank account and since she had the account numbers, she could manipulate the funds from one account to another. This wasn't a normal practice, but every once in a while she would take some funds from the company's account and add it to her personal account. She figured that since she didn't make a good wage, she was entitled to a little extra from time to time. A bonus if you will. Since her uncle didn't check the account or handle the finances, she knew he wouldn't miss it. Plus he didn't have a need to check it because he trusted his favorite niece. He handled the store and the customers; she handled the ordering of products and the finances. That was how they set things up when she started working there right out of college.

When she was done transferring the funds to her account, she turned the computer off and headed out the door to her car. She hadn't eaten anything since breakfast, so she thought about stopping by Croaker Spot for a little food and some karaoke. She loved doing karaoke and the men at Croaker Spot had a little something going on. She had already met a couple of fine brothers there. Unfortunately, nothing really developed out of those meetings other than a few dates. She was looking for that one special man that would just sweep her off her feet. She wanted that prince charming who would adorn her with any and everything that her heart desired. She needed that one person who would whisk her away to a better life. She had set the bar pretty high and she was determined to have it her way. That was one of the reasons she was making sure she had a little something for a rainy day stashed away. It didn't matter how she got it as long as she stacked her bank account. She was determined to live the good life no matter how she acquired it. It was all about using the perfect bait to catch the perfect fish. So far all she had dealt with were guppies.

She was on a quest to get in where she fit in. If she kept doing what she was doing for about 3 more years, she would acquire enough money to live like she truly wanted to live. She had already accumulated a little over ½ million between her paychecks and the transfers from the company's account. She made sure that she didn't spend money frivolously because she didn't want anyone to wonder where she was getting the money from, especially her Uncle Herbert. So, she made sure that she drove the same old car, lived in the same apartment. She kept everything simple. The cruise would be her most extravagant purchase in a while. That was covered because everyone knew that she had been planning to take this vacation with her girls for years. Now it is finally here. She was going to have the time of her life on this cruise. Hopefully she would meet her prince charming too. After finishing her meal and singing some karaoke, she decided to call it a night. She paid her bill and went to get in her car, when a nice looking young man was pulling in to the space next to hers. He got out, looked over at her, smiled and said "Hi." She noticed the most beautiful smile that she had seen in years. She spoke back … "Hi, how are you this evening?" "I am fine, thank you. How are you doing?" "Things are well, I can't complain. Who would listen anyway?" "You never know. I am sure there are plenty of people that find what you say interesting" "Is that so?"

" I most definitely would. It is a shame that you are leaving. I am about to have a drink or two and sing some karaoke." Cashmere thought to herself, this brother sure is fine. She hadn't seen him here before. The Jaguar that he was driving had New York plates; maybe he was in town on business. At any rate, she didn't think a drink would hurt. "You know, I wouldn't mind having a drink." "Great, let's go." She got out of the car and walked over to him. "I'm Cashmere and you are?" "I'm Simeon. It is a pleasure to meet you Cashmere." "Likewise, Simeon." The two of them walked into Croaker Spot. One of the waitresses gave Cashmere a funny look.

Then she noticed Simeon standing next to her and understood exactly what was going on. They sat at a table close to the stage area. "Do you sing Cashmere?" "If you're deaf, I would sound really good." "That's funny; I take that as a no." "You would be correct. I wish I could sing. Don't get me wrong, I do love karaoke, but I know my limitations. I take it you can sing." "I'm okay." "Are you being modest?" "I can carry a tune, that's about it." They ordered drinks and Simeon looked through the karaoke book. He looked up and noticed her smiling at him. He couldn't help but to smile back. He had a feeling that she was thinking the same thing he was thinking, which was that there was an attraction between them. The waitress brought their drinks. Simeon got up to put his song choice in the bowl. Cashmere took that opportunity to take a look at how nice he looked in the slacks he was wearing. She was quite pleased with what she saw. Walking back, Simeon noticed her looking at him. He couldn't help but smile because he knew she had been checking him out. He hoped that she liked what she saw. He sure as hell liked what he saw. She was his type of woman, tall and thick with plenty of curves to enjoy. Her smile was infectious. He hadn't seen a smile so radiant like that in a while. Sitting back down, she asked him "So what song are you going to sing?" "It is a surprise." "Okay, you better be good. Don't have me in here waiting for you to sing and find out you can't." "Oh, is that the only reason you are here?" Cashmere couldn't help but smile some more. "Well, I am also here for a drink too." "Oh, you got jokes." "I'm trying to tell ya." There have been some good singers up there so far. It seemed like the place was packed with people who could really blow. "The next singer coming to the stage is Simeon. Come on Simeon and show us what you got." The karaoke host said. Simeon got up and went to the stage. "Good evening everybody." The music started and the women seemed to pay quite a bit of attention to Simeon. He broke out with Kem's "Love Always Wins". Cashmere was amazed the brother could blow. It was like she was listening to Kem himself. His voice was more than nice. The women were staring at him and he was staring at Cashmere. It made her feel good that she had his attention, when all eyes were on him. His voice, his looks, his gestures towards her made something come alive in her. He had awakened her sweetness.

Twenty Six

After trying to get over the tragic events from earlier in the week, Stephanie knew that she needed to focus her efforts on making sure the grand opening of Rains was more than a success. She had hired all the staff for the evening.

Matthius and his men had finished all of the maintenance that needed to be done. She was expecting one more vendor delivery, and then everything would be completed. She was two days out and everything seemed fine. There was one thing that she remembered she hadn't taken care of yet. That was picking up her attire for the big night. She ordered it months ago. She got the call last week that it had arrived at the store. She had been meaning to get by there and pick it up, but with all the things that had happened as of late, it totally slipped her mind until now. She quickly picked up her keys and ran out to her car to go to Macy's on Midlothian Turnpike to pick up her dress. This dress was sure to be an eye catcher. It was gold with a sheer black lace overtop. The best part was that it came with matching shoes. That was the deal clincher for her. She already had all her accessories. She had bought them several months ago.

There was one piece that she had that was very special to her. Her grandmother's diamond necklace, which was left to her when she passed away a few years back. She had worn it a couple of times before, but this was the most special occasion that she would adorn it. Plus, if she wore it, it would feel like her grandmother was there with her. She would be nothing less than stunning on the night of her grand opening to say the least. When she arrived at Macy's she walked straight to the counter and after giving her name, she asked for her dress. The girl at the counter asked her to come with her. They walked together over to the manager's office. The cashier told her manager that Stephanie was there to pick up her dress. The manager looked at the cashier and said "Thank you, I will handle this." Then she gave the cashier a look that said ... you can leave now. The manager looked over in the corner of the office, where the dress was hanging. "Is there a problem?" Stephanie questioned. "Well, we received the dress, we noticed that the size was incorrect, so we sent it back. Then we received another dress today and unfortunately the size and the color are incorrect." "So, let me get this straight, you've received two dresses and neither of them are correct? I need my dress for an affair that I am attending in two days. How are you going to make this right?" "Well, we were hoping that you could pick out another dress, on the house of course." "I'm not sure you realize, but matching shoes were included with the dress. It took me two weeks to decide on the perfect dress. Is there any chance you can rush to ship the right dress?" "Ma'am, I can't guarantee that it will be here in time." "I would think you would be able to overnight it."

"We can definitely try." "Here is what you will do for me, since this is your error. You will ask them to overnight my dress and also I am going to pick out another dress, accessories and shoes, just in case you can't get my first choice here in time. I expect Macy's to make this right." "Yes ma'am, we will absorb the cost of the replacement dress, accessories and shoes, if your dress doesn't make it in time. We are very sorry for the inconvenience that we have caused you." Stephanie walked away very upset. This is just crazy. What else can go wrong today, she thought. The last time she thought of that question, someone held her father hostage. After getting back to the restaurant, she concentrated on positive thoughts, so that nothing negative would invade her life for the rest of the day. She took time to check and double check her "to do list" to make sure that she had everything covered for the big event. One thing she didn't need was some other form of debauchery in her life to have to worry about.

After all the bad that had happened, she desperately needed some greatness to intervene with the quickness. It was time for things to take a turn for the better! Clearly, they couldn't get any worse.

Twenty Seven

It was a day away from Stephanie's gala affair and Tammy still hadn't gotten her outfit together. She went to her walk-in closet to look for something fabulously stunning to wear to the opening. One thing Tammy loved was dressing nice; her closet was full of magnificent clothes that she had purchased. Everything that she needed to complete the perfect ensemble: gowns, purses, shoes, dresses, skirts, suits, necklaces, bracelets, earrings, hats, shirts, lingerie, panties and bras. She was going all out to show her girl that this was a spectacular event and that she was pleased to be there sharing it with her. She decided on a red satin spaghetti strap gown. She also pulled out her matching red satin high heels. She laid out her diamond tennis bracelet, along with her diamond earrings and necklace. She was sure that this ensemble would be a winner, especially since it made her girls look magnificent. She knew that Rico would just go crazy when he saw her in this outfit. That was mostly her intention. She wanted to look great, but she also wanted to make Rico yearn for her! Deep down she wanted more of what Rico gave her when they made love. She needed to feel his body against hers. Just thinking about him made her sweetness come alive. No man had ever made her sweetness sing like Rico did! She doubted that any man could handle her the way he did. He definitely knew what he was doing and she wanted him to do it again and again! She could almost feel the sensations that he had sent through her when he ravaged her. Her fibers tingled from just the thought of how great this man had made her feel. Clearly, she yearned for him as much as she wanted him to yearn for her. Rico had her mind, body and soul. The brother had handled his business, she was all about him! Speak of the devil ... There was a text from Rico.

Rico: Have you eaten?

Tammy: Not yet. Why?

Rico: I'm at Layla's. Come on over and I will buy you dinner.

Tammy: That's nice, but you don't have to do that baby.

Rico: I know I don't. I want to, plus it will give me a chance to see you.

Tammy: OK. Give me a minute to freshen up and I will be there.

Rico: Cool … I can't wait to see you. Tammy: Be there in about 30.

Rico: Great, I'll see you then.

Tammy began to get excited knowing that she would see him soon. If all went well, maybe he would come over after he was done at Layla's. She put on something that would entice him a little. She pulled out a snug fitting black skirt and a low cut gold blouse. She sprayed on some of her favorite perfume. She touched up the make-up and the hair. One last look in the mirror and she was ready to go get him!

When she walked in Rico was helping a customer, but she didn't go unnoticed. In fact, she saw him smile at her, while looking her up and down. As soon as he was done, he walked over to her and said "You look great, thanks for coming." "Thank you Rico." He noticed how lovely her attire was. She saw him gazing at her shirt. She smiled knowing that he approved of what he saw. "What would you like for dinner baby?" "I would love a huge helping of you." "I can definitely give you that." "I know you can." "What can I get you to eat from here?" "I am in the mood for a nice thick cut of steak. I think I will have the t-bone dinner." "Sounds good, I will get this ticket started for you." Please do. You've already gotten something else started." She watched Rico walk away, enjoying the view in front of her. All she could think was that she would have him all to herself before the night was done. Meanwhile, Rico walked away thinking that he would enjoy all of Tammy tonight. She looked great to him. It was hard for him to concentrate on anything other than her beauty. It was a good thing that he had an apron covering his rising manhood or else Tammy and everyone else would have seen just how excited she made him. Rico brought the t-bone dinner to Tammy with a glass of sweet tea. She smiled and said "Thank you." Rico, this looks great." In turn, Rico stated "Yes, it does." He smiled at Tammy and asked "May I escort you home tonight?" "That would be very nice. I would love that!" "I have to help close up, take your time and enjoy your dinner." Rico walked away, as a huge smile graced his face. He could feel Tammy looking at him. He knew she was probably smiling too, so he turned around to catch her looking. When she noticed, she burst into laughter. Rico had a way of making her feel great about things. She felt secure with him.

After closing up, they walked back to Tammy's. Approaching the door, under her porch light, Rico pulled her close to him and said "Tammy, I love you with all my heart!" Before she could respond, he placed his lips upon hers. Tammy placed her hands on his face and pulled him into her kiss even more. As their lips parted, Tammy looked deep into Rico's eyes and said "I love you too baby!" All they both could think about was being together. They both knew that this relationship would turn out to be much more than what it was now. Or, at least they hoped it would.

Twenty Eight

Stephanie arrived at Rains a couple of hours before the event was to begin. This was it, one of the biggest nights of her life was about to take place. Everything was in order; the staff was in place and putting the final touches on the preparation for tonight's grand opening. The guest would be arriving soon. She went to her office to finalize some last minute things. She noticed a package on her desk. Her first thought was not tonight, this can't be happening tonight. She reluctantly picked up the package and read the contents. "I know something you don't know. You may see me tonight, but you won't realize it. I could be standing next to you at any moment." Signed Guess Who. Great, this was all she needed, right now. She had hoped that since she hadn't received any packages in a while, that they had stopped coming. Now, she knew that this wasn't over. Not only was it not over, but her stalker was threatening to be at the opening tonight. Luckily, she had hired a security service just in case something went wrong. She would make sure that they were on alert for anything or anyone suspicious. She tried to push the letter to the back of her mind, which was hard. She was feeling very uncomfortable about all of this.

She knew she had to regain her focus and concentrate on getting through this evening. She made a promise to herself that if she got through this night without a hitch; she would get the police involved tomorrow morning. With that promise, she put the letter back in the package and slid it in her desk drawer. She looked up and Matthias was standing in the doorway. "Is everything okay Stephanie?" "Yes Matthias … Why do you ask?" "It's just that you look like you have seen a ghost." "I am fine, Matthias, thanks for asking though." "Okay, you're welcome. Just a final note, everything is all set and ready to go for tonight. I wish you the best of luck too!" Matthias walked away and Stephanie looked up at him with this quizzical look on her face. She thought back to the last time the note appeared, he was around then too. Could this be coincidental? Was she just thinking too much about this? Matthias seemed like a nice enough guy, maybe paranoia was starting to set in.

Security arrived and Stephanie briefed them on the situation. She told them to be very alert and keep a close eye on her at all times. She also let them know that she would try to stay close to one of them at all times, but if she got distracted to make sure that someone was close to her. The last thing she needed was to have some nutcase in the same room with her to cause her harm. The media had started to show up along with some of the guests. They were all outside waiting on the red carpet underneath the bright lights. The doors would open in twenty minutes, and then Richmond would get a chance to see Rains in all its elegance and grace. Stephanie took that time to walk around and make sure that everyone was in place and everything was set. She went into the office and said a quick prayer. She returned to the front of the restaurant. Looked at the hostess, security, servers and said "The moment has come. Unlock the doors and open Rains!" The staff began to clap; one of the security officers walked over to the doors and unlocked them. Before the first guest could walk in, the entire staff shouted "Welcome to Rains!" The guest started filing in two at a time. The hostess welcomed everyone and directed them to their tables, where their name cards were placed. The place seemed to fill up rather quickly. People were chatting with one another, the waiters and waitresses were taking orders. There were even some people at the bar already, ordering drinks to get the night started. Cameras were flashing all over the place. Then it happened. Stephanie opened the kitchen door, walked out to the dining area and the guest stood up, clapping erupted all throughout the room. People were cheering and yelling her name. Video cameras swung in her direction, microphones were shoved in her face. She felt on top of the world. She felt as if her life was meant for this particular moment. The smile on her face couldn't get any bigger. She looked around the room and saw all of her favorite people in place. Her parents were there, Char, Cashmere, Tammy and Rico. There were friends that she hadn't seen in years that had come out to celebrate with her. She walked around thanking everyone and mingling to make sure that everything was more than acceptable. She took extra time at her parents and friends table because they knew of her struggle to get to this point. They had journeyed with her, so this was their evening as well as hers. She looked around the room and everybody seemed to be really enjoying themselves. They were eating, drinking and chatting among themselves. The night had turned out to be a success, nothing crazy had happened either.

Nothing could be better in her life than this moment! Everything that she had worked for, everything that she had dreamed about for the longest time was coming into fruition. She looked around at all the happy faces. She looked around at the interior of Rains. She looked around at all the good times that were being had and couldn't help but to feel good. She felt that she had done the right thing in opening this restaurant. She finally felt that she had found her purpose in life.

As the last guest left the restaurant, she smiled and said "Thank you and please come again!" as she had said to every guest as they exited. Security closed and locked the doors, she turned to the staff and said "Thank you all for your help and for making this an unbelievable event! Matthias, please bring out the case of champagne. This is for all of your efforts. This is for you! Please drink up and enjoy. Tomorrow, we will do it all over again. Thank you again … thank you, thank you, thank you. I could never have done any of this without any of you!" Champagne glasses clinked, they all began to enjoy the fact that the hard part was now over. The grand opening was clearly a success.

Richmond had embraced Rains!!!!! All they had to do was clean up tonight and do it all over again tomorrow.

Twenty Nine

Cashmere woke up the morning after Stephanie's grand opening. It was a great evening. She had a wonderful time. But, her mind was consumed by thoughts of Simeon. She had wished that he could have been there with her, but he was back in New York. They had a great time at Croaker Spot; she enjoyed his conversation and his singing so much that they exchanged numbers. Simeon had promised to keep in touch. It had been a few days since they had met, so she wasn't tripping when she hadn't heard from him. She knew that he was busy with his music. She also knew deep down that she would hear from him sooner or later. Simeon didn't know it, but he had captured a piece of her. She went in the kitchen to get a cup of coffee to help start her day. She wondered what the day had in store for her. She figured she would talk to Stephanie sometime today to let her know what she thought about the opening. She thought about possibly going to The Crib tonight as well. Maybe her girls would want to roll out with her. One thing is for certain, she needed to stop by and check on Ingrid today. Something just didn't seem right about her lately.

Ever since she had started talking about that "D" character, she seemed somewhat different. Something just didn't sit right with Cashmere about the whole situation. Although their relationship wasn't the greatest, she felt like she knew her sister well enough to know when something wasn't right with her, even if Ingrid didn't realize it for herself. After finishing her coffee, she decided to pick out something to wear for the day. She showered, put on her clothes, and checked her phone to see who might have called or messaged her. She had gotten a call from Uncle Herbert, the message was about her coming in to cover for him because he had an appointment that was emergent. She called him back to let him know that she would be there as soon as she could. This actually worked out in her favor; it was about time for her to move some more money over to her account. She could do it while he was there, but she didn't want to take that chance. It was easier for her to do it when he was not at the store. She got there about twenty minutes later. "Hi Uncle Herbert, how are you?" "Hey baby, I am fine and you?" "I am fine, thanks for coming so quickly." No problem." "I shouldn't be too long, maybe an hour or so." "Okay, I'll be fine. I have some paperwork to catch up on anyway." That's great, thanks again. See you in a little while." "Bye, you're welcome Uncle Herbert." When Uncle Herbert left, a couple of customers came in and browsed around. She helped them to see if they were interested in a specific clock. Her uncle sold clocks from all over the world. Some of them were very rare. All of them came with a hefty price tag. That's why his store did so well. If he sold one or two clocks a week, the profits were outstanding. Most of the store's money was made on the special orders that they received. They browsed a little longer and decided to place two orders for two Russian clocks. Cashmere took their information, ran their credit cards for the payment. She told them that their shipment should arrive in six to eight weeks. If by chance the shipment didn't arrive in that time, they needed to contact the store and they would check on the purchases for them. She was glad when they left; they spent nearly forty five minutes in the store. Cashmere knew her uncle would be returning soon. She still had to make the transfer. She looked around to make sure that she was the only one left in the store. After making sure, she went to the office, pulled up the stores account, typed in her account number, and input the amount to transfer. The whole transaction took a matter of minutes. When she looked up she saw her uncle coming back into the store. She hurriedly closed out of the bank accounts, clicked on the inventory screen to input the information on the clocks that she had just sold. When he entered the office, he asked "How did things go while I was away?" "They were great, I sold two Russian clocks." "Great, thanks for looking after the store for me." "You're welcome. How did your appointment go Uncle Herbert?" "The appointment … it went well, thanks." "What was the appointment concerning?" "Well, I am considering opening up two more stores, one in New York and the other in Los Angeles. I figured this store is doing so well, that it is time to expand.

I want to capture the New York and Los Angeles markets as well." "That's great. How soon are you looking to expand?" "I will have the New York store open in three to four months. The West coast store will be open in four to six months." "That's great Uncle Herbert. Those two new stores will take us to a better profit margin." "Well, we will be flying over budget for about six months, but I believe after the sixth month we should break even. I anticipate the profits to start hitting by the eighth or ninth month." "Do you already have employees for the stores?" "I have employees for the New York store; I've already signed a year's lease for the building. We will start to set up the store shortly. I have to fly out to L.A. in a couple weeks to scout some stores to see where I want it to be. So far I am looking at West Hollywood, Bel Air and Malibu." "Where is the store in New York?" "It's in Manhattan. We already have everything in place.

We are just waiting on the opening day." "Uncle Herbert, how come this is the first time I am hearing about any of this?" "Well Cashmere, I wasn't sure if I could pull it off, so I didn't want to mention it until I was certain that it would be a go." "Okay, well it just seems like you would have told me about it during the consideration process. I'm happy for you though." "Have you given any more thought to your future?" "What do you mean?" "Well, I know you don't want to work for me forever, do you? I figured you would want to make use of that Cornell degree." "Well, it's funny that you mentioned that. I was just thinking the other day about my future. I do have plans for my future." "Do they include working with me?" "Well, yes, until I land my dream job." "That's great because I may need you to do some traveling in the near future." "Traveling?" "Yes, I will need you to go to check on the other stores from time to time. I just need you to make sure that things are being done right. I don't trust anybody as much as I trust you Cashmere." "Uncle Herbert, thank you so much!" After talking with her uncle, Cashmere left the store and headed home. She couldn't help but to feel bad about what she had been doing to him. She really didn't have a choice though or so she thought. She was tired of living the poor life, she wanted her riches and she wanted them now. The openings of the two new stores would surely put some more money in her bank account, but it would take months for that to happen. She figured she had enough to walk away now, but she didn't want to cause suspicion, nor did she want to miss out on the money that would come her way, when the stores opened. Her plan had been working well so far and now Uncle Herbert was playing right into her hands. It couldn't get any better than this. When Cashmere got home, she poured a tall glass of Moscato, dropped a strawberry in it and added some orange juice. She sat on the couch, turned on the stereo and listened to the radio. All she needed now was a chance to let the Moscato ease her nerves, so that she could try and feel better about the deceit that she had caused in her and her uncle's life. The sad part was that she knew that she had gone too far to turn back now. Although she knew she was wrong, her desire for a better life wouldn't let her stop.

Thirty

Tammy woke up in Rico's arms the next morning with a smile on her face. Because the night before she had seen her girl Stephanie at the highest point of her life so far. She had her man on her arm to celebrate the evening with her. It was a great night for all. Rico made it an even better night, when they got to her place. He made earth shattering love to her, taking her body to places that she had only dreamed about. He made her sweetness sing her song over and over again. She felt him stir a little, easing her backside against him; she felt his manhood take that familiar form that she craved again. Rico cupped her breasts as he inhaled the sweet scent flowing from her hair. He placed soft kisses alongside her neck. Tammy enjoyed the sensation of the kisses, she felt his breath close to her neck with every kiss. She wanted to feel him inside her again. She eased him down so that his back was against the sheets. She began planting soft sensual kisses along his muscular chest. She licked his nipples and eased her lips further down until she was face to face with his manhood.

She looked up at Rico, parted her lips and took his hugeness in her mouth. She enjoyed the way he felt between her lips. Her desire was to please him so that he would share his gift with her. Positioning herself above his manhood, she lowered her sweetness so that it would kiss and welcome his manhood again. As he slid inside her, she began to moan from the filling of his manhood. His manhood consumed her entirely. He filled her to the point of satiation. He took her body far beyond ecstasy with every magnificently precise stroke. He reached up and caressed her sweet breasts. His touch sent electrical sensations throughout her body. She began to moan heavily, her body began to writhe as did his. Her urges began to increase, increasing to a point of an uncontrollable force. She tried to mask it to enjoy his penetration longer. He also tried to hold out to enjoy her sweetness as long as he could. The feeling was too great for either of them to withstand any longer. In unison, they brought one another to the height of their lovemaking by singing each other's songs for one another. Tammy fell to Rico's chest; he embraced her and held her very closely. Her body felt good against his flesh. His body seemed to come alive from her touch. They had embarked on something even more special than they themselves knew. They both looked into one another's eyes and felt their special connection take on a deeper meaning, dive to a deeper depth. "Good morning Rico." spoken softly by Tammy. "Good morning baby. You feel so good to me. I love making love to you. " "I love the way you make love to me, baby. I love the way you love me for me."

They both got up, Rico took a shower, while Tammy went to put a pot of coffee on for them to enjoy. When Rico was done showering, Tammy took her shower, Rico eased back into the bathroom unnoticed. Pulled the shower curtain back, got in the shower with her. After pulling the shower curtain closed, he got down on his knees, positioned her right leg over his shoulder and tasted her sweetness. The water cascaded down her body onto him. The wetness of the water, the steaminess from the heat made it even more intense for Tammy. Her sweetness was gearing up for an encore performance. She placed her hand on the back of his head to push him closer to her sweetness. Rico's tongue went deeper into her sweetness, driving her more and more close to performing her sweet song for him again. She couldn't hold out any longer, his tongue was driving her mad with ecstasy. Her song began to sing, it sang loudly and harmoniously. Rico rose from his knees, kissed Tammy and they showered together, caressing and kissing one another until they were done.

They finally got to their coffee, which was much needed after the night they had, as well as the action packed lovemaking session that had just taken place. With every step Tammy's sweetness reminded her of just how much lovemaking they made. Her sweetness was throbbing from all the pleasure that Rico had bestowed upon her. Her sweetness had an ache that she hadn't experienced before. It was an ache that she wanted to experience much more often.

They enjoyed their coffee, had some breakfast, and then they parted ways for the day. Rico needed to stop by The Crib for a meeting and Tammy wanted to go by Rains and have some lunch with her girl Stephanie. She figured she would call Char and Cashmere too. They all could meet for lunch, chat about the opening, then go from there. She sent her girls a text, asking them to meet her at Rains around one.

Meanwhile Rico drove over to The Crib, thinking about Tammy the entire way. He loved the way she smelled when he got close to her. He loved the kisses from her soft lips. The way she smiled when they were together. Her style, the way she carried herself. She possessed every quality in a woman that he desired. His desire for her was grander than it had ever been for any woman before her. She made him feel like a man. She made him feel like he could accomplish anything in life. She was what he had been missing in his life for a very long time. In short, it was at this point that he realized that she completed him.

Tammy pulled up to Rains a little before one. She was the first of the girls that had made it. Stephanie was in her office, going over some research paperwork for entertainment. She wanted to add something special to the weekend business. She thought it would be great to have some singers on Friday and Saturdays, and some spoken word or even some jazz on Sundays.

Thirty One

Cashmere and Char both pulled up at the same time. They joined Tammy and Stephanie at a table in the back by the kitchen. Stephanie told them about her idea to have some entertainment on the weekends. They all thought it was a wonderful idea. The only issue was that Stephanie was not very familiar with the entertainment scene in Richmond. She didn't have a clue as to what acts would be best for her place. Tammy told them that she could ask Rico since he and R.J. had acts appearing at their club almost every night. This was going to be exciting for Rains. There was a crowd of people starting to gather by the bar area. Stephanie looked up and just smiled because she knew that people were embracing Rains. She had hoped that it would become a staple in the Richmond area. Others were coming in the door, being seated at tables. The serving staff was starting to get busy taking orders and serving meals. Drinks were starting to fly out of the bar area. Chatter and laughter was starting to be heard throughout the establishment. Char looked over at Stephanie and congratulated her for following her heart and making her dream come true. It would seem that three out of the four girls had accomplished what they set out to accomplish. One was still treading water trying to turn her dreams in to a reality. Char was telling the girls about her most recent photo shoot in Spain. It was shot along the beautiful beaches of Madrid. Cashmere was telling the girls about her uncle's plans to expand the business. Tammy told the girls that Rico was easily becoming everything that she wanted in a man. He was saying and doing all the right things to penetrate her heart. He had already been occupying her mind all day, every day for the better part of a month or so. It was plain to see that she was more than serious about Rico. Yet, it seemed almost as if she was still being very cautious of their relationship. As if, she wasn't exactly sure how he felt. Although, he hadn't given her any reason to think that he wasn't just as serious as she was. They had told one another that they loved each other a couple of times, made love several times, and yet she still was a little leery of totally letting her guard down. The more she and the girls talked the more she started to realize that it wasn't really about Rico. It was more so about her. It was about the past relationships that had betrayed her heart when she let her guard down. It was about the men before Rico that loved her body, but not her mind. It was about every indiscretion any man before Rico had committed against her. That was the factor that was keeping her from embracing Rico's love totally. Her mind was far too focused on her love of the past to maintain her heart in the present. She knew that she had to conquer her past to enjoy her future with Rico. Just how was she supposed to do that though? How could she begin to start this manifestation? She reached out to her girls for an answer. They all tossed out ideas, hoping to find a perfect solution. The one thing that was agreed upon was that Tammy had to talk to Rico and tell him just how she felt. Maybe if she was honest with him, he would be able to understand and help her through this. Cashmere started to talk about Simeon and how they met at Croaker Spot. She told them how well he could sing and just how good he looked in a pair of slacks. Of course the girls wanted to know when they were going to meet him. She had to tell them that he didn't live in Richmond, so she wasn't really sure when she would see him, much less when they would meet him. All she knew was that she really wanted to see him again. Stephanie just kind of glanced at Cashmere with a quizzical look on her face. Cashmere noticed the look, but didn't question it, because she knew what the look was all about. It meant that she and Stephanie had to have a conversation about that kiss that they shared.

Cashmere had pretty much dismissed it, thinking that it was just something that happened, but it appeared that Stephanie was still thinking about it.

Maybe she felt that there was more to it than just a moment between them. Either way, they had to straighten it out before it got out of hand. She knew that if she didn't talk to her soon, this would get out of hand and the other girls would get involved. This wasn't something Cashmere wanted to discuss over lunch with the other girls. She also knew that Stephanie had a way of being very outspoken when she wanted to be. She didn't want to have to put her in her place. Stephanie thought she was tough, but Cashmere knew she was tough! She didn't want to have to deal with Stephanie like that, that's why she wanted to handle it one on one with her. Cashmere excused herself from the table and went to the bathroom to check her makeup. She was hoping that Stephanie wouldn't follow her there. After walking in she looked in the mirror, added more lipstick, and sprayed on a little more perfume. On her way back out, the door swung open and Stephanie was walking in. "Cashmere, what's going on girl? How are you these days? Kiss any other females lately?" "Look Stephanie … what happened between us was." "Was what Cashmere? What happened between us was what?" "It was just something that happened, that was it." "Oh, so you just go around kissing your friends, like it's nothing?" "Look Stephanie, don't blow this out of proportion. It was just something that happened. Let's leave it at that, okay?" "Sure Cashmere, I'll just forget that our lips touched intentionally. I'll just act like nothing happened, for your sake." "Great, that would be wise for both of us." With that Cashmere shot her a stern look which said "Don't mess with me!", then walked past her and headed back to the table to rejoin Tammy and Char. Stephanie went to her office to take a phone call, the others continued to enjoy their lunch. When Stephanie rejoined them, her attitude was in check and she was ready to deal with Cashmere again. Luckily, Char or Tammy didn't realize what was going on between them. Things were back to normal for the girls. For now...

Thirty Two

After wrapping up the luncheon with the girls, Stephanie went to make sure that all her customers had everything they needed. She made sure she thanked them for choosing to eat at Rains. After that, she made her way to the kitchen to ensure that all was well. It had become part of her daily routine. She enjoyed talking with the staff. They always had something interesting or entertaining to say. Not to mention that they all seemed to love their jobs. That made Stephanie very happy, since she single handedly hired each one of them. She went to her office to catch up on some paperwork, before she could even sit down, her phone started vibrating. She looked down and it was her mother texting.

Tiffanie... Hello, how is your day going?

Stephanie... Going okay, thanks. I had lunch with the girls a little bit ago. Just started going over some paperwork now. How are you?

Tiffanie... I'm fine, thanks baby. Your dad and I were thinking about going out of town in a couple of days.

Stephanie... Oh, where are you going?

Tiffanie ... We're thinking about driving down to Florida to visit your uncle.

Stephanie... Why are you driving? Wouldn't you rather fly?

Tiffanie... Your father and I want to spend some much needed quality time together. So, we are going to take our time and drive down.

Stephanie... Mom, is everything okay?

Tiffanie... Yes baby, everything is fine. We just want to enjoy each other, while we still can.

Stephanie... How long are you going to be gone?

Tiffanie... We're thinking about 2 weeks. Can you check on the house for us, please?

Stephanie... Of course I can do that mom. I'll stop by after work today, so we can catch up.

Tiffanie... Great, thanks baby. We'll see you later tonight.

Stephanie... You're welcome mom. See you later!

After texting her mom, Stephanie couldn't help but wonder if her parents were okay. It worried her that they wanted to drive to Florida. It had only been a couple of weeks ago that her father had been held hostage in the bank. It worried her that they would be on the road all alone. The hostage scare was still too new for her to get over. She had been trying to move forward and she thought she had, until she heard about this road trip. That brought it all back. Now she would have to worry about them making it to and from Florida safely. She had hoped to be able to talk them into flying, instead of driving. That was the reason why she mentioned stopping by tonight. She needed to get a feel for how they were really doing. She needed to make sure that they were okay. She knew that the hostage situation was still on their mind, because it was still on hers. She was sure that it was still on everyone's mind, everybody was just being really quiet about it. Hoping to make it a bad memory. No one wanted to keep bringing it to the light, they were hoping that it would just go away and their lives could get back to being normal. The one certainty about their lives was that they would never be normal again. This one horrific event has changed all of their lives so much that it would take them a long time just to be able to deal with it. Stephanie couldn't help it but tears started welling up in her eyes. Those tears strolled down her face like millions of raindrops falling from the sky. As much as she tried to hold them back, they just seemed to keep coming. She thought that she had cried them all out, when she saw her dad again.

And then as if she needed it at this precise moment, Matthius showed up at the door. She quickly tried to wipe away the tears before he noticed.

Unfortunately, that didn't happen. He not only noticed the tears, but he asked "Are you okay Stephanie? Do you need anything?" She struggled to get herself back together as quickly as she could before she answered him. "I'm doing okay Matthius, thank you for asking." "Are you sure Stephanie? If you need anything, I would be more than happy to help." Stephanie tried to hold back, but before she knew it she screamed at Matthius "*I AM FINE! I SAID I WAS FINE THE FIRST TIME YOU ASKED ME! DON'T ASK ME AGAIN!*" Matthius just stared at Stephanie in complete shock. He couldn't believe that she had yelled at him like that. He turned to walk away and heard "Matthius, please come back. I truly am sorry for snapping at you like I did. I'm not fine. To tell you the truth, I have a lot on my mind and things just came to a head when you asked how I was." Matthius walked over to Stephanie, put his hand on her shoulder and said "Don't worry about it. I know you didn't mean it. I was just concerned and wanted to help, that's all." "I do appreciate you Matthius, thanks." She stood up and gave Matthius a hug. He hugged her back and said "If you ever need me, just let me know. I will be there for you!" "I truly appreciate that Matthius, thank you so much." She slowly pulled away, while he paused to look deeply into her eyes before he let her go. "Try and have a nice day, Stephanie. I will see you later on." "Okay, thanks. You too, Matthius." She watched him walk away and wondered if she had opened the door to something unintended. Matthius had looked in her eyes with a look that she hadn't seen from him before. It was a look of desire. Up until this point, their relationship had been strictly professional. Now she was beginning to think that it wasn't strictly professional from his point of view. Could he have been flirting all this time and she hadn't realized it? Was she oblivious to his attention to her, all this time? One thing is for certain she was more than aware of it now. She wasn't sure how she would react to him when she saw him again. She only had two choices; one was to talk to him about what happened between them. The second was she could just let it go and hope that she was wrong about the whole thing. Deep down she knew that she wasn't wrong about any of it. She felt the hug he gave her and saw the look in his eyes when he looked at her.

She gathered some papers, her phone, and her purse and decided to take a ride to Pocahontas State Park in Chesterfield, just to gather her thoughts about her day. She also wanted to review the paperwork to verify that she had everything covered. She loved going to the park, just to chill and spend some time with herself. It was the one place that she could just let her thoughts flow uninterrupted. Unfortunately, she had so much on her mind these days. There were some good things and some bad things. Either way though she knew that she had some stuff to figure out and adjustments had to be made in her life to accommodate some of them. Hopefully Matthius wouldn't be one of them. She didn't need any additional issues to deal with right now. Her life was full of enough issues for the time being. Luckily, she had some goodness come her way as well. She decided to head to her parent's house to talk with them. Her mind was feeling freer, she didn't have the frustrations that she had when she first left the restaurant. She felt like she could deal with her parents now and not break down in front of them like she did in front of Matthius. The ride to her parents was very relaxing. She had time to process her thoughts on what she wanted to say to them. She even thought about their replies and came up with responses to them as well. She knew that she had to be very prepared to have this conversation with them.

Thirty Three

On her way back to the crib, Cashmere thought about what had happened between her and Stephanie at Rains. She knew that this wouldn't be the end of it. Stephanie would make sure she brought it up again. Hopefully, it wouldn't be around the others though. She didn't want to have to answer any questions about why it happened to Tammy and Char. As far as Cashmere felt, it was just something that happened, they both got caught up in the moment, or so she thought. It wasn't as if either of them had a thing for women. It was truly unexplainable. Maybe Stephanie was jealous because she didn't really have anybody in her life romantically. Then Cashmere thought, neither do I really.

She had met Simeon, but nothing had really transpired between them since. She had hoped that he would contact her, but he hadn't yet. She wanted him to contact her though. She wanted to see him again. She wanted to hear his voice again. He left an impression on her that was hard to forget. She wanted a man in her life; she wanted to know if he was the one for her. His conversation was smooth, his game was on point. The brother looked nice too. And he could blow! Her imagination had run wild, many a nights on what it would be like to have him all to herself. Maybe he would sing her name when they... She pulled up in her driveway, went into the house, and poured herself a glass of Moscato. It had been a couple of weeks since she met Simeon. She decided that waiting was overrated now. She pulled out her phone, clicked on his name, the phone started dialing.

"Hello."

"Hello, may I speak to Simeon, please." "This is he."

"How are you Simeon, this is Cashmere."

"Cashmere, I am fine and you?"

"I am well, thanks."

"That's good to know. It is funny that you called, I was just thinking about you."

"Really? You were thinking about me?"

"No doubt."

"Well, if you were thinking about me, why haven't you called?"

"My bad ... I was meaning to call. I just had so much going on, I hadn't had a chance."

"Wow ... really? You haven't had a chance to call a sister, send a text or anything? Maybe I haven't really been on your mind then."

"Seriously, I was just talking about you to my engineer." "Your engineer?"

"Yeah, I'm in the studio right now. That's what I've been doing since I got back to New York."

"Well, don't let me disturb you. I just wanted you to know that I enjoyed meeting you and it would be nice to chat again sometime soon."

"No doubt, I feel the same way. I should be back in Richmond at the end of the month. I can also give you a call tomorrow, if you want."

"Yeah, tomorrow would be fine. I'll talk to you then."

"Okay, stay sweet Cashmere."

"Sweeter than you know baby, sweeter than you know."

"Very nice, I will call you tomorrow"

"Bye Simeon."

"Bye Sweet Cashmere."

She hung up the phone and a big smile spread across her face. She now knew that he was feeling her too. She could stop wondering. And the brother was coming to Richmond at the end of the month. She had to get her stuff together, things had to be right. She wanted to make sure that he had the time of his life with her. When she was done with him, he wouldn't be able to stop thinking about her. He would have to call several times a day to get his fill of her. Her imagination took her places that she wished they could explore together. Now she knew that it was more than a possibility. She knew she would get to enjoy Simeon and he would definitely get to enjoy her.

There was a knock at the door. When Cashmere opened it, she saw Ingrid standing on the other side of it. "Hey girl, come on in." "Hey sis, how are you these days?" "I am good, thanks." "How are things with you?" "Things are well, thanks." "What are you doing here?" "I just thought I would stop by and spend some time with my big sis." "Okay, I hear that. I appreciate you thinking of me." "Of course, you're my big sister." "So, what do you want to do?" "I was thinking maybe we could go hang out a little. Maybe go to a movie or something." "A movie would be cool. I could do a movie." "Great, let's roll out and decide what movie we want to see when we get there." "Girl, we have smartphones, we can decide now or on the way." "That's fine, we can do that too." "I'm down for something funny." "Funny would be wonderful." Cashmere pulled up Fandango on her phone and checked to see what comedies were showing." Once they decided, they got in the car and drove to Cinebistro at Stony Point for the three forty five showing. After getting there they got popcorn with lots of butter, a classic mojito and watermelon mojito. They settled in their seats and awaited the movie to start. By the time the movie started Ingrid was starting to feel the effects of her classic mojito. Cashmere looked over at Ingrid and noticed that she didn't look like herself. She looked like she had something on her mind.

Rather than ask her about it at the movies, she decided to just enjoy the movie and ask her about it at a later date. Plus she knew that Ingrid wouldn't admit to anything bothering her. She just wanted to enjoy spending time with her sister. Hopefully the movie will be good too.

Thirty Four

On the way home, Tammy thought about stopping by The Crib to surprise Rico. But she didn't want him to think that she was stalking him or anything like that, so she decided to drive down to Petersburg since she hadn't been there in a while. She drove past Club Char Les-Manze on Melville Street, continued past Petersburg High School on Johnson Rd. Then she ended up rolling down Crater Road towards Blandford. She decided to drive past Virginia State University because it had been a while since she had been over that way. After crossing the bridge and driving up the hill by VSU, she decided to take the back way home because she loved driving through Ettrick, Matoaca and Chester with those winding roads and beautiful homes tucked away in the woods. Driving through Sandy Ford Rd., and Bradley Bridge Rd., were her favorite stretches of road to travel. She had her sunroof open, jazz pumping out the speakers as she just cruised those roads enjoying the smell of fresh air and taking in the beautiful sights along the way.

Once home she changed into some shorts and a t-shirt for comfort. She grabbed an orange, peeled it and turned on the television to chill with a good movie for a little while. It had been some time since she just sat and enjoyed some solitude. So she was taking advantage of the opportunity while she had a chance. She had forgotten how good it felt just to be alone. She had spent so much time with Rico and her girls that she hadn't had any time just for herself.

She hadn't had any time to just think or evaluate her situation with him. She enjoyed spending time with him; she enjoyed the attention he supplied her with as well. The love making was in a class all its own. She tried to think if there was anything that he had done to give her reason to wonder. There wasn't anything that crossed her mind. He had been more than perfect to her. He made her feel very special. He made her feel truly desired. That was a feeling that she wasn't use to anymore. She welcomed that feeling again! She thought that she would never feel like this again about a man. Rico had changed all that for her. He had made her see the beauty of falling in love again. Her realization of this brought a big beautiful smile to her face. She felt honored to have his attention, his love and his adoration. She would hold it close to her heart for as long as he would let her. Her heart felt good again. It felt full of love as well. She wanted to shower him with all this love. She wondered if he could handle all this love she had to give him. Could he handle all this love that had been building up in her for years with no one to give it to? Could her heart withstand another failed relationship? Was she just assuming that this relationship would end like the others? Rico had been perfect up to this point. Maybe she was just thinking way too much now. Her mind was feeding her scenarios that had yet to happen with him. She had to turn her thoughts off, if she didn't she would become paranoid and mess things up between her and Rico. This was part of the problems with her past relationships. Her heart had been all but destroyed before, she sabotaged the rest of her relationships because she was constantly paranoid that all her other boyfriend's would break her heart too. She began to follow them around, show up at their places all times of the night. Her behavior just always seemed to get out of hand and they would end up leaving her because of her paranoia. She hoped that she could control it this time. Rico had proven that he deserved that much at least. She knew that she had to maintain control, so that Rico wouldn't walk away, like the others did. Tammy realized she was over thinking the whole thing and decided to just let their relationship grow and run its course naturally. Everything would be okay as long as she could keep from being paranoid. Clearly Rico was the best thing that had happened to her in a very long time. She wanted him to know just how much he means to her. Ever since he entered her life, she was much happier. It's because of him that her heart now smiles again.

Speak of the devil; Rico was calling Tammy to see if she wanted to get together tonight. Although she really wanted to see him, she declined because she thought it might be best if she was alone tonight, especially since she had been thinking emotionally about their relationship for the better part of the day. She didn't want to come off as being unpleasant to him. So, she told him that she was going to rest for the night and they could probably get together tomorrow. As soon as she got off the phone with him, she felt wrong for not seeing him tonight. At the same time, she knew it was for the best. She was sure that he had sensed something wasn't right with her, what's more is, she was thankful that he didn't ask about it. She didn't have a clue as to how she would try to explain it to him. Not for fear that he wouldn't understand, but because he would wonder why she was worried about it now, when it could be dealt with, when it happens, if it happens. Then she started to wonder why he didn't ask about it? Did he care? Did he know her well enough to tell when things weren't right with her? This took her to a whole new series of thoughts. Her head was bursting with thought's, her body was overwhelmed with emotions. She decided to just have a glass of Moscato and stop thinking about Rico and relationships for the night.

Thirty Five

Stephanie arrived at her parent's house ready to enjoy a pleasant evening with some much needed conversation. Stephen and Tiffanie were in the kitchen making dinner and listening to the Isley Brothers, when she came in. "Mom, Dad, I'm here." "We're in the kitchen dear." replied her dad. Stephanie walked in the kitchen and just started smiling, because it had been sometime since she had seen them in the kitchen together. It was because of them cooking together that she learned to love cooking. She wanted to help, but she didn't want to interrupt the good time that they were having together. Besides this was something that they needed in their relationship, especially right now.

Stephanie sat down at the island, poured herself a glass of sweet tea from the pitcher that was in front of her. She always enjoyed her mother's sweet tea. It was simply the best sweet tea ever, even better than her own. Growing up she had always loved her mother's sweet tea. Every time she had it, it took her back to her childhood and the great times that she had growing up. She looked up and her parents were slow dancing and smiling. They were feeling the groove of the Isley Brothers flowing through their speakers. Stephanie got up and went to attend to the food, so that it wouldn't burn while her parents were cutting a rug. When her parents stopped dancing, she gave them a great big hug. They hugged her back; her mother asked "What was that for baby?" "Because things seem to be getting back to normal between you two, what's more is, y'all seem to be more in love than you were before everything happened. It just feels so good to see the two of you happy again!" "Baby, we have always been happy. I will admit that the bank thing scared the hell out of both of us.

We didn't know if we would see one another again. The whole thing made us rekindle our love for one another. We have a deeper kind of love now. And we decided to live every day to the fullest." stated her dad. "Is that why you guys are taking a road trip to Florida?" "Yeah baby, we want to spend some good quality time together. It's nothing like being on the open road with the one you love!" "Dad, you are such a romantic. Honestly, I can think of plenty of things that would be more romantic, than a road trip." "See baby, that's where you are misunderstanding the whole thing. It's not really about being romantic; it's more about spending uninterrupted quality time with your mom. We are going to take our time driving to Miami. We are going to enjoy ourselves and not have a care in the world. If we want to stop along the way and see the sights, then that is what we are going to do." "I see daddy, so this is more of a therapeutic vacation?" "If that's what you want to call it baby, so be it. To us, it is more of a much needed vacation, along with an opportunity to see your uncle." "Okay daddy, I understand. Will you please call me every day so that I know the two of you are okay?" Before her parents could answer Stephanie gave them both a look ... "Yes, baby, we will contact you once a day, so that you won't worry." her mother said. "Thanks mom. When are you guys leaving?" "We are leaving in a couple of days." replied her dad. "Okay, please call me when you get on the road." Baby, I know you are worried about us, but we will be fine. We will call you, but to be honest Stephanie, we are not going to spend a lot of time on the phones during this trip. We just want to spend time together and have some fun. I hope you can understand that. "Yes daddy, I understand. I still want to hear from you though." "Young lady, please do not forget who the parents are in this scenario." "I know daddy, I just want to make sure that the two of you are okay. You know you would ask the same of me." "She does have you there Stephen. Baby, I will call you in the mornings before we hit the road. Is that okay with you?" "Yes mom thanks. I appreciate it." Stephen just shook his head because he couldn't believe his ears. He understood and appreciated his daughter's concern though. He knew that she really was coming from the heart. Deep down, he knew she was right, he would expect the same thing. He couldn't help but to think that they had raised her well. Although he was playing the tough role, his little girl got close to his heart with that one. She is his pride and joy. The bottom line is he would do anything for her. She knew it too; Stephanie also knew how to work her daddy very well. It was her father who fronted the money for the restaurant, her house and her car. She agreed to pay him back everything when Rains was very profitable. He didn't have a problem with fronting the money for any of it because he knew she was a savvy business person and an excellent cook. He considered it an investment in his child's future happiness. As did she, although she had every intention of paying them back!

Thirty Six

Uncle Herbert announced that the New York store had opened last week. He told Cashmere that he needed her to go to the store in a couple of days to make sure that everything was exactly as they should be. This was just the opportunity she needed to get to know Simeon a lot better. She could see what he was really about. She wondered if she should let him know that she would be in New York in a couple of days or just contact him when she got there. If she contacted him when she got there, would he be happy to see her? Or would she find out that he had someone else? Either way, she was on her way to the Big Apple for a week. Although it was a work trip, she would make sure she found a chance to have a great time, especially if she was with Simeon.

After getting off the plane in New York, Cashmere took a cab to the Hilton Garden Inn Manhattan, where Uncle Herbert had booked her room. When she checked in and took the elevator to her floor, she was surprised by the bottle of champagne, which was waiting for her. Her first thought was that Uncle Herbert was pulling out all of the stops for this trip. She picked up the phone to call her uncle to let him know that she had arrived and to thank him for the champagne. Suddenly there was a knock at the door. She peeked through the peep hole and saw the most beautiful sight ever. She opened the door to see Simeon standing in the hallway. "Simeon, how did you know I was here? I'm sorry ... come in." "Well, to be honest, my sister works at the front desk and she saw your registration. She told me that you would be checking in tonight." "Wait, so you told your sister about me?" "Yeah, we are very close." "Very nice, I guess that means that you do like me." "Of course, I told you that when I was in Virginia." "I know, but I wasn't sure if you really meant it." "Oh, I definitely meant it." "Well, at least I know where the champagne came from." "I wanted to make sure you had a little something to welcome you to New York." I appreciate that, this definitely works. Would you like a glass?" "Sure, that would be nice. So, I am hoping I can show you around my city while you are here." "I would love that Simeon. I was really hoping to get to spend some time getting to know you better." "My feelings exactly Cashmere." Simeon stepped closer to Cashmere, put his hands on her waist and pulled her close to him. He looked in her eyes and said "I have wanted to do this since the first day we met." Then he softly placed his lips against hers, taking in the softness of her tasty lips. She placed her arms around his neck, pressed her lips against his and enjoyed the sensual spark between them. His lips felt good to her. She let her hands slide down his back until they rested just above his backside.

Simeon enjoyed the way Cashmere felt in his arms. He inhaled the sweet smell of her perfume, which took his mind to wanting to explore more of her. She felt good, smelled great and kissed fantastically. The feel of her body pressed against his made him need her right then and there. He wanted to enjoy her, all of her. Right when their lips parted, Cashmere's phone rang. "Damn ... hello." "Hey, Cashmere, just calling to see if you made it to New York yet?" "Yes, Uncle Herbert, I got here about an hour ago. I am already in the room." "Good. So, once you are settled, please go to the store and meet with the manager and the staff. Please go over the books with the manager. Show them how we do things here in Virginia. On Wednesday, I want to have a teleconference with them, please set that up as well." "Okay Uncle Herbert, I will take care of everything." "Great, give me a call tomorrow and let me know how things go today." "Got it." "Okay, I'll talk to you tomorrow." "Bye Uncle Herbert." Cashmere pressed the end button on her phone, looked at Simeon and said "Sorry for the interruption but duty calls. We will have to continue this later on tonight." "What time do you think you will be free? I have studio time tonight." "I'm not sure, probably around 7:00 or 8:00." "I have to be at the studio at 7:30. I should be done around midnight. I hope that's not too late." "That won't be too late, as long as you are worth the wait!" "That's funny because I was just thinking the same thing about you." "Please believe, I will definitely be worth the wait. You don't have a clue what I have in store for you Simeon." "Oh, I am going to enjoy you Cashmere!" "I hope so. Unfortunately, I have to get ready to go to the store." "I understand, I need to go run some errands anyway." Cashmere walked Simeon to the door; she kissed him again before he left. She wanted to feel the softness of his lips again. Simeon pulled her closer so that he could feel her body against his again. After he left, she did a little happy dance. She was truly excited. She enjoyed kissing him. She knew that she would enjoy all of him later. She went into the bathroom to touch up her makeup and hair.

Fortunately, the store was just a short walk away from the hotel. Cashmere took in the sights as she walked up the street to the store. Before walking in, she glanced inside the store to see how things were going. Since the employee's didn't know what she looked like, she decided to go in as a customer to see what type of service she would get. After walking in and walking around for a few minutes, one of the sales people walked up to her, introduced himself as Ali and asked if he could help her with anything. After talking with Ali, she noticed that he seemed to be very knowledgeable about clocks. He was very professional and to be quite honest, she thought he was very, very attractive. She finally introduced herself to the staff. She was happy to know that Ali was the manager because that meant that she would be spending a lot of time with him going over the books, schedules, policies and whatever else she could come up with to keep his attention, at least for a little while anyway. The store was beginning to get busy, Cashmere watched to see how the staff reacted as the customers began to pour in. She was very impressed with the way the staff was handling the customers. They were providing the best customer service possible. They were very informative and sold a boatload of clocks. Ali was manning the cash register and taking all orders for special clocks. She introduced herself and stood behind the counter with Ali and helped with orders when he was busy. She got a good whiff of his cologne and it smelled great to her. She looked over at him, taking in his smooth skin, finely manicured goatee and sexy bald head. She found herself fantasizing about kissing Ali. "How are you enjoying New York?" Ali asked.

There were several seconds that passed before Cashmere answered because she was so busy fantasizing about him that she really hadn't noticed that he was talking to her. "New York is a great city from what I've seen so far." "Well, I hope you have a great time while you are here." "Thank you. I have a feeling that I will have a wonderful time here." She smiled at Ali and he smiled back.

Little did he know that she was hoping he would help her enjoy New York. After closing the shop for the night, Cashmere and Ali went into the office to go over the schedule and books, as her uncle had asked. Ali sat down at the desk, pulled out the schedule to show Cashmere. Cashmere leaned in over his back. She eased her face along the left side of his face. She was close enough to inhale his cologne. To her surprise he didn't move away. He continued to tell her about the employee's and their schedules as if nothing had happened. This brother was hard to read is what she thought. She knew that he felt her ample breasts on his back, yet he didn't even budge. There wasn't any reaction at all. It was as if he didn't even feel them. So, she moved in a little closer. Not only was her breast on his back, but her face was close to his face. So close that if she turned her face to the right just a little bit, her lips would touch the side of his face. Still, there wasn't a reaction. She wondered what the deal was? Was he just trying to be nice? Did he realize that she was coming on to him? Since her advances were not being acknowledged, she decided to cease and get back to business. "So, the store has been open for a few weeks. It seems like the staff was well trained, but I wanted to go over the books as well. Herbert wanted to make sure that everything was up to par." After talking with Ali about the schedule and the books, Cashmere felt more than confident that he knew exactly what he was doing. She felt that he would take very good care of her uncle's store. "Okay Ali, I think I have seen enough for tonight. We can call it a night." "Are you sure you've seen enough?" "What do you mean?" "Well, I figured there was something else that you wanted to see, since you were flirting with me earlier." "Oh, so you did notice that?" "Well, of course I noticed it. How could I not feel all that on me?" "So, why the late reaction then?" "Well, to be honest, I was trying my best not to be enticed by your advances. I figured we could take care of business first, when the opportunity presented itself again, then I would take advantage of it." "Oh, is that what you thought? How do you know the opportunity would present itself again?" Ali laughed a little then said, "Well, not to be cocky or anything, but you initiated it in the first place and you are still here. So, I figured the offer was still on the table." "Oh, you did, did you? Well maybe I am pulling the offer off the table." "Okay, thanks for going over everything with me tonight. I should be leaving. Have a good night." Ali got up, headed to the office door, and turned around to look at Cashmere again. "Have a good night Ali. I will see you tomorrow." With that Ali opened the door and said "Good night Cashmere." He left and she locked the door behind him. After going over some paperwork, she went back to the hotel. The night air was brisk, she enjoyed the walk back. It gave her a chance to think about Simeon. She hoped that she would see him tonight, especially since Ali declined her advances. She really didn't know what to make of him.

He was fine, but he didn't respond the way she expected. He resisted her, which was something that she was not familiar with happening to her. To be honest, it bothered her, but she knew that Simeon would be there to take care of her needs, which would make her forget about Ali.

Thirty Seven

It was a beautiful morning when Tammy awoke. The sun was shining, birds were chirping outside her window. She jumped in the shower, put on some clothes and decided to go by Layla's Cafe for some breakfast. When she got there, she saw Char sitting at a table. "Hey girl, how are you doing this morning?" "Hey Tammy, I'm fine girl. How are you these days?" "I'm fine, got a lot on my mind." "Like what?" "Well, things are getting really serious with Rico and I. I am starting to get nervous; you know how I can get." "Tammy no. Don't do this again. Rico is a good man. He adores you. Not to mention he is fine." "I know Char; I don't want to ruin it. I'm not doing it intentionally. I just can't help feeling this way when things get serious." "I know where this is coming from Tammy. You have to get over that jerk. He was not the right man for you. You finally have the right man and you are still holding on to what was done to you in the past." "I am trying to get over it. It is just taking me some time to deal with it." "Some time ... Tammy, you have been dealing with this for years. You may need some professional help getting over this." "Come on Char, I don't need any professional help to get over this." "Well, if you don't need professional help, why are you still dealing with it then? Why have you chased off every man since that fool hurt you? Here's a better question ... why are you scared that you may lose Rico over it, if you don't need any professional help?" All Tammy could do was look at Char because deep down she knew that she was right. This demon had been haunting her for far too long. She had let it affect her life for too long now. She knew it was time to get a handle on this before she lost Rico. "Does he even know about this Tammy?" "No, I haven't told him about it yet. It was on my mind all last night. He called to see if I wanted to get together, but I just didn't feel like it because I knew it wouldn't be fair to him." "Tammy, it is already starting to affect your relationship with him. You need to get a handle on this really soon, before it's too late." "Char, you don't think I know that already? If it was that easy to do, I would have done it already." "Hold on a minute ... there's no need to get an attitude. I am just trying to help you. "Char, I'm sorry. I know you are just being a friend. I do appreciate you. I am just really worried that I may mess this relationship up. Rico means the world to me. I don't want to lose him." "I don't want to see you lose him. That's why you need to do something about it, so that it doesn't happen." "Girl, you are right. I am going to get over this and move forward with Rico. Thanks for always having my back." "Good, I hope so. If you need me, don't hesitate to call me. You're welcome. It's what we do!" Char paid for her meal, left a nice tip and left to go to the airport. She had to fly out to Atlanta for a fashion show. Tammy thought about the conversation that she had just had with Char. Realizing that Char made a lot of sense, she vowed to make sure that she got over this situation very soon. She pulled out her phone and called Rico.

Rico ... Hey baby. How are you?

Tammy ... Hey baby. I am fine, thanks. How are you doing?

Rico ... I am missing you, that's how I am doing.

Tammy ... Awe, that is so sweet. I am missing you too baby.

Rico ... We should do something about that.

Tammy ... I agree. We should do something about that soon.

Rico ... I was thinking about going to Chesdin Landing today. How does that sound?

Tammy ... Isn't that a private course though?

Rico ... Yes. Do you play golf?

Tammy ... A little bit. I am not very good though. How are we going to play there if it is private?

Rico ... I have some friends that live out there, so I go there when I can. Do you want to go?

Tammy ... Oh, very nice. There are some beautiful homes out there. I would love to go. Don't beat me too bad though.

Rico ... Don't worry. It will be fun. I'll pick you up in an hour or so.

Tammy ... Okay, that sounds great. See you soon baby.

Rico ... See you soon baby.

After hanging up from Rico, Tammy paid her tab for the eggs and bacon that she ordered and headed home. When she got home she got her golf clubs out of the garage, changed into her golf gear, sprayed on some sexy perfume and waited for Rico to show up. Rico rang the doorbell exactly an hour after talking to her. One thing about him, he was always on time. He loaded her golf clubs in the car, opened the door for her to get in and they were off to Chesdin Landing. Rico opened the panoramic roof, put on some reggae, and looked over at Tammy who was showing some thigh, which caught his attention. They talked on the way, when they arrived Rico got the clubs out of the car and they walked into the golf house. After getting their cart, they headed out to the course to get started. Tammy wanted to see just how well Rico golfed. She was curious about his athletic ability anyway. Rico let Tammy go first with a couple of practice swings; he wanted to check her form to see if he could help her be a better golfer. After her first swing, Rico noticed that her hands weren't positioned correctly and she wasn't swinging all the way through her swing.

He quickly walked up behind her to show her the proper hand positioning. Of course Tammy enjoyed him being so close to her. Not to mention he smelled wonderful to her. Once she had that down, he demonstrated how to properly swing through her swing. Tammy was impressed with Rico's golf knowledge so far. She stepped up to take her swing for real this time. Rico was standing a few feet behind her checking out her hand positioning; which was correct.

Tammy's swing was full; she had great follow through as well. The ball sailed for a great distance. Rico was impressed with how far she was able to hit the ball. Tammy had some power behind her swing. Rico stepped up to take his swing. Tammy took notice of his stance, his form and his swing. When Rico hit the ball it sailed magnificently for almost two hundred yards. Rico made sure that he hit it as far as he could because he knew that Tammy was watching.

Watching him ... she most certainly was. "Baby that was a great shot." "Thanks baby, I put a little something on it." "Oh you definitely put something on it.

Remember I said don't beat me too badly." "Baby, I am sure you will do fine. Play your game." Tammy went to take her second shot, which was about one hundred and fifty yards from the hole. She smiled at Rico, and then said "Watch this baby." She swung a mighty swing, the ball sailed high and far, landed, then rolled straight into the hole. "Yes!" Tammy dropped her club and ran straight to Rico. She jumped in his arms with utter excitement. He caught her as if he was catching a feather out of the air. He swung her around, once or twice and then placed his lips on hers. She kissed him feverishly, because she was feeling the rush from her great shot. Rico moved in to take his second shot. The swing was strong, maybe stronger than it needed to be, because the ball rolled past the hole by about two feet. Rico took his 3rd shot, which was the sinker. Tammy couldn't help but smile because she knew that she was winning so far. All she had to do was keep it up, and then she would be victorious. She would be able to brag about it to her friends, what was more; she would be able to brag about it to him. Chesdin Landing was a spectacular place to play golf. The views were amazing. The course was pristine at best. Rico felt at home on this course. Tammy was starting to feel comfortable there as well. They played through the rest of the holes, when they were done, Rico tallied up the points. He had won by only a few strokes. Tammy proved to be a better opponent than he had anticipated. Although he was happy about Tammy playing a great game, she was tired and ready to relax. They got in his car and drove a couple of blocks, then Rico pulled into the driveway of a huge two story brick house. They got out, walked inside, Tammy said "This is really nice. Is this where your friend lives?" "Tammy, I have to be honest with you. I do have friends that live in Chesdin Landing, but they don't live here." "Okay, well, whose house is this?" "This is my house Tammy. I bought it a couple of years ago." "Rico, this is very nice, but why didn't you tell me you lived in Chesdin Landing?" "I'm not really sure. I suppose it was because it doesn't really matter." "You don't really like talking about yourself, do you?" "Not really. I try and live as low key as possible." "I suppose I understand, but if you don't open up to me, how am I ever going to really get to know you?" "Baby, you are getting to know me. I think you know me very well!" Having said that Rico pulled Tammy close to him and kissed her with much intensity. She put her arms around his waist and kissed him very lovingly. "Now, please give me a tour of this place." "Okay, I'll show you around."

Thirty Eight

After leaving her parents, Stephanie drove to the restaurant for a staff meeting. The restaurant has been open for a month now. Business was thriving. They had a good amount of regulars that frequented often. It was now time for Stephanie to introduce some acts for nightly and weekend entertainment. She had auditioned several acts over the last couple of weeks and decided on three of them to perform from Thursday to Saturday. She wanted to let the staff know of the upcoming changes. Also, she wanted to discuss how business had been going since the opening. Stephanie started the meeting by thanking everyone for their service and great attitudes for the past month. She told them of her intentions to bring in acts three nights a week. The staff was very receptive to her idea. In fact, they were excited about the whole thing.

Stephanie was very happy that the staff was excited about the entertainment. She let them know that business had been great since the grand opening. She also complimented them on their professionalism and great work ethics.

Stephanie ended the meeting with a couple of bottles of Moscato for the staff to enjoy. While they were enjoying the Moscato, she went to her office to finalize the entertainment rotation. When she sat down she saw an envelope on her desk with her name written on it. Hesitantly, she picked up the envelope, opened it, but she knew what the contents contained before she pulled it out. They read the same as the others had read "I know something you don't know!" This time though, the sentence was repeated five times. At the bottom of the note there was another sentence that read "You are going to find out soon." Of all the notes that she had received, this was the most scary note of all, because it indicated that something was about to happen.

Stephanie began to get really nervous. She got up, closed her door and sat back down at her desk. All she could do was cry. She didn't know why anyone would want to do anything to her. She knew that she had to do something about this before something really bad happens. There was a knock at the door; she tried to wipe her tears away before saying "Come in." When the door opened, it was Matthius standing on the other side. He came in and shut the door behind him. Noticing almost immediately, that she was not herself. He asked if she was okay. She tried to act as if everything was okay, but just couldn't pull it off. She told him that she had been receiving strange letters for some time now. He asked what was written in the letters. Stephanie handed him the letter to read for himself. Mathius couldn't believe his eyes. "Stephanie, do you have any idea who or why someone would do something like this to you?" "No, not at all. I really don't know what to make of it." "Have you called the police yet?" "Not yet, I was about to do it when you knocked on the door." "Do you want me to sit with you while you make the call?" "No, I don't think that is necessary. I can manage on my own." "Are you sure Stephanie, I really don't mind." "Yeah, I'm sure Matthius. Thank you though." "You're welcome. Okay, I will leave you alone, so that you can make the call." Matthius opened the door and walked out, closing the door behind him. He lingered outside the door for a few seconds to see if Stephanie was really going to call the police. Stephanie noticed Matthius' shadow outside her door. This was puzzling to her, but she quickly disregarded it and called the police to report the letters. The police department said that they would send someone out as soon as possible. After getting off the phone with the police, she gathered all the letters, so that she could give them to the police when they arrived. She put the letters in a manila folder and headed outside to meet the police. She didn't want to alert the staff that something wasn't right. When the police showed up, he walked up to her and introduced himself as Detective Cruz. "Is there some place we can go to discuss this?" "There is a coffee shop next door. I would rather not do this in front of my staff." They walked over to the coffee shop, ordered a couple of cups of coffee and sat down to discuss the situation. Detective Cruz started his line of questioning with "When was the first time you received a letter?" "I believe the first time was about two months ago. I have received letters on my car, taped to the restaurant door and on my desk." The letters that were on your desk, how did they get there?" "I believe one of the staff members put them on my desk, because they had my name on them." "May I see the letters?" Stephanie handed Detective Cruz the manila folder. Detective Cruz looked at the letters intently. He noticed that some were hand written and others were computer generated. "Why didn't you contact us when you received the first letter?" "Well, to be honest, I really wasn't disturbed by it at that time. I had a lot going on; I guess I sort of dismissed it." "What made you call today?" "Well, the latest letter seems to indicate that something is going to happen. I feel threatened now. I don't want anything bad to happen to me or anybody that I know." "Well, I am glad that you called. This is definitely a serious matter. It appears that you may be in real danger. We will start an investigation right away. Unfortunately, we will have to designate a policeman to follow you around, just in case someone tries to harm you." "Follow me around ... what exactly do you mean? Will they have to come to work with me too?" "Unfortunately, yes. I will have them follow you in an unmarked police car." "Detective Cruz, I am not sure that I am comfortable with having someone follow me around everywhere I go." "I assure you, they will be as discreet as possible. The alternative is not to have someone around to help you when something happens to you." "Isn't there something else that can be done? This can't be the only way to handle this." "I understand your concerns. There is another opportunity; we can place you in protective custody, while we investigate. Hopefully, we will be able to solve the case before too much time passes." "Protective custody how does that work exactly?" "Well, we would put you in a secure safe place for an allotted time. You would not be permitted to leave or have any contact outside of the house." "I don't think that will work either. I just opened a business and I need to be there to make sure that things go the way they should." "I understand that this may not be the opportune time to do this, but we are concerned for your safety. We have to do one or the other. We can't keep up with the same course. If we do, something will surely happen to you." "I just don't see how I can do either right now." "Ma'am, I really don't think you see the seriousness of these letters. Someone is stalking you, possibly trying to do harm to you." "Detective Cruz, I do see the seriousness of the letters. That is why I called the police."

"Well, if you see the seriousness, then let us do our job and protect you." "May I have a couple of days to think about it?" "Here is my card. Take a couple of days to decide. Give me a call when you have made your decision. In the meantime we will start the investigation. We may be contacting you with questions along the way." "Thank you Detective Cruz, I appreciate you understanding my concerns. I will give you a call in a couple of days. Feel free to contact me whenever you have questions or concerns." "You're welcome. Thank you as well. I will be in touch." Detective Cruz got up and exited the coffee shop. Stephanie finished her coffee, and then went back to the restaurant. She went back to her office, signed some paperwork, then grabbed her purse and left for the day. She drove home thinking about the meeting she had with Detective Cruz. Deep down she knew that she would have to either agree to have the police follow her or go into protective custody. Neither of the situations suited her life well, at this point.

The bottom line is that if she didn't do either of them, she would probably end up hurt or worse dead. When she got home, she walked upstairs to her room and saw another letter placed on her pillow.

Thirty Nine

When Cashmere got back to her room, she called Simeon to see how he was doing in the studio. The phone went to voicemail, so she left a message. "Hey Simeon, it's me Cashmere. Give me a call when you get this." She was tired and desired a shower, so she went to the bathroom and took a nice long hot shower. Her thoughts of Ali and Simeon kept her busy while she cleaned herself. After towel drying, she decided to lie down and watch a little television. She turned the light off, so that the only light shining in the hotel room was from the television. Cashmere folded the pillow in half, and then laid her head on it, so she could watch the television in comfort. After watching television for a little while, she found herself nodding off. She hadn't realized how tired she was. The shower relaxed her in such a way that sleep was simply inevitable.

When Cashmere woke up the next morning, she noticed that her phone was blinking. She had voice mails from Simeon and Uncle Herbert. She called Uncle Herbert back first to give him an update on what she learned the day before, at the shop. After talking to him, she called Simeon back. Again, the phone went to voicemail. Perhaps he was still asleep from a late night in the studio. She decided to get her day started. She wanted to get some breakfast, then she would go by the store to check on things again. Plus she wanted to see Ali again. She wondered if he thought about her, like she thought about him.

Something was different about Ali though. She couldn't quite put her finger on it. Nevertheless, he had her attention.

Cashmere decided to start her day. She did her hair, got dressed, sprayed on some perfume, and then headed out to breakfast. She decided to have breakfast at Les Halles, and then she would continue to the store to observe the staff again today. After finishing her breakfast, she paid the check and walked to the store. It was a nice morning out, the air was crisp. Cashmere enjoyed her leisurely stroll up the street. When she walked into the store, she was happy to see that they were busy helping customers. It appeared to her that Uncle Herbert was accurate in his choice to open a store in Manhattan.

Business seemed to be more than profitable these past couple of days. Cashmere walked behind the counter to help with the purchases, so that Ali could help on the floor with the clock sales. She observed the staff being more than professional. They all went out of their way to make sure that the customers got their questions answered and were very happy with the service provided and their purchases. When the shop slowed down, Cashmere took that opportunity to call Uncle Herbert to tell him that the store and the staff was a positive decision. She let him know that she was impressed with everything that she had seen thus far. Of course, Uncle Herbert was glad to hear the news. The information made him feel a lot better about moving forward with the Los Angeles store too. After getting off the phone with Uncle Herbert, Cashmere went to the office to review the earnings for the past couple of weeks. The numbers were fantastic. Each day the profits seemed to increase. There was one slow day in the last ten days of business. That was very impressive to Cashmere. She wondered if this was because the store was a novelty to the neighborhood or if business would continue to be this profitable. Manhattan definitely seemed to be a hot bed for specialty clock connoisseurs. After Cashmere had lunch there was another rush of customers that were looking to purchase clocks. Business just seems to be getting better and better for this store. At the end of the day Cashmere got the staff together and told them that she was very happy with what she had seen so far. She told the staff that they had moved many clocks over the past couple of weeks.

There were several specialty orders made that were for a substantial amount of money. The numbers looked great! Cashmere and Ali locked up the store after the employees left. They stood outside the store talking for a few minutes. After saying good night, Cashmere began to walk away.

"Cashmere!" said Ali. When she turned around he was standing right there. He put his hands on both sides of her face and pulled her close to him. He pressed his lips against her soft full lips. She was reluctant at first to kiss him back. Then she gave in and reciprocated his advances. She placed her arms around his neck and let her lips explore his. His lips felt good to her, she enjoyed the softness of them. When their lips parted, their eyes told the story of their mutual desire for one another. "What prompted you to do that?" "It just felt right. It has been something that I have wanted to do since yesterday." "Now, that you have done it. What happens now?" "Well, what do you want to happen Cashmere?" "Ali, I am leaving New York tomorrow morning, so if you are interested in spending any time with me, it needs to be tonight." "I understand, would you like to go out for a drink?" "There is a nice bar at my hotel, we can go there." Cashmere and Ali walked slowly to the hotel enjoying some conversation and laughter.

Once they got to the hotel bar, they grabbed a table close to the door. The waitress came over and welcomed them, then took their drink orders. While waiting for their drinks, they chatted about everything under the sun. The waitress brought the drinks over, Cashmere and Ali were having such a great time talking and laughing together, that they barely noticed her putting them on the table. Ali reached over to touch her hand. She held his hand, looked in his eyes, and realized that she was having a great time with him. They continued to hold hands and talk the night away. Before they knew it hours had passed and the bar was getting ready to close for the night. "Cashmere, I have had a great time getting to know you. You are a very nice person and I would love to get to know you a lot better." "Ali, I have had a great time with you as well. Honestly, I would like to get to know you better as well." "Why does it sound like there is a "but" behind that?" "Well, because there is a "but" behind it." "Well, are you going to tell me?" "Well, I am sort of seeing someone else." "Sort of, what does that mean?" "It means she has a man!" They both turned around and Simeon was standing there. Cashmere's eyes grew big, she couldn't believe her eyes. She wondered how long he had been at the bar. Had he seen them enjoying themselves? This had just gotten very uncomfortable. Simeon looked at Cashmere and said "What the hell is going on here Cashmere?" "You seem like an intelligent young man. I am sure that you can see we are on a date." Ali stated. "I'm not talking to you player. I am talking to Cashmere." "Simeon, please don't get this twisted. Ali and I are co-workers. We had some drinks together to celebrate a great day at work." "Oh Cashmere, is that all this is? My bad, I thought we were on to something here." "Cashmere, please tell me that this clown is not telling the truth." Simeon said. "Simeon, I am not going to lie, I am attracted to him. I am attracted to you as well. I have only seen you once since I have been in New York. For some reason when I call you, you are not available to talk. So, I'm not sure what you and I have together." Okay, I told you I would be in the studio. So, you decided to get involved with this clown because my phone went to voice mail? "Look son ... I'm not going to be too many more clowns!" Ali stated with a little attitude. "Simeon, we never decided that we were a couple. I know we were moving towards that, but we hadn't made that decision yet." "Wait ... wait ... wait Cashmere ... are you saying that you want to be with him?" Ali asked. "Ali, I really like both of you. I don't know who I want to be with. I do know that I have known him longer than you. I was excited about coming to New York because I knew he was here. Then I met you and was naturally attracted to you. So, right now I am a little confused." "Confused? You are a little confused? This is some foul shit Cashmere. When we met in Virginia, I thought I had met someone really special. I really liked you too. Since you are confused, I will decide for you. You can have this clown!" Simeon walked off to leave the hotel. "Simeon!!!! Simeon!!!!" Cashmere shouted.

Forty

Rico took Tammy by the hand and guided her to the kitchen to start the tour. He showed her the subzero freezer, and the Vulcan stoves. He poured her a glass of Moscato to enjoy on the tour. They went out to the family room, which led to the patio. Once at the patio he showed her the pool with the wet bar at the opposite end of the pool. He showed her the jacuzzi, then they walked back inside, he took her to the game room, which had a pool table, ping pong table, poker table and dart board. After that, he took her to the theatre, which had sixteen seats, another bar and a huge movie screen. He walked her back towards the front door, where they ascended the spiral staircase to the second floor, where all five bedrooms were hidden. Tammy was impressed to say the least. She knew that Rico was doing well, but she had no idea that he was doing as well as this. Rico's home was beyond beautiful. Quite frankly, it was one of the nicest homes she had seen in some time. After showing her around, they adjourned to the kitchen again, where Rico began to prepare something to eat for them. Tammy continued to look around the room, noting the beauty of his home. "Rico, this is a really nice home." "I am glad you like it, baby. It feels really good to have you here with me." "That is truly nice to know. I would love to be here more often." "I would love that too. It would be nice to have you around more often." Tammy walked over to Rico and put her arms around his waist, ran her hands up his muscular chest. She kissed him on the neck. His words made their way to her heart and she wanted to let him know just how much she appreciated him sharing them with her. Rico turned to her and kissed her passionately on the lips. She returned the passion that had been building up inside her with her kiss.

It was clear that Rico felt the same way for her that she felt for him. Their relationship had turned into something wonderful. Rico was more than what she expected in a good man. He was everything and more than she ever wanted in a man. She looked at Rico who was still cooking dinner for them. The kitchen smelled wonderful. Whatever he was making, she couldn't wait to try. After golfing, she was more than ready to taste whatever culinary greatness that he was concocting in the kitchen. "How long before dinner will be ready baby?" "We still have another fifteen or twenty minutes before it will be ready?" "Would you mind if I took a shower real quick?" "That depends." "Depends on what baby?" "Whether I can join you or not." "Baby, if you join me the food will burn." "Oh, I guess you have a point there. Maybe we can take a shower after we have eaten." "Really?" "Yeah, I was thinking it might be more interesting if we showered together." "Rico, of course you can join me baby. I would love to shower with you." "That sounds good to me. Would you like another glass of wine baby?" "Yes, I would. Let me get it though. Do you want something baby?" "Actually, I would love some Tennessee Honey right now." "How many rocks with that baby?" "Two or three would be fine, thanks." "You're welcome baby. I got you. Don't worry." "I'm not worried! I'm too happy to be worried baby." "Is that so? What's making you so happy?" "You are baby. You are my source of happiness." "Rico, I feel the same way. You are my source of happiness too. I believe you bring out the best in me." After giving him his drink, she pulled Rico closer to her and hugged him very lovingly. He enjoyed the way she felt in his arms. It was a feeling that he just couldn't get enough of. He rubbed his hands up and down her back. Just the feel of his touch sent a sweet sensation through her body.

They sat down to dinner. Rico lit some candles to ensure a romantic setting. She made him feel special and he wanted her to know that she was very special to him too. After enjoying their dinner, Rico put on some music for them to enjoy. They cuddled up on the couch; she laid her head on his chest. She inhaled the sexy fragrance that emanated from his masculine chest. After unbuttoning his shirt, she placed little kisses along his chest. Rico rested his hands on her back, while she traced the outlining of his chest with her finger. Her well-manicured nails glided across his chest like a little sharp sword etching her way along his sexiness. Just the touch of his skin directly beneath her fingernail made her feel a sweet sensation. She looked up and her eyes met Rico's, igniting a spark between them. This relationship just felt right between them. The whole day seemed to just flow effortlessly. The golfing was a great surprise, sharing a romantic dinner and now resting in each other's arms, everything seemed to just fall into place. Tammy loved spending time with Rico; she loved the way he made her feel. What's more is that she loved the way he felt. She enjoyed rubbing his chest and thighs. Rico enjoyed her touches more than anything. Well, there was something that he loved more than her touches. And that was making love to her. The way she received his lovemaking was natural. She was the object of his affection. She reciprocated his lovemaking with great sensual desire. Her body was his throne and he was definitely the king of his throne! Having said that, Rico looked into Tammy's eyes and asked "Would you like to take that shower now?" "Only if you shower with me." "I would like nothing better." She kissed him softly on the lips. He pulled her closer and reciprocated her kiss with the same amount of passion as she provided to him. Her lips tasted like the sweetest nectar known to man. They both climbed the stairs up to the second floor. They went to Rico's bedroom, he showed her the shower which was spacious enough for six people to shower at once. There were eight shower heads coming from many angles. There was one giant shower head that hung from the very center of the shower. There was definitely more than enough room for them to do whatever they wanted to do in there. Tammy stepped in the shower and Rico followed with much anticipation of enjoying her. He walked up behind her and put his arms around her. She leaned her neck over to the left to give him more access to her neck. Rico placed kisses alongside her neck. The water cascaded down their bodies creating a very romantic feeling between them. She turned to face Rico and kissed him on the lips. Rubbing her hands up and down his back, she felt the muscles of his back as her hands moved slowly up and down him. Rico pulled her closer to feel her body against his. The trickling of the water between their bodies made for a more enjoyable experience. Rico let his hands slide down to Tammy's ample rear. He squeezed both cheeks and enjoyed every moment of it. Rico lathered up some soap in his hands and rubbed it all over Tammy's body. Tammy began to feel a wonderful sensation cruise through her body. Rico's touches were more than welcomed, her body reacted from all the pleasure that she was receiving from him. He moved his hands slowly up and down her body. He caressed her breasts as the soap ran between his fingers. He took extra care to rub her sweet spot. She felt her sweetness begin to stir. Tammy lowered her hand to hold his manhood. His manhood responded instantaneously as she slid her hand up and down his shaft. Rico reached around her legs and lifted her up, placing her against the shower wall. He entered her slowly, pushing himself all the way inside her. She wrapped her arms around his neck to hold on. Rico bounced her up and down penetrating her deeply. With every stroke she felt herself getting closer and closer. His stamina was strong, Rico buried his face in between her breasts.

Pleasing them to no end. She kissed the top of his head. Rico laid down on the shower floor and Tammy straddled him. She took as much inside of her as she could. The water streaming down on them, the bathroom was slightly steamy from the warmth of the water. Rico and Tammy were steamy from the lovemaking. Tammy began to ride him faster and faster, her breasts were bouncing up and down. She could feel Rico getting harder and harder inside of her. She knew that he was getting closer. He knew that she was getting closer as well. Their energy was peaking; their bodies were yearning for release.

Tammy let out a loud moan and collapsed on top of Rico's chest. Rico pulled her face up to his and kissed her passionately. "Oh baby, thank you that was great." "You're welcome Tammy. It was wonderful." "You always make great love to me." "I love the way you feel when we make love, baby.

Forty One

Stephanie couldn't believe her eyes. What's more is that she couldn't believe that someone had been in her house. This was getting out of control. She was terrified; she pulled out her card for Detective Cruz. She called him to tell him what she had found, then ended the call, because she knew that he wouldn't let her stay at her house any longer. She called Tammy to tell her about the letters. Tammy didn't answer so she left a message.

Stephanie ... Tammy, it's me. I need to talk to you when you get this. I received two more letters today. One was in my house! Call me when you get this!

Right when Stephanie pressed end on her phone, she heard a noise downstairs. She wasn't sure what it was, but she knew that she should be the only one in the house. She made her way down the stairs, slowly, cautiously. She heard the sound again, this time it was much louder. She knew that meant that she was getting closer to whatever was causing it. She went into her office and noticed that there was a drawer opened on her desk. Papers were all over the desk and floor, as if someone were looking for something. She looked up and saw that one of the French patio doors leading outside was open. She quickly closed and locked it. Again, she pulled out Detective Cruz' card, dialed his number and awaited his answer. He picked up after the second ring.

Detective Cruz ... Cruz here.

Stephanie ... Detective Cruz, this is Stephanie. Someone was in my house!

Detective Cruz ... Are you okay Stephanie? Are they still in your home?

Stephanie ... I am fine, just a little freaked out! No, they are not here any longer.

Detective Cruz ... Stay on the line. I am on my way. Tell me what happened.

Stephanie ... I came home and found a letter in my bedroom. Then I heard a noise downstairs in my office. When I went to investigate, I heard it again. Then, I noticed that my desk drawer was open and papers were all over the place. I also saw that one of the doors leading outside was open.

Detective Cruz ... Okay, did you touch anything? Are you sure that there isn't anyone else in the house?

Stephanie ... Yes, I touched the letter and I closed the door.

Detective Cruz ... What did the letter say?

Stephanie ... Detective Cruz, the letter said "It is time to show you what I mean!"

Detective Cruz ... Are you sure that you don't have any idea who might be up to this?

Stephanie ... No, I don't have a clue.

Detective Cruz ... I need you to really think about this. I believe that it might be somebody that you know, either in your past or in your life now.

Stephanie ... Why do you think that?

Detective Cruz ... They know your every move. They know where you're going to be and when you're going to be there. They know where you live, which makes me think that you may have invited them in at some point and time.

Stephanie ... I never thought about that.

Detective Cruz ... Okay, I am pulling up now. I will be at your door in a couple of minutes.

Stephanie ... Okay, I'll open the door.

They both pressed end on their phones. Detective Cruz got his notebook and two extra clips for his Glock. He exited the vehicle and walked up to Stephanie's door. Stephanie was looking through the peephole and opened the door as soon as she saw him. Without hesitation, she flew into his arms. "I'm sorry, I shouldn't have done that. I was just so relieved to see a safe face." "No problem Stephanie, I totally understand, I probably would have done the same thing, had I been in your shoes." "Be thankful that you are not. This is not a good place to be." Stephanie stepped back to allow Detective Cruz room to enter her home. "Please come in." "Thank you very much Stephanie." Stephanie led Detective Cruz to the kitchen. "Please have a seat. Would you like some coffee or tea?" "Coffee would be fine, thanks." "How do you take it?" "Sugar and cream, please. Do you mind if I ask you a question while you prepare the coffee?" "No, not at all." "Great! Do you remember when you arrived at your home?" "I believe it was about 7:30." "When did you notice the letter?" "It was a couple of minutes after I got home. I went straight to my room." "Okay, when did you hear the noise?" "I heard the noise a couple of minutes after I saw the letter." "Is there more than one way to get downstairs from the second floor?" "Well, I do have a deck off of my bedroom that has a stairwell that leads downstairs." "So, it is possible that whoever was in your bedroom, heard you come in and went down the balcony stairs to your office, while you were reading the letter?" "Yes, it is very possible." "Did you hear anyone outside?" "No, I didn't. I didn't hear anything until I heard the noise in my office." "Okay, can I take a look at your bedroom?" "Yes, it's this way." Stephanie led Detective Cruz up to her bedroom and showed him where she found the letter." She pointed to the exact place where she found the letter on her pillow. "Where is the letter now?" "I have it here." Stephanie handed the letter to Detective Cruz for him to review. Detective Cruz took the letter from Stephanie with his gloved hand, looked over the contents and placed it in an envelope marked evidence. Detective Cruz looked around the bedroom for any other signs or clues that could possibly aid him in his investigation. "May I please see the balcony stairwell?" "Yes, it is right outside these doors." Stephanie opened the doors and they both walked outside. "Have you touched anything out here since you called me?" "No, I haven't been out here since yesterday." "Great, I am going to take a look around." "Okay, take your time Detective Cruz." Detective

Cruz took out his flashlight and looked around the balcony. He noticed something on the balcony underneath the table. Upon taking a closer look, he recognized the item to be a gold cuff link. He put the cuff link in another evidence bag. "Stephanie, do you recognize this cufflink?" After looking at the cuff link Stephanie said "No, it does not look familiar to me." "Okay, thanks. We will find out who it belongs to and let you know." Detective Cruz walked down the stairwell very slowly, he was looking all around to see if there was anything else that looked out of place. "In my professional opinion, it looks as if the perpetrator entered the household, went directly upstairs to your bedroom, and placed the letter on your pillow. They then heard you enter the house, got scared, went out the bedroom doors, down the stairs and entered your office, while you were up here. The noise you heard was them either entering the house and searching for whatever it was that they were looking for. Then they heard you coming downstairs and ran out of the door to get away before being seen." Stephanie put her face in her hands and started to cry. Finally, she was letting out everything that had been building up inside of her since all this began. Detective Cruz walked over to her and put his arms around her, then said "There's no reason to cry, we will make sure that whoever is doing this to you, will be caught" "Thank you Detective Cruz, I really appreciate it. I'm sorry for crying in front of you. It's just too much for me to handle right now." "I understand Stephanie. I will make sure that you never have to deal with this again! You have my word on that." Detective Cruz pulled out his phone and called in for a surveillance detail to protect Stephanie until they caught the intruder. Stephanie did not object this time, because she knew that he was right. Once the detail arrived, Detective Cruz gave specific instructions to them to make sure that nothing happened to her.

Forty Two

Cashmere looked at Ali and said "I'm sorry, I can't do this." She walked away, leaving Ali standing there. When Cashmere got to her room, she fell on the bed and just started crying. She knew she had messed things up with Simeon. It hurt her to see him walk away and not look back. This wasn't at all how she expected her trip to go. She knew she had to try; she had to do something to make him see that it was really him that she wanted. She wiped the tears from her eyes, picked up her phone and dialed Simeon's number. The phone just rang and rang, then went to voicemail. After leaving a message, she put the phone down; laid back on the bed and started crying again. All she could think was that Simeon was gone forever. Cashmere grabbed her phone again; she decided to send him a text.

Cashmere ... Simeon, please call me. I am really sorry. I know I messed up, please give me a call.

She waited a few minutes for a reply. There wasn't one. She figured he wanted to reply but wasn't sure what to say or possibly was too mad to reply right now. Either way she hoped that he would reply sooner or later, she really wanted to talk to him again before she left New York in the morning. For now Cashmere had done everything that she could to reach out to Simeon. Now, it was on him to get back in touch with her, if he wanted to do so. She laid back down, checked her phone to see if she had received a text from him, then ended up drifting off to sleep. It seemed like it had been a couple of hours since Cashmere had drifted off to sleep when she heard a knock at her hotel room door. At first she wasn't sure if it was a knock, when she heard it again, she got up, straightened her hair, went to look out the peephole and noticed that there wasn't anybody there. She opened the door, looked down the hall and saw a man walking away. "Excuse me ... did you just knock on my door?" "Yes I did." When the man turned around, she was surprised to see that it was Simeon standing there. She ran directly to him and hugged him right away. "Hold on ... you have some explaining to do." "I know, I am just glad to see you. I am glad that you came by." "I came by to hear what you had to say, since you were blowing my phone up." "Okay, that's fine. Come on in and we can talk." Cashmere reached for his hand, but he did not offer his hand to her. Cashmere looked at him, she understood his hesitation, and then started to walk towards her room. He followed her into the room, ready to hear what she had to say. He had already made up his mind that if her conversation wasn't right, then he wasn't going to go any farther with this relationship. Cashmere was just glad that she had a chance to talk to him again. She knew she needed to convince him that she was sorry and wouldn't make a mistake like that again. Simeon sat in a chair by the window, Cashmere sat at the desk, turned her chair to face him. She looked at him; she saw the hurt in his eyes. It was hard for her to look at him, knowing that she was the cause for all his pain. "I'm listening Cashmere!" "I know Simeon; please give me a moment to get my thoughts together." "Really, I would have thought by now that you would have had time to get your thoughts together." "Listen Simeon ... first let me start by saying how sorry I am that I was interested in someone else. Honestly, I really wasn't sure where we were going though." "We may not have solidified our relationship Cashmere, but we both knew that there was something there. We knew that we were more than friends." "I know, but you weren't returning my texts or calls, I guess I had developed doubts about your intention for us." "Cashmere I told you where I would be. When I am in the studio, I turn my phone off, because I don't want any distractions. Maybe I should have told you that, but it didn't dawn on me to do so." "Simeon, I understand that. I am glad that you told me because I really thought that you were ignoring me or maybe there was someone else." "Cashmere, I was far too excited to see you when you arrived. There isn't anybody else in my life. I wanted you to be the one in my life. So, the reason you were with that clown is because you thought I had someone else?" "Yes, I was weighing my options, because I hadn't heard back from you. I won't lie, I was attracted to Ali and I thought that if I couldn't have you, then I needed to move on." "You don't think that you should have talked to me about this before you decided to move on?" "Simeon, I tried to contact you several times and I didn't hear from you. I really didn't know what to expect from you. Let's be honest here, we barely know each other." "Okay, I give you that, but I'm not going to lie, you had my attention until tonight." "And now?" "Now, I don't honestly know. It all depends on how I feel after we are done talking." "Is that so?" "Yes, it is." "Well, how are you feeling now?" "I am not sure. I really liked you, and then you disappointed me." "Come on Simeon, you are here for a reason. Why don't you just admit that you are still interested?" "It's obvious that I am still interested. If I wasn't I wouldn't be here." "Okay, so what are you going to do now, then?" "I am going to think about what I have heard tonight and make a decision." "And when will you let me know?" "You will know when I let you know." With that Simeon got up and said "Good Night." Just like that he was gone.

Cashmere couldn't believe he just left like that. She waited to see if he would knock on the door again. It didn't happen though. Simeon was gone; she was hoping it wasn't forever though. Something deep inside her told her that Simeon would be back in her life soon. He was just making it difficult for her right now. She decided to go to bed for the night, she had an early morning, she needed her rest. She had way too much excitement for the night. She drifted off to sleep. The next morning when she awoke, she jumped in the shower, got ready, headed out the door with intentions of stopping by the store to check on things before she flew back to Virginia. She walked by the store, looked in the window and saw Ali. She decided not to go in, but to walk away, so that she didn't have to face him right now. When she walked away, Ali looked up to see her leaving. He wanted to run after her, but decided to just leave things as they were.

When Cashmere returned to the hotel, she hailed a cab, got in and headed to the airport. Her flight back to Virginia was due to leave in a couple of hours. When she got there, she checked her bags, went to get some coffee and sat down to read the paper. Not really paying attention to her surroundings, she heard a voice "Do you always drink coffee in the morning before you catch a flight?" She looked up and Simeon was standing in front of her. "What are you doing here Simeon?" "I'm here to catch a flight." "Oh where are you going?" "I have some business in Virginia that I need to take care of." "Is that so? What business is that?" When Cashmere asked that question, she was hoping that he was going to say that she was the business that needed to be taken care of.

"Let's just say that I have to take care of something. May I sit?" "Sure. That would be nice." "Thank you very much." Simeon pulled the chair out and sat down directly across from Cashmere. "You look very beautiful today Cashmere." Simeon's eyes lingered over Cashmere's beauty as he complimented her. "Thank you Simeon. I appreciate you noticing." "You're quite welcome Cashmere." They looked into each other's eyes for a few moments, then Simeon said "Look Cashmere, I am going to just put this out there, so that we are both on the same page. I like you a lot. I came here to let you know just how much I want you. So, if you want, let's forget about last night and move forward from today on." Cashmere looked at Simeon, she couldn't believe her ears. She thought that she had lost him forever. She took his hand and said "I would like nothing more than to move forward with you Simeon." He leaned over and kissed her with inviting lips.

They both got up and boarded the plan for Virginia together.

Forty Three

When Tammy checked her phone, she saw that Stephanie had left her a voicemail and text message. When she listened to the voicemail, she instantly got worried. She called Stephanie back and she answered right away.

Stephanie ... Tammy, I am so glad you called me back.

Tammy ... Are you okay?

Stephanie ... Physically I am fine, but emotionally, I am a wreck.

Tammy ... Please tell me you called the police!

Stephanie ... Yes, I did call the police. He just left here a few minutes ago. There is a surveillance detail outside my house right now.

Tammy ... Well, that's good. At least you can get a good night's sleep.

Stephanie ... That would be nice. I haven't slept well for a long time now.

Tammy ... What happened Stephanie?

Stephanie ... I came home and there was a letter on my bedroom pillow. Then I heard a loud noise downstairs. When I went down there, they ran out the door. There were papers all over my desk and floor, as if they were looking for something.

Tammy ... What do you think they were looking for?

Stephanie ... I don't have a clue. I wish I knew. Detective Cruz found a cuff link outside on the balcony. Hopefully he will have some information soon.

Tammy ... I hope so Stephanie. I am sorry that you have to go through this.

Stephanie ... Thanks, me too. Thanks for calling me back too.

Tammy ... Girl don't even mention it. You know I am here for you.

Stephanie ... Okay, well I am going to try and get some sleep. It's been a hell of a day.

Tammy ... I hear you girl. Good night.

Stephanie ... Good night!

After Tammy got off the phone from Stephanie, she couldn't help but to feel sad for her friend. She looked at Rico; her face alerted him that something wasn't right. By this time, Rico knew her facial expressions. When she told him what was going on, he asked "Do you want to go see her?" "I'm not sure right now. I don't want to make her feel any worse than she already does." "I can understand that. Well, let me know if you change your mind, we can go there and have some drinks later, if you want." "I'll think about it. If we do, I think we should invite Char and Cashmere too." "Maybe the three of you should go. I don't want her to feel awkward with me there." "Baby, I want you to go though." "I know you do baby, believe me I want to go too. I just think it would be better for her, if her girls were there for her. She doesn't need any extra pressure from me." "You are so sweet baby. What did I do to deserve you?" Tammy smiled at Rico and blew him a kiss, which he graciously caught in his hand.

Tammy went outside to gather her thoughts before she called her girls. Stephanie was certainly going through it these days. First her father was held hostage in a bank, now she had a stalker in her home. She needed her girls now, more than ever. They all had to be strong for her though. They couldn't walk in there and turn into waterfalls in front of her. That wouldn't be good. They needed to show strength, so that Stephanie would display strength too. The girls agreed to go over to Stephanie's to try and make her feel better.

When they arrived Stephanie was already nursing a glass of wine. "Girl, what is going on? How are you these days?" Char asked. "Things could be better. I just don't feel safe in my home anymore. The truth is I don't feel safe anywhere that I go now. This fool has gotten me spooked. He could be outside lurking in the bushes for all I know." "If he is outside, your surveillance detail will get him. They were on us as we walked up to the door. We had to give our names before they would let us ring the doorbell. They even checked us to make sure that we didn't have any weapons on us." Tammy said. "Well, I kind of liked that part though." Cashmere said. They all burst out into laughter. "I needed that. I haven't laughed like that in a minute. Thank you for that." Stephanie said with a smile. "Girl, fill some of those glasses up. Wine makes everything better." Char said. Stephanie pulled out another bottle of Moscato, and poured a round for everyone. They toasted to great friendships and forever sisterhood.

Forty Four

After hanging with her girls, Stephanie decided to take a nice hot shower and get ready for bed. The day had been very draining and exhausting. Although she knew that the police were outside her door, she still had a hard time falling asleep. It just didn't sit well with her, knowing that someone had been in her house, in her bedroom, no less. How was she supposed to sleep soundly tonight with all that has happened, especially today? Stephanie tossed and turned for a couple of hours before falling asleep. She couldn't help but to wake up throughout the night, especially when she saw a light in her backyard. It startled her at first, and then she realized that it was one of the surveillance details checking the perimeter. Surprisingly, Stephanie fell back to sleep with ease.

When she woke up, she couldn't help but to still feel tired. Her body still felt drained, she needed something to bring her back to life. She decided to do the one thing that she does best. She decided to go to the restaurant and cook some breakfast.

When she arrived, of course the surveillance detail was in tow. She quickly entered the restaurant, went to her office to check her messages. Not noting anything emergent, she went into the kitchen, gathered some pans and utensils to cook with, and then went into one of the coolers for some items to cook. After cooking her breakfast, she sat down at one of the tables in the dining area to enjoy. When she was done with her meal, she went back into the kitchen, cleaned her dishes, put her pans and utensils away, and then went back to her office. While in her office she made her weekly orders of produce, meats and linens from some of her vendors.

Her phone rang, it was a call from Detective Cruz. Stephanie hurried to answer the phone.

Stephanie ... Hello Detective Cruz.

Detective Cruz ... Good morning Stephanie. I just called to see how your night went?

Stephanie ... Well, to be honest. It was hard for me to get to sleep with everything that happened yesterday.

Detective Cruz ... I understand that. I spoke with the surveillance detail this morning and they stated that there wasn't any activity around your home last night, other than three female visitors.

Stephanie ... That's good to know. I woke up last night and saw a light in the backyard. I realized that it was your surveillance detail and went back to sleep. Yeah, some of my girls stopped by to check on me.

Detective Cruz ... I am sorry if they disturbed you. I will speak with them about being more discreet.

Stephanie ... No, that's okay. You don't have to do that.

Detective Cruz ... Are you sure? I can have them make an adjustment. It's really not a problem.

Stephanie ... I am certain. They were only doing their job.

Detective Cruz ... Okay, sounds good. I understand that you are at the restaurant? Did you notice anything out of place or another letter?

Stephanie ... Yes, I am. I didn't notice anything. So far everything seems in order.

Detective Cruz ... Great, sounds good. We sent the cufflinks and the letters out for testing this morning. Hopefully, we will find out something soon. I will keep you posted.

Stephanie ... Thank you so much Detective Cruz.

Detective Cruz ... You're very welcome Stephanie. Have a good day.

Stephanie ... Thanks, you too.

When Stephanie got off the phone with Detective Cruz, she felt a lot better about the evening before. She knew that he was working diligently on solving this case. That gave her the confidence she needed to keep her head up and persevere through the days ahead.

The staff started to come in for work. They quickly got into place and you could smell the goodness coming from the kitchen. Stephanie loved to open her office window and door, so that she could smell all the food that escaped the kitchen. She could sit in her office for hours and just bask in the sweet smell that permeated from in there. That's one of the reasons she wanted a restaurant, because not only did she love to cook, but she loved the smell of great food! The greatest accomplishment for her was seeing someone happy from enjoying one of her meals. That was the fuel that she needed to drive her to success. She was filling up on that fuel. So far, her restaurant was doing exceptionally well. Diners were packing the place nightly. Her choice to have entertainment on the weekend's had proven to be a great idea. She couldn't be more pleased with her restaurant right now. If only the rest of her life was as sweet as this. Although she has gone through some things, she knew that things would get back to normal soon enough. Everyone has to go through their struggles in life, it was her turn now. She just wished that her struggles didn't have to be so dangerous, so life threatening. Why couldn't she have maybe a flat tire or be late on a bill? Why did it have to be so severe? She knew that it would be over soon. Hopefully, no one would get hurt. Especially her.

She thought back to the night before when her girls showed up to check on her. That brought a smile to her face. It relieved her mind of all the stress and issues that she had been going through. At least for a little while anyway. She took comfort in knowing that there was someone around her at all times. At first, it seemed kind of intrusive, but she quickly realized that she would rather have intrusiveness over danger any day. By now whoever was stalking her, knew that she had called the police. Hopefully, they would back off and leave her alone now. They would be stupid to continue now that the police were involved. She figured by now that the surveillance detail would be hungry, so she instructed her staff to make some eggs, sausages, bacon and toast for the detail. They all had barely finished eating when someone said "Is this what you are supposed to be doing?" They all turned to see Detective Cruz standing there. "Tell me how is it that I could walk in here unnoticed by any of you? Suppose I was the stalker, some of you would be dead now." With that being said, they all got up and went back to their post. "I'm sorry, it was all my fault. I thought that they needed something to eat. Something to keep their strength up." Stephanie said with a smile. "Ma'am, I totally understand, but they are seasoned officers and should know better than that. I do appreciate you taking care of them though. Next time, if there is a next time, please don't feed them all at once." "Oh, I am ma'am now? You know you can call me Stephanie, to be honest I prefer it." "Yes Stephanie, I am aware. I will make sure that I call you that from now on." "Please do. Now, would you like some breakfast as well?" "Well, if it is not too much trouble. I would love to taste your cooking." "Oh, you want me to cook it for you? You do know I am the owner, right?" "You are the owner of a restaurant, so that means you should be able to cook." "Okay, since you obviously feel like you deserve a meal cooked by me, please follow me." She walked off, knowing that Detective Cruz was definitely going to be behind her. When she got to the kitchen, she pulled out some more ingredients. "Have a seat, I will whip you something up real quick." "How do you know what I want?" "Easy, you want whatever I make for you.

That's how it goes at Rains!" She smiled, he smiled back. "Okay, I guess you have a point there." "Don't worry, I am going to make you my favorite breakfast. If you don't like it, I will eat it. You don't have cooties, do you?" "Okay sounds fair enough." Stephanie made an omelet with ham, mushrooms, cheddar cheese, smoked gouda and spinach. She made the bacon crispy, poured a mixture of orange and pineapple juice. She laid two pieces of sourdough toast with butter on the plate. "I hope you enjoy it." Detective Cruz looked at the plentiful plate. Everything looked so good that he didn't want to eat it. It was a vision of beauty unveiled upon a plate. "Thank you very much." "Come on ... eat it. You are taking too long." Detective Cruz eased a forkful of omelet into his mouth. His facial expression gave off an instant look of satisfaction. He chewed the omelet slowly, meticulously, as if he was tasting each and every morsel of it. He tilted the juice towards his mouth and let the orange/pineapple mixture make its way down his throat. He had never expected such a great taste. All he could do was smile, for he was now in food heaven. "Well?" Stephanie's voice broke him out of his food trance. "Sorry, this is definitely delicious. Thank you again for making this for me." "I am glad you like it. Now get back to work." "Oh, you got jokes." "You didn't know. You better ask somebody." They both laughed, as Detective Cruz continued to enjoy his meal.

Forty Five

As Cashmere and Simeon settled into their seats on the plane to Virginia, she was happy that he was sitting next to her. She had taken a huge chance at losing him, with her infatuation with Ali. Lucky for her, Simeon was able to put her mistake behind him, he knew what he wanted, and she was it. He was playing for keeps now. He knew that he had to step his game up because if he didn't Cashmere may be easily persuaded to be with someone else. He wasn't about to have that. He wasn't about to go through that bull again.

Cashmere looked over at Simeon and smiled. She couldn't help to think about how fine he was. She wanted him way more than he knew. Her thoughts of making love to him had consumed her. She wanted to touch him so she reached over and grabbed his hand. He reciprocated by wrapping his fingers around her hand. Her skin felt soft, she smelled wonderful too. Her perfume was sweet and sensual. Simeon knew that he was going to have her as soon as they got to Virginia. He had made his mind up that he was going to give her all that he had in the way of lovemaking. He was going to put it on her so that she wouldn't even think about another man again. He was determined to make her his or at the very least she would want to be his! He wanted all that she had to offer and believe me; Cashmere had a lot to offer. He looked over at her, focusing on her sexy juicy lips that were covered with lipstick, his eyes moved down to her ample chest. He was quite pleased with what he saw, it didn't hurt that she was showing some cleavage either. Then his eyes cascaded down to her thick thighs that were looking very good in those tight jeans she was wearing. When Simeon looked up, he saw Cashmere looking at him and smiling.

He knew that she saw him checking her out. The part that he missed was that while he was checking her out, she was checking him out as well. She had positioned her eyes on the bulge that was showing in his pants. Simeon placed his hand on her thigh and squeezed her leg softly. She smiled, leaned over and kissed him gently on the lips. After kissing him she placed her hand on his thigh and ran her hand up and down it.

After the plane landed, they got off, and picked up their bags. Simeon rented a car, then they drove to Cashmere's place. Once they arrived at her house, they both knew what was going to come next. For Simeon, he was going to claim his prize. For Cashmere, she was going to finally have Simeon the way she wanted him. As they were walking in, Simeon couldn't help but to look down at what she was working with. He knew that it wouldn't be long before he was enjoying her. The way she swirled her flavor was more than enticing. Simeon was enjoying the way her flavor swirled before him. Before they could get in the door good, he had her up against the wall, kissing her full juicy lips. She ran her hands down to his buttocks and his hands were all over her. They both felt good to one another. Simeon pressed his body against hers, as he felt her great sized breast against his chest. Her perfume permeated his nostrils, which enticed him all the more. Cashmere began to feel warm from all the heat that was transpiring between them. Simeon had his hands full with her sweet booty as Cashmere was kissing his neck. Simeon buried his face between her breasts, which sent jolts of electricity through his body. She was so soft and she smelled divine. He couldn't help but want her more! She pulled his face to hers and kissed him softly at first, then with more passion. She bit his bottom lip and uttered the words "Come with me." She guided him to her bedroom. They both fell on the bed; she got on top of him, continuing to kiss him. He ran his hands up and down the back of her thighs concentrating on her ample buttocks. She started unbuttoning his shirt and kissing his chest. He rolled her over and kissed her sweet lips. He started unbuttoning her shirt; revealing more of her for his eye pleasure. They were everything that he had imagined them to be. He quickly buried his face between them again. She cupped the back of his head and eased him closer, so that his face was submerged between her cleavage. She began to feel warmer, her heat was building. "Simeon, I want you so badly. Please take me!" she urged. Simeon unhooked her bra, pulled it off and exposed her full breasts. She removed his shirt enjoying the view of his athletically chiseled chest. She rolled him over and began to kiss his nipples while rubbing her hands along the sides of his chest. The ripples along his six-pack felt really good to her touch. She couldn't wait to explore more of him, what's more is that she couldn't wait for him to explore more of her. She was really ready for him. Her body was on fire from his touch. His touches felt like little kisses all along her body, introducing ecstasy to anything in its path. He had her right where he wanted her, but she wouldn't dare let him know. She didn't have to let him know. He knew exactly what he was doing. He knew exactly what he was going to do to drive her even wilder. Cashmere was in for it tonight. She unbuttoned his pants and was eager to release what was hidden behind his jeans. She couldn't wait to see, to feel all that he had to share with her. She felt his manhood pressed up against her. Simeon was truly into this, he wanted to give her more than she bargained for; he was prepared to give her that knock out sex. He unbuttoned her jeans, slid them down and tossed them across the room. Her body was mesmerizing. Her thighs were thick, waist curvy and her breasts were very ample. Simeon was about to climb that mountain and enjoy her wholeheartedly. He started with a simple kiss to her ankle, moving his way up, he placed kisses along her thighs. He continued moving up, where he noticed her burgundy panties. "You won't need these any longer." he said as he slid them down and tossed them across the room too. He eased his way between her legs parting them as he slid closer to her sweetness. The time had come; he was face to face with her sweetness. She was waiting to see if he was going to have a taste. To her surprise, he not only tasted her but he drove her to a roaring climax. She could barely contain herself. All she could think was this was just the beginning. He made his way up to her sweet lips. She looked him deep in his eyes, she gasped when she felt him go inside her. She felt him within her. He felt great inside her. He was giving her that good good that she had needed for some time now. As he penetrated her sweetness, he kissed her lips with extra sensuality. He was giving her what she needed. She began to feel her sweetness start to tune up for another climax. He rose up and put her legs over his shoulders, driving himself deeper inside of her. "Arch your back baby." he told her. She did as she was instructed. Simeon began to thrust harder and harder. He wanted her to feel him as deep as she could. He needed her to know that she belonged to him. She received him entirely, enjoying every thrust as if it was the very last one. Truth be told she couldn't resist any longer. He couldn't contain himself any longer. He had succeeded in letting Cashmere know that she was off the market. All she could do was roll over and close her eyes. Simeon looked at her and thought to himself "That's what I'm talking about. Good night Cashmere."

He got up, went to the bathroom and took a shower. When he returned Cashmere had started snoring. He couldn't help but to laugh as he turned on the television to chill while she slept.

Forty Six

Tammy called Char and Cashmere to see if they had time to get together with the girls tonight. Char answered and said that she would love to get together.

Cashmere's phone went to voicemail. Tammy wasn't sure if she had made it back from New York yet, so she left her a message. "Cashmere, what's up girl? Call me when you get this. We are planning a girl's night out tonight." Tammy was worried about Stephanie because she knew that Stephanie was in more danger than she was letting on. Tammy thought back to when Stephanie first told her about the letters, she warned her then to contact the police, but she wouldn't do it. She was glad that Stephanie had finally taken her advice and contacted them. The surveillance detail made them all feel better about it, but the stalker was still out there. Tammy decided to call Stephanie back to make sure that she was still okay.

Stephanie ... Hello.

Tammy ... Hey girl, I just called to make sure that you are okay.

Stephanie ... To tell you the truth I am still a little scared. This is just way too crazy.

Tammy ... Yeah, it really is. I wish you had called the police when this first started.

Stephanie ... You're right, I should have. I didn't really believe that it would turn into something like this. I thought that it would eventually go away. Now that the surveillance detail is with me, I feel much safer. Detective Cruz is on top of everything too.

Tammy ... I know you did. Oh, Char is down to get together tonight.

Stephanie ... What about Cashmere?

Tammy ... I left her a message. I haven't heard back from her yet. I think she may still be in New York.

Stephanie ... Oh okay. I thought she was supposed to get back this morning. She might be sleeping.

Tammy ... Well, I am sure she will call sometime today. How are your parents?

Stephanie ... Yeah, I am sure she will too. My parents are doing okay, thanks.

Tammy ... That's good. Okay, I will call you later.

Stephanie ... Okay girl. Talk to you soon. Thanks for calling to check on a sister.

Tammy ... You're welcome. Talk to you soon. Bye.

Stephanie ... Bye.

Just as Tammy was putting her phone down, Rico walked up behind her. He did it so quietly that he startled her a little bit. She jumped just a little. "I'm sorry babe; I didn't mean to scare you." "It's okay baby. I am just a little nervous about what Stephanie is going through." "Is she okay?" "No, she is still a little scared. They haven't caught him yet. I hope tonight relaxes her a little bit." "I hope so too. Where are you planning to take her?" I thought we would start out at Croaker Spot, and then roll over to The Crib for some drinks." "It sounds like it is going to be a great night." "I hope so. Are you sure you don't want to go with us?" "Yeah baby, I am sure. I think this is something that you and your girls need to handle without a man around." "Okay, will I see you after?" "Of course baby. If you want." "Do you want me to come by your place or will you come by mine?" "I'll come by your place baby. I don't want you to have to drive too far. I am sure you will be feeling good when you leave the club." "Yeah, you're right. Here." "What's this?" "This is a key to my place." Tammy looked at Rico and smiled. Rico took the key, placed it on his key ring and said "Are you sure?" "Of course I am sure. I want you to have it. I've actually been carrying it around since last week." "Oh, I see you have thought this through." "Yes I have. I love you Rico and I want to spend as much time with you as I can. You make me very happy and I hope that I make you happy as well." "Baby, you have no idea how happy you make me. I thank GOD for you walking into Layla's Cafe that day." They hugged and kissed, when they stopped kissing, they looked at one another again and couldn't help but to kiss again. That kiss ended with a nice long hug. Rico walked over to the couch, turned on the television to watch the news. That was one of his morning rituals. He always watched the news because he wanted to make sure he was aware of what was going on in the world. Tammy brought a couple cups of coffee in to the living room. She handed Rico one of them and sat beside him on the couch. Tammy couldn't help but to smile. She felt really good about her and Rico. She was really happy that he accepted the key too. She had been very nervous about giving it to him; she didn't want him to think that she was moving too fast. They both sipped their coffee. She couldn't help but look at him and smile. He made her so happy. She felt complete with him in her life.

Rico looked at her and smiled, letting her know that he was just as happy with her as she was with him. She moved over to him and he held her in his arms as they continued to drink their coffee and finish watching the news. She laid her head on his chest; he gently kissed the top of her head. That kiss brought a smile to her face. Rico could be so romantic. She loved that for such a masculine man, he could show his sensitive, romantic side too. Rico loved the way that Tammy felt lying against him. He loved the way her body felt, the way she found comfort in him. It was something that he had wanted for a long time. Now he had it with Tammy and so much more. After the news went off, Tammy laid in his arms a little longer. She was enjoying it for as long as she could. She felt like she could spend the rest of her life in his arms. He certainly wouldn't object since he loved the way she felt in his arms. The way she would rub his chest when she laid on it, was simply wonderful to him. Her hands were soft and truly felt great against his chest. It was a touch that he not only liked, but one that he desired often. Tammy enjoyed feeling the muscles beneath her fingers as she let them roam all over him. His body was like a Picasso painting to her. Each muscle was like a carefully thought out brush stroke. She took her time running her fingers along his body. He was in heaven. Each fingertip gliding over his skin took him to greater heights. Her touch was simply mesmerizing to him. He enjoyed her slow steady fingers gliding alongside his body. Total relaxation overcame him. Before he knew it, she had rubbed him into an unanticipated slumber. Tammy kept her fingers moving along his body to continue relaxing him. Plus he felt good to her as well. Her sweetness had started reacting to the feel of his skin.

Forty Seven

Stephanie was more than ready to see her girls tonight. She really needed some girl time right now. What she really needed was the comfort of a man in her life. She had grown tired of being alone. She wanted someone to fulfill her lonely nights after work. She envied Tammy's relationship with Rico. She adored the love that her parents had for one another. She wondered why she didn't have a love of her own. Was she too consumed with work to allow someone into her life? Or was it that she hadn't met the right man yet?

Whatever it was, she was missing out on love. That was one part of her life that needed to change, especially now. She didn't want to go through this ordeal alone. She wanted someone to comfort her. Someone to tell her that everything would be alright. She needed the soothing touch of a loving man, a man that only had eyes for her. She knew that she had a lot of love to give to someone special. They would never know it though because she was too busy building her restaurant to give anyone a chance at her love. Of course that wasn't her intention. It was just how things seemed to pan out for her. She knew that it wouldn't always be this way, but when would things change for her? When would Mr. Right come into her life? When would she be swept off of her feet? Stephanie decided to go to the kitchen to make some sweet tea so that she could sit out on the patio to enjoy it before she got ready to start her day. While she was sitting outside she noticed one of the surveillance detail walking by on his patrol of her place. He waved and she waved back. She offered him some sweet tea; he graciously declined and wished her a good day. She was sure that he was thirsty; he just didn't want to bother her, since it was clear that she was relaxing. She watched him walk around the house, and then she heard the doorbell ring. She got up to open the door; looked through the peephole and saw one of the police officers standing in front of Char. When she opened the door the officer immediately asked "Do you know this person?" "Yes, this is my friend Char, she is welcomed here." "Okay, ma'am you may enter the home. If it's okay with you, we would like for one of us to be in the house with you, while she is here." "I don't see the necessity of that. I have known Char for some time now." "I understand ma'am, but we need to do our job too." "I understand. I tell you what; we will be on the patio. You can meet us back there and secure the area from a distance." "Yes ma'am, I will see you in the back in a few minutes." Char walked past the officer and entered Stephanie's house. "Girl, I see they are still on the job." "Char, I can't believe I have been receiving threatening letters for several months now. At first they were being left at my restaurant, the other night someone was in my house and I found one on my pillow in my bedroom. To be honest, I am glad they are around. I feel a little safer these days." "I am so ready to go out tonight, so I can take my mind off of all this. I need some sort of normalcy in my life again."

"Damn Stephanie, I can't imagine going through all this." "I know, it is a burden that I wouldn't want you or anyone else to have to deal with. You have your own life to worry about." "I understand Stephanie, but you know we are your girls. We are here for you, just like you are here for us." "I know and I appreciate that. The truth is I was hoping that it would just stop. Would you like something to drink or eat?" "I'll take some of that sweet tea that you have." "Good, I want some more as well. Go ahead out to the patio and I will bring some out." "Sounds good Stephanie, thanks." Char went out to the patio, sat down and saw the policemen about twenty feet away from her. When Stephanie came out with the tea, she also had some strawberries that she had chopped in halves. She sat down and noticed the surveillance team watching them from afar. She decided to sit with her back to them so that she didn't have to keep looking at their faces. She knew that this was necessary, but it was such an inconvenience. It was a good thing that she wasn't romantically involved with anyone right now. They would surely want to be around, if she were. No telling what would happen then. "So Char what's going on with you?" "Well I am flying out to Hawaii next week for a photo shoot. Then two weeks later I will be in

Italy." "That reminds me, the cruise is three weeks away too. I hope that this craziness is over by then." "What if it isn't? How will that affect your trip?" I am not sure, they will probably tell me that I shouldn't go or that one of them will have to go with me." "That would not be cool Stephanie. You guys have been planning this trip for a while now. Aren't you supposed to be driving down to Cape Hatteras with the girls?" "Yes, that's the plan. I will talk to Detective Cruz about it to see what he thinks." Detective Cruz, who is that?" "He is the detective that is in charge of my case." "Why does that name sound so familiar to me?" "He was the lead detective on the bank robbery case with my parents." "That doesn't seem a little strange to you." "It hadn't until you just mentioned it." "Maybe it is a coincidence. As long as he takes care of the situation, it's all good." "I think I will still ask him how he ended up with my case, just to be on the safe side." "Let me know what he says." "You know I will girl. So what time are we supposed to be leaving tonight?" "Will you have to take your surveillance with you tonight too?" "I really hope not, but I am pretty sure they will have to be near." "This really is an inconvenience in your life." "I know it is, but to tell you the truth I feel safer knowing that they are around. I just don't like being babysat." "Well hopefully it will be over soon and you can go back to living a normal life." "That's just it; I don't want a normal life. I want a spectacular life." "What makes for a spectacular life to you?" "For me, it is a successful business, someone to share it with, the ability to travel and enjoy life without questioning the cost." "All that sounds great to me. You have a semi successful business. You've always had money. Now you need someone to share it with." "Well, I haven't always had money. My parents have money; I want to get my own money. As far as my business, I figure it will take me about five years to establish another restaurant. Once I have my second restaurant, I will be ready to start traveling." "Hopefully you will meet someone really special between now and then." "Yeah, hopefully sooner than later!" Both Stephanie and Char burst into laughter. Char looked over and noticed the police officer smiling; he was looking in their direction, so she naturally thought that he was smiling at them. "Why do you think he is smiling so much Stephanie?" "He sees two beautiful women that he can't have." "Girl, I know that's right. Although, he is kind of cute." "Char, I am sure in your line of work, you have seen some drop dead gorgeous men." "Of course I have, but that's different." "Why is that?"

"Because they are just as concerned with being beautiful as I am. I like a man that doesn't spend all day in the mirror, if you know what I mean." "I can understand that. I guess you see quite a bit of beautiful men that are more concerned with their looks than they are with anything else." "Exactly, I want a man that is not concerned with all that. I want a man that just loves to have fun, someone who is spontaneous, intelligent, and God-fearing." "What ever happened to the guy that you met at the grand opening?" "Oh he still lives with his mother; I'm looking for a man, not a boy trying to pretend he's a man!" "Wait, he still lives with his mother?" "Yeah girl, I could just see it now, we go back to his place to get a little cozy and his momma comes out in her housecoat, asking if we would like some sandwiches. Oh hell no. If you don't have your own, I can't come out and play." "Damn, that's a shame. I thought he was cute too." "Yeah, he was cute, but he wasn't ready to be a grown up. And I don't have time to wait for him to grow up. No woman should have to do that. He should already be a man when he comes to me" "I feel you Char. I believe that if a woman can take the time to get her life together, the least a man can do is the same. Now don't get me wrong there are quite a few men out there that have their stuff together. Unfortunately, there are a lot of men that aren't even close to having their stuff together, and those are the ones that always seem to want to approach me." They both just started laughing again. They were sure that the police officer thought that he was the basis of their amusement.

Forty Eight

When Cashmere started to stir, Simeon looked over and started smiling. She opened her eyes, he moved over closer to her. "Did you sleep well?" "How long was I asleep?" "You were asleep for only a couple of hours." "I guess I was tired from the flight." "That might have been it or it could have been that knock out sex that I gave you." "Oh you are full of yourself today." "Oh okay, so you didn't get that good good last night?" "Simeon, the love making was nice, but I fell asleep because I was tired from the flight." "Sure, yeah that's it. You were tired from the flight. It didn't have anything to do with all that you received this morning, either." "I already told you that it was nice. You handled your business. Is that what you want to hear?" "Thank you. Yes, that's exactly what I want to hear." All Cashmere could do was smile. "You are truly something else Simeon." "Now that you know ... what's on our agenda for the day?" "Well, I have to go to the office sometime soon to meet with my uncle." "When are you doing that?" "I'm not sure, probably around two or three." "Okay, how long will you be there?" "Damn Simeon, you ask a lot of questions." "Well, I am just trying to plan out my day too. I figured I would get some time in the studio while you were meeting with your uncle." "You have studio time in Richmond too?" "Yeah, there are a couple of producers in Richmond that I am working with." "Oh, so this trip was about your music and not about me?" "That's not at all what I said. I came here to make you mine. I figured since you were going to be busy, I could take care of some stuff too. Is that wrong?" "No, it's not wrong; I just don't want it to turn out like the last time." "Neither do I. Obviously you need undivided attention." "Oh, you had to go there. That's not fair." "Okay, you're right. Sorry about that." "It's all good. I am going to jump in the shower." Cashmere walked to the bathroom, just as naked as she was when she was born. Simeon couldn't do anything but admire her very sexy body. It instantly brought a smile to his face. He wanted to go get in the shower with her, but he knew that would only delay things. He also knew that he would enjoy her later on tonight. He got his clothes out of the suitcase and looked around for an ironing board and iron. To his surprise he heard Cashmere singing while she showered. He actually liked what he was hearing. She had a very nice tone to her voice. Simeon was already attracted to Cashmere, now that he knew she could sing, he was much more attracted to her. As Simeon was getting dressed Cashmere walked out of the bathroom with a towel wrapped around her. Even in the towel, she looked very entrancing. She noticed him smiling. "Do you like what you see, Simeon?" "I most definitely do like what I see. I may have to pull that towel away and enjoy what is underneath." "Oh, no sir. You are already dressed and ready to go. We wouldn't want to make you late for your studio session." Cashmere walked up to him and kissed him on the lips, then walked away quickly so that he wouldn't grab the towel from her. "Could you please go to the kitchen and fix us a couple of sandwiches and some sweet tea?" "Ah, sure. I guess I can do that." Simeon walked away knowing exactly what Cashmere was up to. She was trying to get rid of him so that she could get dressed without him trying to ravish her again. She couldn't deny that she wanted him. She knew that she wouldn't resist him, especially since he truly handled his business. Her body was still throbbing from earlier. He could have her whenever he wanted her, she didn't want him to know that though. Not yet anyway. Simeon returned with their lunch, Cashmere was fully dressed and looking fabulous. "Let's eat at the table. That way we can be comfortable." "Okay, after you." Cashmere walked ahead of Simeon and he enjoyed the view from behind.

After finishing their lunch, she began to gather her things to head to the store so she could meet with Uncle Herbert. "Do you need me to drop you off at the studio?" "No, I'm good. I rented a car, remember?" "Oh okay, well when will you be done?" "I tell you what, when you are done, call me and I will wrap things up and meet you back here." "Great, that sounds good. It shouldn't be more than a few hours." "Okay, I will see you later on then. Have a great day!" Cashmere walked up to Simeon, put her arms around his neck and kissed him very passionately. "I am glad that you are here with me baby." She turned and walked out the door. Simeon took out his phone and dialed Sammie's, one of the producer's numbers...

Simeon ... I'm on my way.

Sammie ... Okay, see you when you get here.

Simeon ... Cool.

Sammie ... Cool.

Simeon pressed end on the phone, got another glass of sweet tea, and then gathered his lyrics from his suitcase. He opened the door, walked down to get in the rental. Within minutes Simeon was there. He went down the hall to the last studio on the left. "What's up Simeon?" "What's going on with you Sammie? It's good to see you man." "Yeah, it's been a minute since we put in some work." "No doubt, I got some hotness here for you. Been working on some things since the last time we spoke." "Cool, I can't wait to hear what you've come up with. I know it is hot." "I think so, I am pretty proud of it. I think it fits your style very well. I hope you have some new material." "Oh for sure ... I have written four new songs since I was here last. I just need something that really cracks to lace it with." "Hell yeah ... you are in luck then. I have been saving some tight tracks for you." "Now you have me excited, queue them up. How many tracks do you have ready?" "I have six tracks ready. You can pick the four that you want; I have other projects that I can use the other two on." "Oh I get first pick?" "Yeah, you know how we do man." "That's what I'm talking about fam. That's what's up." "You can have them for two points apiece." "Damn Sammie, you are always about business." "Hell yeah, there isn't any other way to be. Do we have a deal?" "Yeah, deal." "Okay, we will settle the paperwork after you pick your beats." "Okay, that's cool." Sammie queued up the music.

When Cashmere walked in the store, it was busier than normal. Everybody was on the floor slanging clocks, even Uncle Herbert. He nodded at me and motioned for me to go and help a browsing customer. I acknowledged and headed in their direction. I noticed a line at the cash register; this reminded me of when I was in New York. Uncle Herbert's businesses were really doing well. He had a keen mind for business. She wondered why he hadn't noticed the missing money over the years or had he noticed it and just not mentioned it, hoping that it would turn up as easily as it disappeared. She looked over at Uncle Herbert and he was all smiles, helping the customers with whatever they needed. His whole life was these clocks. He lived and breathed them for as long as she could remember. She remembered back to when she was a kid; he would come over to the house for a get together and would always end up talking about having a chain of clock stores one day.

Everybody thought he was crazy, but he was determined to do it. She couldn't help but to feel proud of him and ashamed of herself at the same time. When the store cleared out, Uncle Herbert walked over to Cashmere... "How did the trip to New York go?" "Uncle Herbert, things went quite well. The New York store seemed to be busy every day that I was there. The staff seems to be very knowledgeable and engaged in their work. They all seem to get along very well too." "That's great to hear. How were the finances and what about the manager Ali, does he seem like a good fit?" "Oh Ali, he seems very knowledgeable." "And?" "There's no "and"." "Are you sure? "Yes, I am sure." "You don't seem like it. I will take your word for it though. I trust you Cashmere; you are my flesh and blood." "Okay, thanks Uncle Herbert, I love you too!" "Good, can you do me a favor and handle the floor; I have some clocks that I need to order." "Yeah, but I thought ordering the supplies was my job." "It is, but there are some special items that I need. I really don't want to trouble you with them." "Uncle Herbert, is everything alright?" "Of course dear, why wouldn't they be?" "I don't know, you just seem a little strange, all of a sudden." Uncle Herbert looked at her, then turned away and headed through the office door. She wondered if that look was a look of disappointment. Whether it was or wasn't, something was different about Uncle Herbert, she had to watch her step from here on out.

Forty Nine

While Tammy enjoyed relaxing in Rico's arms, she knew they both had things to do today. She needed to run some errands before meeting the girls and Rico had a meeting with R.J. before the club opened tonight. Although it was hard for them to let go of one another, they knew they had to get their day going. Tammy was first to move away. Then Rico followed suit. They both wanted to just sit back down on the couch and enjoy the rest of the day in each other's arms. The more time they spent together, the harder it was getting to be without one another, even if it was for only a few hours. Their bond had strengthened so much since the day they met. It was as if they had been made for each other. As if it was their destiny to be together. Rico jumped in the shower, while Tammy got her things together. When Rico was dressed, they both headed out to his car. By the time they got to Tammy's place, Rico was wishing they were still at his place. He was enjoying having her there. He walked her to the door, and then gave her a very nice kiss, before she closed the door. This was the part they both had been dreading. They knew that it would only be for a few hours, but those few hours would seem like an eternity to them.

Tammy went straight to her bedroom, took off her clothes and jumped in the shower for a nice long hot relaxing shower. All she could think about was the great time that she had with Rico the night before. She wanted to spend all day with him, but knew that she needed to check on Stephanie, plus she missed the rest of her girls. This night was going to be all about Stephanie. She was truly worried about her. The one thing that she knew for certain was that Stephanie needed her girls right now. She may not realize it, but she did. She didn't need any more craziness in her life. She had way more than her fair share of craziness so far. When Tammy got out of the shower, she noticed that her phone was ringing. She answered it and Cashmere was on the other end.

Tammy ... Hey Cashmere. What's going on girl?

Cashmere ... I saw that you called. I heard your message. I have a friend in town, I was thinking about bringing him with me.

Tammy ... Well, I am not sure if that is a good idea.

Cashmere ... Why is that?

Tammy ... Well, we are getting together because Stephanie needs our help. I don't think it would be a good idea to bring someone else along with you. It might make her uncomfortable.

Cashmere ... Okay, well in that case, I can only come for an hour or so. It wouldn't be right to leave him alone for too long.

Tammy ... I understand. I'm just glad you can make it at all.

Cashmere ... You know I wouldn't miss it, especially if one of my girls needs me.

Tammy ... I know. I was thinking about getting together at about 6:00, is that cool for you?

Cashmere ... Yeah, that's fine. Where are we meeting?

Tammy ... We can meet at Croaker Spot or at my place. I'm good with either.

Cashmere ... Let's meet at your place. We can talk to Stephanie there. When y'all go to the club, I will come back home.

Tammy ... Okay, that sounds good. See you then.

Cashmere ... Great. See you at six.

Tammy ... Bye.

Cashmere ... Bye.

When Tammy hung up the phone she felt good that Cashmere was going to be around tonight. Cashmere was the one person that could talk some sense into Stephanie. She wouldn't hold back. She would say whatever was on her mind. Tammy loved her directness, her no-nonsense approach. She was the type of person that everyone needed in their lives at some point or another. Stephanie was about to get a big dose of Cashmere tonight. That's exactly what she needed to get her mind back on track. Nobody really knew what Stephanie was thinking these days. She had immersed herself in her work, it seemed like she was trying to forget everything that had happened. No one could blame her, if that was the case.

Tammy sent text messages to Char and Stephanie, letting them know to come to her place at six tonight. Both Char and Stephanie replied that they would be there.

Tammy was hopeful that the evening would be fun for all of them, especially Stephanie. When the girls arrived at Tammy's, they all were dressed to impress. Four beautiful women, all gathered in the same place at the same time for the same purpose. The night started off as usual with some Moscato and the girls sitting around just catching up with one another. Tammy had made some hors d'oeuvres to get them through their conversation before going to Croaker Spot. There was laughter in the air, up until Cashmere blurted out "Stephanie ... What is going on with you? How come you didn't tell us about the stalker guy?" Stephanie looked directly at Tammy. "Stephanie, I was worried about you. I thought you needed someone to talk to about all of this.

You didn't sound so well the last time we met." Tammy stated. "So, you called them and asked them to talk to me? What is this an intervention? I don't think I am in need of an intervention!" "This is not an intervention. This is just friends getting together to help out another friend. You are our girl and we love you." "If I wanted everyone to know, I would have told them myself. I can't believe you did this Tammy. You are supposed to be my girl." "What are you talking about Stephanie? Are you drawing a blank? Cashmere is the only one that wasn't there the other night. I am your girl; we all are your girls. That's why we are here to help you through all of this." "Help me through what? What is it that you think you can do to help me?" "Sometimes people just need to get stuff off their chest.

Maybe if we talk through it, it will make you feel a little better about everything." "I don't think I need to talk to anyone else about this." "Stephanie, cut the crap. You know you need your girls right now. Stop tripping and start talking!" shouted Cashmere. "Okay, maybe Cashmere didn't say that the best possible way, but she is right. You need to get all your feelings out.

That way you release whatever stress or tensions you have built up inside you." Char said. "I really don't think I need to talk about anything. I told you, I have already talked about it. I told Tammy, I talked to the detective on the case. I think I have talked enough about this. As a matter of fact, I am done talking. I hope y'all have a great night. I'm going home!" "Really Stephanie ... is that where we're at? You're upset and want to leave because we care about you and want to help you through this?" "No Cashmere, I am leaving because I feel like I am being put on the spot! I don't really want to hang out tonight because of it." Stephanie got up and left, slamming the door behind her. Char, Tammy and Cashmere were surprised at her reaction. They all thought that they were doing the right thing by wanting to help her. "Oh damn." Cashmere said with a puzzled look on her face. They all knew that the next time they talked to Stephanie; she was going to have some words to say about this. "So are we still going to the club ladies?" Tammy asked "I'm still down to go if you two want to roll." Char said. "Yeah, I need some fun right now. Let's do it." Tammy said. "I won't be making it to the club tonight. I have something else to attend to tonight." Cashmere said. "That's right she has a friend in town!" Tammy said. "Oh, do tell Cashmere, do tell." Char stated with a slight smile on her face. "There's nothing really to tell. Simeon, the guy I met at Croaker Spot is in town from New York. We are spending some quality time together." "Quality time, is that what they're calling it these days?" Char said. The girls started laughing.

Cashmere wished them both a safe night and left to spend time with Simeon!

Fifty

When they got to The Crib, it was packed as usual. Of course Rico had made sure that they had their customary V.I.P. section, stocked with all the goodies that they loved. Tammy looked around for Rico, but he wasn't anywhere to be seen. She wondered if he was in the office. Char poured a tall glass of Moscato, dipped a strawberry in some chocolate and enjoyed the tastiness of it all.

Tammy decided on vodka and cranberry juice to start her evening off. She couldn't help but to think about Stephanie. She started to feel bad, but deep down she knew that they had her best interest at heart. She only hoped that Stephanie would feel the same way after a couple of days. "Tammy, what's on your mind?" asked Char. "I was just thinking about Stephanie." "We tried to help her. She wasn't ready to accept it yet. Don't worry. We've known Stephanie forever, she'll come around." "Yeah, I guess you're right. I'm about to go out here and get my dance on." "I hear that. Do your thing girl." Char said while laughing a little. Both of them went out to the dance floor and started dancing together. Slowly but surely, some guys walked up and started dancing by them. Tammy slowly walked away, while Char danced with the three of them, before deciding to walk away as well. When she returned to the table, R.J. was there checking on the girls to make sure that everything was to their liking. Char thanked R.J. for the great spread that he had laid out for them. They felt like royalty when they were there. R.J. and Rico always made sure that they were well taken care of. They really went out of their way to take care of them. "Is Rico around?" Tammy asked. "You just missed him. He left a little bit ago." replied R.J. "Oh okay. It sure would have been nice to see him before he left." "I think he was thinking the same thing as you. To be honest, I believe he was waiting for you to get here." Tammy couldn't help but to let out a big smile. She knew that it would have been a wonderful treat to see Rico tonight. She had to admit there were some nice looking brother's in The Crib tonight. None of them caught her eye like Rico did though. Tonight wasn't about her and Rico. It was supposed to be about Stephanie, but since she caught an attitude and didn't want to participate. It was going to have to be about her and Char. Char was pouring another drink, while Tammy was enjoying some chocolate covered strawberries. Attention was rising from the gathering of men that were checking them out. They both knew that it was Char that was drawing the attention. It always went down that way, because they recognized her as a celebrity. The funny thing is they would look, but they wouldn't approach. They were all intimidated by her status, which is totally understandable. What they didn't know was that Char was more attracted to the boy next door type, rather than the celebrity types. She knew the celebrity game all too well, since she was one of them. So, you see, she was really caught in a catch twenty two because she wouldn't give the celebrity types the time of day, but the boy next door guys wouldn't approach her either. It was a pity too, because she saw some guys that she would be interested in getting to know or at the very least chatting with. Unfortunately, they would never know, because they would never approach her. Tammy decided to take Char's mind off the fact that the men would not approach her by continuing the conversation about Stephanie and the way she reacted tonight. "I can't believe she acted so stank tonight." "She should have known that at the very least, we had her best interest at heart." replied Char. "To me, it just doesn't seem like her. Something else must be up, something that she didn't want to share with us." "You think so Char?" Tammy questioned. "Yeah, why would she act that way, if it wasn't like that?" Char said. "I tell you what, now that you mention it, she has been acting funny, since we were all over her place last month. I thought it was all about her parents and the stalking thing. Now I realize that it might have started a little before that." Tammy commented. Speak of the devil; Stephanie was walking over to their table. She had decided to grace them with her presence. "Hey girl, I'm glad you decided to come after all. We're glad to see you!" Char exclaimed. "Well, I thought it over and I realized that some of you actually had my best interest at heart.

So, I wanted to come and hang out with you." After saying that she asked where Cashmere was? "Cashmere has a friend in town, so she didn't come to the club." "A friend in town." Stephanie repeated with a hint of attitude. Stephanie sat down at the table, poured herself a stiff drink of vodka and orange juice. Tammy and Char looked at each other in amazement, as if to question what her comment actually meant.

Something was going on between Cashmere and Stephanie that the others weren't aware of. They weren't quite sure if they should ask about it now or wait until another time. They were there to have a good time, they didn't need any drama at the club. You had best believe that they would find out what was going on between Stephanie and Cashmere, especially since they were supposed to go on their trip in a couple of weeks. There was no way that they were all going on a trip together with this drama. They weren't going to let Cashmere and Stephanie's drama ruin their vacation. Furthermore, they couldn't believe that Stephanie and Cashmere had kept something from them. They were like family, no secrets between them. Apparently, there was more to it for her than there was for Cashmere. Because Cashmere never gave any indication that something wasn't right between them. Char looked at Stephanie and noticed that she looked very upset now. When She noticed that Char was looking at her, Stephanie just looked away, continuing to sip on her drink. Tammy looked at Stephanie, noticing the tension on her face, but didn't question it at that time. She knew that this was going to be good, when it came out though. Everybody in the circle knew that Cashmere wasn't to be messed with. If there was an issue between her and Stephanie, it had to be something daunting. "Stephanie, we didn't mean to upset you or hurt your feelings. We were just trying to help. We figured you needed to get some stuff off your chest." Char said. "I love you girl! I do need to get some things off my chest.

Please believe when I am ready, I will do just that. Tonight caught me off guard though. I went home and realized that none of you really meant any harm. I felt bad about how I reacted, so I decided to come out and apologize for my behavior. The investigation is on-going. I am supposed to get an update from Detective Cruz tomorrow." "Well, we are glad that you came out Stephanie. We really are worried about you. The bottom line is that we are all sisters, we have to have each other's back to make it out here." Tammy said. "I totally agree." Char stated, but not before Stephanie rolled her eyes. Tammy saw it as well.

She couldn't let it slide any longer. "Stephanie what is going on? Why are you rolling your eyes?" "I'm sorry, there's just something I have to take care of and I can't get it off my mind." "I'm assuming this is about Cashmere?" Stephanie wanted to tell them, but she knew if she told them about the kiss that she and Cashmere shared, they would go straight to Cashmere with it. She was pissed with Cashmere about it, but didn't really want to deal with her about it in front of the rest of the girls. Oh, how she regretted ever kissing her. She wasn't sure just how she could get away with not telling them. She thought about leaving, but that would only add more fuel to the fire. Plus she didn't want them to think that she didn't want to hang out with them tonight. She knew she needed to get her attitude in check or they would surely press her for details. Before saying anything, Stephanie pulled out her phone and sent a text to Cashmere.

Stephanie ... Look Cashmere, I need to get this off my chest. You may not be bothered by it, but I am. I am a little upset about what went down between us. I don't really want to go there with you, but we need to get this behind us. You kissed me and put our relationship in an awkward place. I am pissed at you and I need to set you straight, so that I can move on with my life.

Fifty One

When Cashmere got up the next morning, she read Stephanie's text. She couldn't believe that she had gone there. Stephanie didn't have a clue the pain that was about to come her way. She had gotten way out of pocket; there was no way that Cashmere would let this go on much longer. Cashmere was trying her best to keep this under wraps, so that there wouldn't be any drama on the cruise. Stephanie was making it very difficult for her though. This was going to end up very badly, if things didn't change, and change fast! Cashmere and Stephanie were quickly going down a horrible path. All Cashmere wanted to do was put it behind her. It appears that Stephanie doesn't want to let it go.

She wondered if Tammy and Char knew about their kiss. If that was the case, it was truly not a good thing. The fear for Cashmere was that this would damage all of their friendships and things would never be the same. What would Char and Tammy think about the kiss they shared? How would she explain that what happened between them was a moment of weakness and vulnerability for her? What would Stephanie say about how she felt about the kiss? Apparently she wanted more than just a kiss between them. Had this been something that Stephanie had thought about before? Did she always have feelings for her? Way too many thoughts were going through Cashmere's mind right now; she needed something to take her mind off of this crazy drama.

That's when she rolled over and saw Simeon laying there still asleep. He was beautiful even in his sleep. All she could do was smile at him. He had gotten in pretty late from a night in the studio, so she didn't want to disturb him. She knew he was tired, so she eased out of the bed, as not to disturb his slumber. She grabbed her robe, went into the kitchen to make a pot of coffee. She sat down at the table, sipping on her coffee, when she heard the bedroom door open. She anticipated his entry into the kitchen. When she saw him walk in wearing only a pair of boxers, her face told the story of her happiness to see him. He eagerly walked over to her and placed a sweet good morning kiss upon her lips. "Good morning beautiful how was your night?" Good morning Simeon, it was interesting. And yours?" "My night was great; I got a lot of stuff taken care of. Why was yours interesting?" "That's great. I'm happy for you.

Well, we tried to talk to Stephanie about some of the things that are going on in her life, she was tripping about the whole thing, so it didn't go as well as we had hoped." "Well, she'll come around sooner or later. You'll see everything will work out." "I hope so; I'm not too sure about that though." "Just have faith. Y'all have been friends for a long time now; surely this won't change that. I'm sure she knows how much you care about her." Cashmere just looked at Simeon, thinking "If only you knew." "Would you like some coffee baby?" "Yes, thank you." Simeon gathered that there was more to this story than she was admitting. He decided not to press the conversation. He hoped that when she was ready to talk about it with him, that she would. Besides, he really didn't want to create a bad vibe between them. They were having a good time together, so there was no need to destroy it. They both sat at the table looking at each other, while enjoying their coffee. Cashmere offered her hand, Simeon gladly accepted it. He held her hand as if it was a rare gem. Her skin was smooth and soft, and he loved every moment of touching her. Her eyes were glued to his athletically sculptured chest. His six pack looked very inviting to her. They both were enticing to each other. She wanted him. She wanted to feel him against her body. She wanted to enjoy him again. It would be her turn to show him what she was working with. Simeon started rubbing on her arm with long, slow, smooth strokes. His touch was simply divine. She couldn't get enough of his touch. Those strokes along her arm made her want so much more. She felt herself begin to weaken from the feel of his touch. Simeon was starting to feel the effects as well. Cashmere got up and sat on his lap, giving him a sensual kiss. Simeon was rubbing on her leg, enjoying what he was feeling. He was enjoying it so much that Cashmere could feel his enjoyment beneath her. Just when she was getting into it, ding dong, bam, bam, bam, somebody was at her door. "Simeon, I will be right back baby." "Okay." Cashmere went to the door, flung it open and was surprised by who she saw.

Stephanie was standing outside her door with much attitude. "Oh, hell naw ...you didn't just come to my crib banging on the door." "Yes I did Cashmere. We have something to discuss. There's no time like the present." "Stephanie, you are tripping. Don't make me go there with you. I am really trying to be cool with you, but you are pushing it!" "Trying to be cool with me. You are trying to be cool with me, maybe you should have thought about that before you kissed me!" Stephanie was getting loud now. This was not going to be cool. "Is everything okay out here?" Simeon asked. "Who the hell are you?" Stephanie screamed. "First of all, there is no need to shout at me. I am Simeon." "Simeon, well Simeon, why don't you go back in the house. Cashmere and I need to discuss some things." Cashmere turned to Simeon "Baby, let me handle this, I will be there in a minute." "Okay baby. And you better watch who you talk crazy to young lady. You don't know me like that!" Stephanie rolled her eyes at Simeon, as he walked away. Cashmere stepped closer to Stephanie and said "Look girl, I don't know what the hell your problem is but you better not ever come to my crib talking ish to me again. Do you understand me?" Stephanie just kind of looked at Cashmere, fear gathering in her eyes now. Cashmere stepped up a little closer and said again "Do you understand me? Before you answer let me tell you this ... you are lucky I have guest or you would be picking your damn teeth up off my porch right now." "I'm sorry." Stephanie said. "You better be sorry. Now get the hell away from me before I lose my cool." Stephanie walked away like a dog with their tail between their legs. She knew she had messed up with Cashmere. When she looked back Cashmere was slamming the door. When Cashmere turned around, Simeon was looking dead at her. "What the hell was that all about?" "Simeon, I am so sorry. I had no idea she was going to come over here like that." "Who the hell was that?" "Baby ... that was Stephanie." "What was she so mad about?" "It's a long story baby." "Why don't you start at the beginning?" "To be honest baby, it's about something that happened a little while ago. I don't really want to talk about it though. It's a little embarrassing." "Well, it seems like you are going to have to talk about it soon. She seemed really pissed with you about whatever is going on." Simeon pulled Cashmere close to him and held her in his arms. He knew that she was battling with this. She instantly felt better from his hug. He knew that it was going to take more than a hug for her to get pass this. This seemed like it was too close to her heart. Her friendship was clearly threatened by this. If she could take it back, she would. Unfortunately though, what's done is done!

Fifty Two

"Last night was quite an experience." Tammy told Rico. "What was the problem baby?" "There seemed to be some tension at the table once Stephanie showed up." "Tension? Between who?" "At first I wasn't sure, but then I could tell that her frustrations were directed towards Cashmere. Whatever it is, it is serious. It seemed like Stephanie was trying to downplay the whole thing, after she realized that we were curious. She didn't want to discuss it." "Well, I hope they work out their differences. I would hate for this to spill over into your trip." "Yeah, I know, that wouldn't be cool at all." "When are you supposed to go on the cruise?" "We are supposed to be going in three weeks." "Oh, that is soon.

What happens if it isn't settled by then babe?" "Well, the trip is already paid for, so we'll just have to deal with it." Rico looked at Tammy with genuine concern in his eyes. He knew how important this trip was to her. It was important to all of them. Tammy's phone beeped.

Char ... Hey girl ... What was all that about last night?

Tammy ... Girl, I don't have a clue.

Char ... Seems like Cashmere and Stephanie have some issues between them.

Tammy ... I hope they clear it up before we have to sail off.

Char ... If they don't, it will make for an interesting trip. That's for sure!

Tammy ... Yeah, especially since we all have to ride together to Cape Hatteras.

Char ... I am glad I won't be there for all that.

Tammy ... Lucky you!

Char ... Alright girl, I just wanted to know what was up. Have a great day!

Tammy ... Alright girl, I'll talk to you later.

When Tammy put her phone down, all she could do was worry about her friends. What was to become of this crazy situation? Would their friendships survive this without being scathed? Tammy started to reminisce over some of the great times that were had by them. She knew that those good times may be threatened going forward. Something had to be done. She couldn't get all the girls together again and try to discuss it, because she was sure that Stephanie would get upset again. Who knew how Cashmere would react, when whatever the problem is, came to the forefront. Tammy had no clue what the drama was all about. All she knew was that it was extremely serious and that their friendship had never been through such a test as this before. Suddenly, her thoughts were interrupted by a sumptuous scent coming from the kitchen.

Rico was in there creating a masterpiece of a breakfast. He had prepared Tuscan style rib eye steaks with vegetable omelets. He even served fresh squeezed orange juice. Had she really been distracted that long that she didn't even notice he wasn't in the room with her? She walked into the kitchen just in time to see him plating her breakfast. He placed it on the table, pulled her chair out for her, and motioned for her to have a seat. After she sat down, he looked at her and said "Baby, I am sorry that you have to go through whatever it is that you are going through. I wanted to do something for you to make you feel a little better, for as long as you can. Please take your time enjoying this breakfast." "Oh Rico, you are so sweet, thank you so much for caring." She placed a little kiss on his cheek. They sat down and enjoyed their breakfast, enjoying conversations along the way. Rico tried his best to take her mind off of the drama that was about to unfold. He enjoyed seeing her smile again. She was so beautiful when she was happy. It was something that he was starting to miss, since he hadn't seen her smile since yesterday, when they parted. When they were done eating, Rico gathered their plates, washed the dishes and poured them some more orange juice. Tammy was smiling again. She was happy. He had succeeded. Their world was good again. At least until she heard from one of her girls. "I was wondering if you would like to go for a ride in the country this morning." Rico asked. "Sure, that would be nice. Maybe we can find somewhere to stop and just chill with one another." "That would be wonderful. Let's get ready so that we can go." "Sounds great, let's do it." They got up, went into the bedroom, took showers, got dressed and were ready to head out the door. Tammy decided that she wanted to drive this time. They headed out in her Lexus coupe. They rode out, reggae was easing through her speakers. Cruising through Virginia's country roads with the sunroof opened. Tammy looked at Rico and smiled. When they pulled over they were in Dinwiddie at the Farmers Market. Tammy had decided to stop and pick up some ingredients for a romantic dinner tonight. She thought it would be nice to cook for Rico, especially after he had made such a great breakfast for them. They walked around the farmers market holding hands. Tammy found some bell peppers, mushrooms, kale, potatoes and asparagus. Rico saw some cashews and tangelos that seemed to call his name. When they were done shopping they walked back to the car and drove off. The reggae was still filling the speakers. Tammy enjoyed riding through those winding country roads. It always seemed to relax her. This time it was especially wonderful, because Rico was sitting next to her. By the time they got home, she was more than ready to cuddle up next to Rico. Rico decided to change into his swimming trunks and dove into the pool. His hope was that Tammy would follow suit and dive in with him. After a few laps in the pool, Rico got out, went into the house and took a shower. When he got out of the shower, Tammy was there to help dry him off. She took her time toweling off every part of his body. She moved the towel slowly over his chest. She eased the towel down between his legs to make sure that his manhood was dry. She smiled when she felt him rise from her touch. Tammy fell to her knees and took Rico's manhood in her mouth. She took her time to please him. It was just a little something to give him something to look forward to later on tonight. When she was done, she stood up and kissed him very passionately. He pulled her closer to enjoy all of her, but she pulled away. "You can have me later tonight." She left him standing naked in the bathroom. He watched her walk out of the bathroom wanting to finish what she had started.

Fifty Three

Stephanie focused on the recent conversations that she had with her girls. She wasn't very happy with the way she acted towards Cashmere. She knew that she was wrong and needed to make it up to Cashmere, but that would be hard, since she was sure that Cashmere would be out for blood now that she had embarrassed her in front of Simeon. She knew that she wasn't about to let her get away with it. In the past, she had seen Cashmere get with people that had crossed her and it wasn't ever a pretty sight. Amends had to be made and made quickly, before Cashmere had time to get even angrier. Stephanie figured that she had until her guest left, and then Cashmere would be at her door to exact her revenge. All she could see in her mind was how Cashmere stepped up to her, ready for battle. She knew that her guest was the only thing that kept her from handling her business right then and there. Now her fear was how she would calm Cashmere down enough to talk this out with her. She needed her to be cool when they went on their vacation, especially on the ride down to Cape Hatteras. There was no doubt that Stephanie had her work cut out for her. She knew she had unleashed the beast, now she had to deal with it. And deal with it she would. She couldn't get this mess off her mind, no matter what she tried to think about, her mind always reverted back to Cashmere and the anger that was building inside of her. She still had to deal with her feelings towards what went down between them. She had secretly developed some sort of feelings towards Cashmere. That was the only answer she could think of to make any sense of why she felt this way towards Cashmere now. Her emotions were all over the place. She felt anger, jealousy, rejection and a need to experience more from her. The only issue was that Cashmere didn't feel the same way. To top it all off, she had a boyfriend or whoever this so-called Simeon was, at her place. It was all good; she would have her chance on their vacation, as long as things were cool between them by then. There was a knock at the door. Stephanie peeked through the peep hole and saw Detective Cruz standing out there. For some reason he did not look too happy. "Detective Cruz, how are you?" "I am fine Stephanie, how are you?" "I am well, thanks." "So, do you want to tell me about you giving my guys the slip the other night?" "What are you talking about Detective? I don't recall giving your guys the slip." "Oh okay, so Saturday night, you didn't go to The Crib to meet with some of your girlfriends?" "Okay, yes I did go there. I didn't give them the slip though. I figured they would just follow me, like they follow me everywhere else." "It's pretty hard for them to follow you when you leave out your backdoor, cross through the neighbor's yard, then drive away in your car that is parked on an adjacent street." "Why would I do such a thing? That is just crazy." "Maybe you did it because you didn't want to deal with having a surveillance team with you in the club. I'm not sure why you did it but I do know one thing, and that is that you should never do anything like that again. Anything could have happened to you." "You sound like my father now." No, I sound like someone trying to keep harm from getting close to you." "Is there a difference?" "I guess not, but if you don't let me do my job, then I won't be able to keep you safe." "Is this you chastising me?" "Someone needs to chastise you!" "Excuse me … I am a grown ass woman. I don't need chastising. Not from you. Not from anybody." "You may not need chastising, but you certainly need to start listening to somebody, before it's too late." Too late? Too late for what Det. Cruz?" "Too late for you Stephanie." He turned away, walked out the door and slammed it shut. She looked out the window as he walked across the street, and talked to the surveillance team. Two more unidentified cars pulled up before he sped off.

There were more cops around now than she ever wanted in the first place. She couldn't make a move without one of them noticing her now. There was something different about Detective Cruz tonight. He wasn't himself. He was more than frustrated about her leaving the detail. She couldn't quite put her finger on it, but something was definitely different about him. She looked out the window again, there were four policemen in her front yard. Two were on each side of the house and there were four more in the back of the house. All of them had their eyes on her house; they were waiting for her to make an attempt to go somewhere, to go anywhere. Detective Cruz had made it so she couldn't make a move without one of his guys knowing that she had done so. It would appear that she had pissed him off beyond belief. Things were about to get real for her. Little did she know that Detective Cruz did not play once his feathers were ruffled. She had definitely ruffled his feathers. He could be a real hard ass when he wanted to be. One thing was for sure, she was about to find out. She decided to take her mind off things by making herself a very nice meal. She pulled out some lovely tenderloin, some asparagus and decided to make a nice creamy risotto. She also decided to have a merlot with her meal.

She prepared the marinade for the tenderloin, after letting it rest in the juices; she placed it in the oven for thirty five minutes. Meanwhile she started to prepare the risotto and asparagus. Once the tenderloin was done, she shocked the asparagus in some ice water and started plating everything. She then poured her merlot, sat down and began to enjoy her meal. It had been some time since she cooked a nice meal at home. Normally, she would eat at the restaurant, since she was there so much. She found it very relaxing to be at home without any interruptions from anyone. Just to be able to enjoy some quiet time. She needed time to just let her mind wander wherever it wanted to wander. No pressures, no deadlines, no special meals to prepare. It was just her and her savory meal. Although it was nice, it would have been much better if she had someone special to share this great meal with.

Fifty Four

After Cashmere dropped Simeon off at the airport, she drove over to her sister's place to check on her. She hadn't talked to Ingrid in a few days. Well, at least since Simeon had been in town. She was way too busy spending time keeping him entertained. She definitely had a great time entertaining him, but she had to get back to reality. She sensed something wasn't right with Ingrid. She needed to find out what was going on with her, which would be a tough task. Ingrid wasn't one to really talk about things that bothered her. She would keep things to herself until they blew out of proportion. Then, it was usually too late to help her with it. Cashmere figured she would try her best to get her to discuss what was bothering her.

When she got there she found Ingrid in her pajamas, sipping on some orange juice. She couldn't even sit down long enough before Ingrid jumped up and ran to the bathroom. Cashmere could hear her having a hard time in there. When she opened the door, she saw Ingrid on the floor bent over the toilet bowl, with her face inside it. She ran over to her, pulled her hair back out of her face. She hated to see her sister sick, especially when she didn't know what was wrong with her. Ingrid got up, cleaned herself up. They both went back to the living room, where Ingrid got some more orange juice. "Girl, what is going on with you?" Cashmere asked. "I don't know. I haven't been able to keep anything down since yesterday. Every time I turn around, I am running to the bathroom, tossing up everything that I've eaten." "Wait a minute ... when was the last time your friend visited you?" "My friend?" "Girl, don't be dumb right now. You know exactly what I mean." "Oh, you mean my monthly?" "Of course that's

"

what I mean. When was the last time?" "Come to think of it, I don't really remember having one last month." "That's it then, you're pregnant Ingrid. You are going to have a baby!" "Pregnant, I can't be pregnant." "I would put money on it. You are going to have a baby." "This is definitely not what I need in my life right now." "Girl, maybe you should have thought about that before you laid down and gave up the goodies. It's all good though, I am going to be the best auntie in the world." "Auntie, if I'm pregnant, I am not keeping this baby." "What? What are you talking about?" "Exactly what I said, I am not ready for a baby yet." "Well, you better get ready!" "We're not even sure I'm pregnant yet." Okay, make yourself a doctor's appointment and let them tell you. I already know." "You could be wrong you know." "I could be, but I am not." Cashmere just looked at Ingrid. She wasn't sure if she was happy for her or felt sad for her.

The one thing she did know was that her sister's life was about to change, if she was pregnant. Then she thought, I may be an auntie. That would make her so happy. She knew that she would spoil her niece or nephew beyond belief.

Ingrid had this very uncertain look on her face. Cashmere could tell that she was weighing her options. She was trying to figure out how this would affect her life. The one thing that Ingrid knew for certain was that her life would not be hers any longer. If she decided to keep the baby, she would live for her child. She would try to be the best mom possible. That was a decision that she would make based on the results of her doctor's appointment. One thing that Ingrid knew was that if Cashmere had anything to do with it, she was definitely having this baby! This was definitely the biggest thing to happen in Ingrid's life. "Cashmere, will you go with me to my appointment? I really would like for you to be there with me." "Girl, of course I will go. Just let me know when it is and I am there." "Great, thanks. I don't think I can do this without you." "You don't have to do this alone. You know we will be here for you. That's what family is all about." "I am so lucky to have you as a sister. You get on my nerves sometimes, but I wouldn't trade you for the world." "Girl please ... you get on my damn nerves, but I do love you." A tear started to well up in Ingrid's eye; she hadn't felt emotion like this in a very long time. Cashmere made her feel better about possibly being pregnant. She didn't want to claim the pregnancy yet, because she really didn't know how she would feel about the whole thing. This could easily be the best thing in her life or the worst of luck. She would be the only one to know the answer to that. And she would know that answer soon enough. The question was ... whether she was ready to make the decision that she had to make. She remembered when she was a tween, all she could think about was getting married to the perfect guy, the house with the white picket fence and having a child or two to raise and love for an eternity. It was important to her to have everything in place in her life, to have worked her plan. Alas, life doesn't always play by your expectations, sometimes life has a plan, all its own for us.

When Cashmere and Ingrid arrived at her doctor's appointment, Cashmere could tell that Ingrid was very nervous. The truth is Cashmere was nervous for her. She knew that this would be a tough road for Ingrid. She knew that Ingrid would need a lot of support to get through this. While waiting in the lobby, Ingrid couldn't keep still. She was tapping her foot, she had to do something to keep her mind off of the possibility of being pregnant. The nurse called her name to check her in; they got her weight and height. Then they asked her to have a seat in the lobby again. About twenty minutes later they called her name "Ingrid, please come with me". The nurse said. Ingrid got up, started to walk over to the nurse, Cashmere followed closely behind. They followed the nurse to the examining room. "Hello Ingrid, I'm Janice, what brings you to us today?" Before Ingrid could answer, Cashmere blurted out "She's pregnant!" "Excuse me, but I believe she is talking to me." Ingrid quickly said. Cashmere just looked at Ingrid. She backed off because she knew that Ingrid was right. "I think I may be pregnant." "Okay, when was the last time you had your menstrual?" It was over a month ago." "Okay, let me take your vitals and we will go from there." Janice put the blood pressure cuff around her arm, then placed the thermometer in her mouth. After writing the vitals down in her chart, Janice said "The doctor will be with you very soon." "Thank you." replied Ingrid. Janice exited the examination room. Cashmere saw the look of nervousness that was plastered all over Ingrid's face. "I know you are nervous, but we will get through this together." She reached out to hold her little sister's hand. "Thank you for being here with me. I really appreciate it." A couple of seconds later there was a knock at the door, the doctor walked in and greeted them. "Hello, I am Dr. Johnson. What brings you in today?" "I think I may be pregnant." "Oh I see, well we can most certainly find that out for you. I will order a pregnancy test for you and we can call you with the results in a day or two. How does that sound?" "That sounds fine. Thank you." "You're most welcome. Janice will be back in a few minutes to get you set up." Cashmere squeezed Ingrid's hand a little tighter, because she knew that she needed the reassurance that everything was going to be okay. When Janice returned, she gave Ingrid instructions on how to complete the test. Then she showed her to the restroom. While Ingrid was gone, Cashmere took the time to say a little prayer for Ingrid. She knew that this would be a long hard road for Ingrid, if she was pregnant. Especially since she knew that she didn't really want to keep the baby. On the other hand, if she kept it, could she take care of it the way a child needs to be taken care of? So far Ingrid had only been responsible for herself, and that had been a struggle for her. This was definitely something that would be an eye opener for her. Hopefully, it would make her a stronger, better person.

Fifty Five

Rico and Tammy decided to take a ride down to Virginia Beach. It was a perfect day for a drive. The weather was sunny, not too hot. There was a cool breeze flowing through the air. On the drive down, Tammy told Rico about how excited she was about the upcoming cruise. This trip had been in the making for a very long time, she didn't want anything to ruin it. Rico knew that she was talking about the situation between Cashmere and Stephanie. He was hoping that their outing today would help take her mind off of their shenanigans. When they arrived in Virginia Beach, they drove immediately to the beach. Rico thought it would be nice to take a walk on the boardwalk.

Maybe stop at some place for a quick drink or do a little shopping. He wanted to take her mind off of Cashmere and Stephanie. The boardwalk was crowded with people enjoying the cool breeze coming off of the ocean, which carried Tammy's sweet fragrance directly to Rico. Rico reached for Tammy's hand, she quickly wrapped her fingers around his. Tammy tried her best to hold back her smile, but she couldn't because she loved the feel of his skin against hers. It made her think about other things that they had done together. It made her think about how he made her body feel when he made love to her. He commanded her body as if it was his kingdom. His attention to her essence was more than superb. He made her body come alive like it hadn't before. She looked at him with happiness gleaming in her eyes. He noticed the sweetness coming from her gaze, which made him give her a very similar look. "Why don't we get a room for the night and see what this town has to offer?" Rico stated. "That sounds fine to me." They both knew that once they got the room, things would get heated.

They kept walking down the boardwalk. Rico pulled out his phone and started looking for hotels in the area. Tammy kept enjoying the scenery. She looked up ahead and thought that she saw someone she recognized, but disregarded it. She knew that she didn't know anyone in Virginia Beach. At least she thought she didn't. Rico found a hotel close to where they were and booked it for the night. He was thirsty so they decided to get something to drink at one of the local stores on the boardwalk. "Babe, why don't we go and check into the hotel? That way we can get comfortable and get ready for tonight." Tammy said. Rico knew exactly what she was getting at, so he quickly agreed. They turned around and started walking back to the car.

Tammy was looking at the ocean and Rico noticed a guy passing by them, looking at Tammy. He quickly dismissed it because he knew that he had a very attractive woman, so he expected men to look at her. Besides, he really wasn't a jealous person. By the time they got back to the car, Tammy couldn't stop smiling. All she could think was how much she loved being with Rico. Everything was so perfect between them! They pulled out of their parking space and drove to the hotel, where they valeted their car. Rico gave the valet a twenty and asked him to keep it out front for him. "Sure thing!" the valet said with a smile. They walked into the hotel, went straight to the front desk. "Welcome to the Sheraton, my name is Henry, how may I help you?" "Hello Henry, we're checking in. The room should be under Rico James." "Yes, Mr. James, I see your reservation here. Your room is ready for you. May I please have your license and credit card?" "Sure, here you go Henry." Henry made a copy of the license for their files. "Here you are Mr. James. Here is your room key as well. You are in our penthouse suite, which is on our top floor. We have taken the liberty of adding those items that you requested." "Thank you Henry, I do appreciate the extra effort!" "No problem at all Mr. James. I hope you enjoy your stay here at the Sheraton!" "Thanks, I am sure that we will Henry." When they walked away, Tammy looked over at Rico and asked "Items, what items was he talking about baby?" "Oh nothing baby." "Yeah okay baby." "You'll see in time baby. You'll see in time!" She just looked at him, wondering what was going on in his mind. Something was up. She knew that she would find out sooner or later. Her curiosity was killing her though. She wanted to know and wanted to know now. She would try and subside her strong desire to ask him again. She respected the fact that he wanted to make whatever it was as special as it could be for her. He was always thoughtful like that. He always found a way to make her feel special. That was one of the many things she loved about him. They were alone on the elevator ride up to the penthouse, so she quickly pulled him close to her and kissed him with great passion. Rico enjoyed the feel of their lips pressing against one another. He pulled her even closer, so that he could feel as much of her as he could. Her body felt great pressed against his. Every curve on her body found a place on his masculine body to enjoy. She could feel his chest muscles pressed up against her, which turned her on so much. Suddenly the elevator stopped and they heard a ding, followed by the elevator voice saying "sixteenth floor". The elevator doors opened slowly and they exited. Rico opened the penthouse suite door, they both were amazed by what they saw when they walked in. The suite was breathtaking. There was a view that overlooked the ocean. Floor to ceiling windows were throughout the suite. Tammy went upstairs and saw a huge bedroom; around the corner was a bathroom with a huge jacuzzi tub. A few seconds later there was a knock at the door. Rico answered it and one of the bellmen walked in with some items on a hanger in white garment bags, as well as some boxes on a bellman's cart. "Thank you, you can put them in the upstairs closet." Rico said as he pointed to the stairs. "You're welcome Mr. James." The bellman began to take the things upstairs; Tammy was walking out of the bathroom by the time he arrived upstairs. "Hello Mrs. James." Tammy didn't correct him, she just replied "Hello." She watched as he put the things in the closet. She wondered what this was all about. Rather than asking him, she decided to wait it out to see what was going to unfold. The bellman made a couple more trips to the closet, then she heard Rico thanking him, when she walked downstairs she saw Rico handing him a tip before he walked out the door. Rico turned to look at her; he couldn't help but to smile at her. She was strikingly beautiful to him. "What are you smiling about Rico?" "Baby, I am smiling about you." "Why is that?" "Please believe, you will see. You will definitely see baby!" Rico walked up to her and kissed her forehead. He went upstairs, turned on the water to fill the tub. When the tub was full, he asked Tammy to come up for a bath. When she arrived, she noticed candles, glasses of wine and Rico was in the tub with his arm extended "Would you like to join me?" "How can I resist?" She took her clothes off and entered the tub with him.

The bubbles cascaded against their bodies like little rain droplets falling from the sky. He handed her a glass of wine and said "Here's to a wonderful evening!" They clinked their glasses and each took a sip. Tammy laid back against the tub and just relaxed, while the bubbles that propelled from the tub did their thing. She realized that she was having the time of her life with Rico.

It couldn't possibly get any better than this. Rico eased closer to Tammy, he took her in his arms, kissed her with heated desire. She kissed him back, eased her hands down his back. The water felt great under her hand and against his back. Rico continued to enjoy her sweet lips, the softness of her breasts pressed up against him. Her body was like a temple of gold to him. He truly enjoyed the riches that her goldmine brought him. He loved to play in her treasure chest.

When they were done enjoying one another, they both toweled off. While Tammy was taking her time in the bathroom, Rico exited, heading straight for the closet. He pulled out the bags and boxes that the bellman had placed in there. He carefully pulled out the bag with one of Tammy's surprises in it. He laid the dress out on the bed, taking time to straighten it out, so that she would get the full effect from the royal blue spaghetti strapped dress that boasted sequins along the top of the breast line. He then pulled the bag off his black six button suit. He also laid it out as well beside her beautiful dress. Now all he needed was her to open the bathroom door and come into the bedroom. He couldn't wait to see her face when she saw the dress. Finally the bathroom door opens, he sees her come out of the bathroom, and she enters the bedroom. Immediately, she looks at the clothing on the bed. "Oh Rico, that is a beautiful dress. I do hope that it is for me." "No, I thought we would switch it up tonight, the suit is for you baby." She gave him a crazy look of disbelief. He couldn't keep from laughing. "Yes, the dress is most definitely for you baby." She walked closer to it, picked it up and placed it against her body. "Yes, I can definitely make this work; I just need some shoes and a few accessories." Rico smiled "Here. Open these boxes baby." He handed her two boxes, one of medium size and the other shaped like a shoe box. She opened the shoe boxed one first, royal blue open toe heels with sequins as well. She was very excited now, she moved on to the medium box, where she found a blue sapphire necklace. Her face lit up with excitement. "Thank you so much baby! I take it you would like me to put this on now." "Well, it would be nice." "May I ask where we are going?" "Yes, you may ask." "I can ask, but you won't answer?" Rico smiled at her and said "That's right. Trust me; it will be worth your while though." She smiled back and said "It always is baby. It always is." They both got ready; looking outstanding when they exited the penthouse. The valet pulled Rico's Mercedes up to the front door. They eased in the car, drove to Catch 31 for a nice meal. Tammy didn't have a clue what the evening held in store for her, she couldn't wait to find out either. They were seated instantly at a nice romantic table for two. Rico looked at Tammy and said "You look stunning baby." "Thank you. You look rather handsome yourself." "Thank you so much baby." The waiter approached the table "Good evening, I will be your waiter for the evening. My name is Jackson. Would you like to start off with something to drink?" Tammy thought the waiter's voice sounded familiar.

When she looked up she realized why. Jackson looked her dead in the face, fortunately for her; Rico was still looking at the menu. Until Jackson acknowledged her by saying "Tammy, is that you?" "Hello Jackson, how are you?" Before Tammy could explain Rico asked "Excuse me and how do you know each other?" "Tammy and I are old friends." "Is that right? Please elaborate." "Rico, this is Jackson. Jackson, this is Rico, my boyfriend." "It's very nice to meet you Rico." "Okay Rico, Jackson and I used to date. He was actually the guy I was telling you about that broke my heart!" "Now Tammy, I don't think that is a fair assessment of our relationship." "Jackson, you can think whatever you desire. I know the truth." Rico could see that Tammy was getting uncomfortable, so before it went any further, he intervened. "Jackson, I am sure you are an upscale young man, who has nothing but the utmost respect for women. Fortunately for me, you decided to step away from this beautiful lady. Now, it is my turn to make her happy. I sincerely thank you for that; please advise your manager that we will not be needing your services at our table tonight. Have him send someone over that we both would be more comfortable with. I am sure that you can handle that. Thank you and have a great night!" With that Jackson didn't hesitate to leave the table. Rico watched him walk over to whom he figured was his manager. Tammy looked at Rico "Thank you baby. That could have been an uncomfortable situation. "You're welcome baby. This is our night; I don't want anything to mess this night up. A few minutes later the manager walked over to their table "Good evening, my name is Fredric; I understand there was an issue with Jackson. He explained the situation to me and I have decided to serve you myself tonight. First off, I will give you a free bottle of wine to ease your discomfort." "Thank you so much Fredric. I think we would like a bottle of Moscato." Tammy stated as she looked over to Rico for confirmation. Rico nodded his head in agreement. "Have you had a chance to view the menu or would you like a few more minutes?" "I think we will need a few more minutes, Fredric." Rico answered.

Fifty Six

When Stephanie awoke later that evening, she realized that she had fallen asleep on the couch. There was a knock at her door. She got up, looked out the peephole and was surprised to see Matthius standing out front. Matthius...What are you doing here? It is almost 9:00 o'clock at night." I'm sorry to bother you at this time of night, but I needed to let you know that there was another letter that arrived for you. It looks like one of those stalker letters again." "Matthius, I appreciate you bringing it, but it could have waited until I got back to the office." Then she wondered where the surveillance team was right now. Then she heard a light knock at the back door. "Hold on for one minute Matthius, I have to put something on." She walked to the back of the house, where she saw the surveillance team. She opened the door and one of them told her that they have been tracking Matthius for over a week now. We think he is the stalker, but we need confirmation on that. Please let him in, we will be right here. When he tries something, we will get him." "Matthius, are you sure?" "We won't be sure until he makes a move. We think that's why he is here." "Are you sure you will be able to get him in time?" "Yes, I am positive." "Okay."

Stephanie went back to the door. Matthius heard her taking the deadbolt off, then she opened the door. "Good evening Matthius, thank you for bringing the letter out to me. I really do appreciate it." "No problem Stephanie, may I trouble you for a glass of water?" "Sure Matthius, please come in. Have a seat in the living room. I will be right back with your water." "Okay, great." Matthius walked in the living room, looking around suspiciously. He took out a handkerchief and a small bottle of chloroform.

He quickly poured some of it on the handkerchief. Hearing her return, he tucked the handkerchief behind his back. When she approached him, she reached out to hand him the water. It was then that he grabbed her arm, pulled her to him. She dropped the glass; it shattered against the table that it hit. He immediately, turned her around, put the handkerchief up against her face. With an instant, three of the surveillance team was on him. They wrestled him to the ground. With a knee in his back, his hands pulled behind his back, they quickly handcuffed him and read him his rights. Another one pulled Stephanie to the side to make sure that she was okay. "Are you okay?" "Yes, I am just a little shook up, but I am fine. Thanks for the quick reaction." "You are very welcome. We will get him out of here right now. I assume you would like to press charges." "You assume correctly!" They opened the door to take him away and Detective Cruz was standing there. "May I come in?" "Yes, please do." Det. Cruz entered; he could see that she was totally scared. She had every right to be scared to; her life had just been threatened. "Thank you and your men so much for everything. I am so sorry that I was not the most cooperative person; I hope you can forgive me." You are very welcome. You weren't really that bad, not all the time, anyway. I am just glad that we got him before he did any real harm to you." "Please let me make it up to you. I owe you that much at least. What can I do for you?" "No, that's fine. It's all part of the job. Thanks for the offer though." "No, I insist. How can I make it up to you?" "Okay, if you insist. How about dinner?" "Sure. Come to the restaurant anytime you want and I will take care of you." "Well, that's not really what I was thinking about." He gave her a smile that displayed those pearly whites. She knew exactly what he meant now, but decided to make him ask for it. "Well, what is it that you were thinking about Det. Cruz?" Now was the time to play his hand. "Well, I was hoping to have dinner here with you one night." "Here, with me? That's what you want?" "Yes, if you wouldn't mind." "How can I be sure that I won't need the surveillance team here?" "Oh, I am a gentleman. You will be safe in my company." "Okay Detective Cruz, I tell you what. Give me a couple days to think about it and I will let you know. How does that sound?" "It sounds better than a flat out no. Okay." With that, Detective Cruz wished her good night and walked out the door. She watched him cross the street and get in his car. He pulled off and she watched the car go down the street before closing the door. Now she understood his rampage the other day. He wasn't reacting professionally, he was reacting emotionally.

Stephanie couldn't help but smile a little at the thought of Detective Cruz being smitten with her. He was a handsome man, standing at 5'11, short brown hair, hazel eyes and a very deep sexy voice. She wondered how she could not have noticed him before now. Was she so consumed with everything that was going on in her life that she had overlooked this fine specimen of a man? Whatever the reasoning, her eyes were wide open to him now. Dinner would be very interesting. She figured she would wait until tomorrow to respond as to when she would have dinner with him. It had to be soon though, because next weekend she was going on vacation with her girls. She figured she would think about it over a nice glass of Moscato. It had been some time since a nice man had been interested in her. No doubt, she wanted to be in a relationship. But she didn't want to appear to be easy. That wouldn't be a good idea. As she sipped her Moscato, she thought about how safe she felt when he was around. She knew that he would protect her from any and everything. Of course that made her feel really good. She contemplated calling him tonight, but she didn't want to appear to be desperate. For now, it was good that he wasn't sure how interested she was. Hell, she didn't really know if she was interested yet. She did however enjoy the thought of having a man over for dinner though. Now the question was what she would fix for him. It had to be something stunning, especially if she decided that she liked him.

Fifty Seven

The days had gone by rather quickly. Excitement was brewing for some in the air, for others it was not so pleasant. When Cashmere arrived at Tammy's house on the morning of the drive to Cape Hatteras, everybody was there except Stephanie. Tammy and Rico had picked up the rental about an hour before Cashmere arrived. Tammy and Cashmere went to put their luggage in the trunk, when they were returning to the house, Stephanie was pulling up. Tammy continued in the house. Stephanie got out of the car, popped the trunk, to get her luggage. Out of the corner of her eye, she saw Cashmere crossing the street. Fear immediately captured her because she didn't really know what to expect. She figured she would expect the worst from Cashmere. The bottom line is that she had every right to go off on her after the way she acted in front of her guest. Cashmere was up on her really quickly. "Look Stephanie ... we have to get something straight. I am not trying to hear your mouth on this cruise. I don't want any drama from you. I hope you understand exactly what I am saying. I am going to let you slide for your earlier buffoonery." "Cashmere, I am so sorry for the way I acted. I felt rejected by you, since there wasn't another opportunity for us. I would like to know why you kissed me in the first place though?" "Well, to be honest Stephanie, I got caught up in the moment. I have always wanted to kiss a girl, so I went for it." "Maybe you should have considered how the other person would react." "Well, I am sorry if I made you uncomfortable or led you on." "Apology accepted, thank you Cashmere." Stephanie rolled her luggage across the street to put it in the rental. She and Cashmere hugged each other, Stephanie was relieved that they had made up and put their issue behind them. Tammy walked out just as Stephanie was closing the trunk. "What is taking you guys so long?" she asked. "Nothing, we were just coming inside." "Okay, whatever ladies, just get in here." They all walked through Tammy's door. She had made some quick egg and sausage sandwiches for everybody. She had orange juice and grapefruit juice as well. The girls ate, and then packed a cooler full of drinks and snacks for the road. They loaded up and started out on their way to Cape Hatteras. The ride was seemingly fun so far; they were talking, and listening to some oldies that Rico had put on a compact disc for their ride down. Stephanie, decided to tell the girls about what had happened to her. "You know I was being stalked, right?" "Yeah, whatever happened with that?" Tammy asked. "Well, I was given a surveillance detail to hang out at my place and follow me around everywhere. Last week, Matthius came to my house." "Matthius, I didn't know you guys were friendly like that." Cashmere commented." "We're not, but it turns out, he was my stalker. He came to my house and tried to drug me. Lord only knows what he would have done to me, had he gotten away with it." "So, what happened?" Cashmere questioned. "Well, he tried to poison me with some chloroform. The surveillance team was on him so fast; I barely had a chance to realize what was going on. They had him on the floor and took him away." "Damn girl, it sounds like you almost lost your life." Cashmere said. "So, the detective on the case wants to get to know me better over dinner." Do tell, what is he like?" Tammy asked "He is very nice looking. Seems to like what he sees." "Come on girl, give up the dirt. We want to know the deal." Cashmere said. "Okay, he asked me to cook dinner for him, at my place. I am very nervous about the whole thing though. He seems like a nice guy. He's very cute too." "Are you going to cook for him?" Tammy asked. "I most certainly am. I just have to let him know." "And when are you going to let him know?" Cashmere asked. "I'll let him know soon. Don't worry; I'll share the juicy details, if there are any." "Girl, you know there will be some details. You have not had a male's interest in quite some time. Especially, if he is as fine as you say he is." Cashmere added. "Okay, you didn't have to go there girl. So Tammy, how are things between you and Rico?" Stephanie said. "Rico and I are fine. He is just so amazing. I couldn't be luckier. We went to Virginia Beach last weekend and had a great time, until Jackson showed up." "Jackson, how in the hell did that go?" Cashmere asked. "Surprisingly, Rico was really cool about it. He politely let Jackson know that his services were no longer needed. In fact, the manager of the restaurant served us the rest of the night." "I bet that was pretty overwhelming for a minute." Stephanie added. "Yeah, I had never been in a negative situation with Rico, so I wasn't sure how he was going to handle it. It was a good thing that Jackson wasn't rude. You know Rico is a big boy, that's one of the things I love about him." Tammy stated.

When the girls arrived in Cape Hatteras, Tammy drove straight to the Lighthouse View Motel. They checked in, got their key and headed up to their room. This was going to be interesting, the three of them together in one room for a couple of days. After they freshened up, they decided to get something to eat. They figured they would walk around to see what was nearby. They stumbled upon the Fish House restaurant. Cashmere had just thought about how long it had been since she'd had some really good fish on the ride down.

Stephanie was ready to try something great; fish was always a favorite of hers. Tammy was just ready to eat, it really didn't matter what they ate, as long as they ate soon. They walked in; the hostess seated them at a table in the far right hand corner of the restaurant. The place was really busy. "That's a good sign." Stephanie noted. It was barely six in the evening and the place was already filled with people. The waitress greeted them and asked if they wanted to start with some drinks or appetizers. Stephanie said "We will start with both, please." The girls ordered drinks, and then decided on their appetizers.

By the time their drinks came, they had also decided on their entrees. They were enjoying their drinks, when their appetizers arrived. Tammy was definitely hungry. She dove into her appetizers right away. Wasting no time with small talk, she quickly devoured her food. "Damn girl slow down, the food patrol will issue you a speeding ticket for eating so damn fast." Cashmere said while laughter consumed her. Stephanie couldn't help but laugh either. It was as if Tammy was eating her first meal ever. Tammy quickly turned the conversation from her to Cashmere ... "So Cashmere, tell us about your new friend that lives in New York." Stephanie looked at Cashmere with a curious eye. "There's really nothing to tell. He's a musician from New York who comes to Virginia sometimes for studio time. He's working on a debut album. I will tell you this though; the brother can sing his butt off." "I bet that's not all he can do Cashmere. Why are you leaving out the juicy stuff?" Tammy stated. "Some things are private ladies." "Yeah okay, they haven't been private before. Why, all of a sudden are they private with this one?" Stephanie asked. "This one is nothing like the others. This one is very special. That's why!" "Oh, is he now? What makes him so very special?" Tammy questioned. "Well, to be honest, it's not as much about what he does or doesn't do. It's more about how he makes me feel. He makes me want to be a better person. He gives me hope and increases my desire to live the best life I can. That's why he is special to me." "You sound like you are in love." Stephanie stated. Cashmere looked at both of them and said "Maybe I am." Then she smiled. Stephanie just looked at her, wondering if she would one day be able to smile like that. When their entrees arrived they were so immersed in conversation that they hardly noticed the waitress walking up to the table. The waitress put their plates on the table and said "Enjoy." "Thank you." The girls said. Continuing to eat, the girls resumed talking about any and everything under the sun. This trip was turning out to be a great thing. So far it was drama free, stress free and just full of happiness. "So, where do y'all want to go tonight? Should we go to a club and see how Cape Hatteras gets it poppin'? Cashmere said. "A club would be cool. We should definitely do that." Stephanie said. "Cashmere, since drinks are on you, we will let you decide where we roll." Tammy said. "It's all good. I can handle that. I heard about this spot called Level 2, that's supposed to be where it goes down." "That sounds good to me." Stephanie said. "Level 2 it is then." Tammy stated. As the girls began to finish their dinners, Stephanie's phone rang.

Stephanie ... Hey Char

Char ... What's going on girl? How is the trip so far?

Stephanie ... Things are going well. We checked in a while ago. We're just wrapping up dinner. Now, we're talking about going out to see how North Carolina does it.

Char ... Make sure you check out Level 2.

Stephanie ... That's where we're going.

Char ... You will have a great time. North Carolina's finest will be there.

Stephanie ... That's good to know.

Char ... Tell the girls I said hi. I have to go get ready for a photo shoot.

Stephanie ... Will do. Enjoy Italy.

Char ... Oh, you know I will girl. Love ya bye.

"That was Char on the phone. She was just checking on us." "I wish she were here though." Tammy said. "Oh, she also said that Level 2 is a good spot to check out." "What time did y'all want to leave?" Cashmere asked. "I would say about 9:00 or 10:00. Let's give the local talent time to get there first." Stephanie said. "That sounds good to me." Cashmere said. As the girls walked back to the hotel, Stephanie couldn't help but to realize just how much fun she was having, hanging with her girls. Everything was cool between her and Cashmere. Tammy was always a joy to be around. The only thing that was missing was Char. When they got back to the room, Cashmere decided to take a nap. She was tired from all the traveling and the meal that she had just eaten. Tammy and Stephanie decided to get their clothes together for the evening.

Stephanie and Tammy burst into laughter, Cashmere woke up and said "What? What's so funny?" You are girl. You are what's so funny. You were snoring your butt off over there." "I do not snore." Cashmere blurted out. "Yeah okay, tell it to someone that might believe you." Tammy said. "Whatever ladies!" Cashmere got up, walked into the bathroom to take a shower. When she came out, the girls were having a glass of Moscato. Tammy poured one for Cashmere and handed it to her. They raised their glasses and said "Here's to true friendship!" "I know that's right, there's nothing like kicking it with my girls!" Cashmere smiled and said. "Let's get ready to do this club thing."

After the girls got back, they laughed and talked about their night at the club. There were quite a few guys in there trying to get chosen, but neither of the girls wanted what they were offering. They all decided to lie down and get some rest, since they had an early morning.

In the morning when they awoke, excitement was in the air. The day had finally arrived, they were going to enjoy themselves beyond belief. Tammy got dressed and took the rental car back to the rental company. The other girls got themselves ready so that when Tammy returned they could check out and head over to the ship. After Tammy returned they checked out and took the hotel shuttle to meet the ship. When they exited the shuttle, smiles were all abound. They grabbed their luggage, walked up the gang plank to board the ship. The ship was beautiful; people were walking around having fun already. When they each arrived at their staterooms, they noticed that they all had a basket with fruit, wine, and chocolate. Stephanie put her luggage in the closet, turned to get her purse and noticed her phone ringing.

Stephanie ... Hello

Det. Cruz ... Hello Stephanie. I hope all is well.

Stephanie ... All is well. I hope you are well too. What can I do for you?

Det. Cruz ... To be honest, I just wanted to check to see if you wanted to do the dinner thing?

Stephanie ... Oh I see. You are quite the persistent one.

Det. Cruz ... I just don't want this opportunity to get away from me.

Stephanie ... Opportunity for what?

Det. Cruz ... Opportunity to get to know you on a personal level.

Stephanie ... Oh I see. Well, I'll tell you what. When I get back from vacation, we can have dinner and see what you are talking about.

Det. Cruz ... Okay that sounds great to me.

The ship's horn blew, slowly the ship started to move out to sea. The girl's met out on the deck, along with the rest of the passengers. Their vacation had begun!

The End

Discussion Questions

1. What were your thoughts on why Tammy's brother Edward was locked up?
2. Could you relate to Tammy's hesitation about telling Rico her profession?
3. Why do you think Cashmere hasn't utilized her Cornell degree?
4. What did you think of Rico when he was introduced as a worker at Layla's cafe, then we found out that he co-owned The Crib? Does it sound like a place that you would frequent?
5. Who did you think was sending Stephanie the notes?
6. What did you think of Cashmere and Ingrid's relationship?
7. How did you feel when Stephanie found out that her father was being held hostage at the bank?
8. What did you think when Stephanie tried to focus on her grand opening, while her father was held hostage?
9. Did you feel the ecstasy between Rico and Tammy when they first made love?
10. Did it surprise you to find out that Stephanie's father had put Tammy through law school?
11. How did you feel about what Cashmere was doing to her Uncle Herbert?
12. Which character did you relate to more?
13. Which character did you relate to the least?
14. Is there a sub-character that you would like to see developed more?

CHAPTER 1

Day one, The Diamond Line left the dock, the girls left the upper deck. They decided to take a stroll around this vessel to check out what it had to offer. They walked until they saw a huge pool. There were people already swimming and hanging out around it. There were lots of kids laughing and playing. There were some adults that were hanging out, already having drinks and getting cozy.

The girls continued to walk around the boat. They ventured upstairs to find several restaurants, bars, a casino and even a couple of night clubs. Cashmere looked at the others and said "It's about to be on tonight in this piece!" Tammy looked at Cashmere smiled and said "I know that's right girl!" "I can't believe we are finally here. We've waited so long for this moment." Stephanie said.

They walked by the ship's bridge and saw the Captain at the helm. He nodded at them and they smiled back. Cashmere's phone notified her of a message. She checked her message and saw something that made her curious. It was from Ingrid … it simply stated "I don't mean to bother you, but call me when you get a chance." The first thing that came to Cashmere's mind was that something was wrong with her little sister. She wanted to text or call her right now, but she was too scared, she feared the worse, of course. She showed the phone to Stephanie … they both had a concerned look on their faces. Stephanie told Cashmere, "You need to contact her right now and see what is going on". "I know, but there is something eerie about her text. I am almost certain it is awful news." Cashmere said. "You will never know if you don't get in touch with her. If it is awful news, don't you think you should know sooner, rather than later?" Chimed Stephanie. The bottom line is that Cashmere knew she needed to contact her. She was just worried about what Ingrid's had to say to her. Stephanie's face began to show much frustration … "Call her now Cashmere!"

Cashmere pulled up the text, read it once more and pressed the phone button. The phone began to dial, Ingrid answered almost as instantly as the phone began to ring. "Cashmere…" Ingrid stated. "Cashmere…" She stated again. "Hey girl, how are you?" Cashmere said. "Well, to be honest, things could be better." "What do you mean Ingrid? What's going on?" "Well, I am in the hospital." "Hospital … what's wrong Ingrid." "I am in labor and it doesn't look good." "Ingrid, what are you talking about?" "Cashmere, the baby is breach and it is premature. It's coming tonight and the chances of survival are very slim." "Chances of survival for who? You or the baby?" Cashmere could hear the crack in Ingrid's voice, when she said "For both of us! She knew she was about to cry. She knew she was about to lose it. All Cashmere could think was, I need to be there with my sister.

Other publishings by William Dance Jr.

Words From Me To You! (Poetry)

The Adventures of Boris and Friends (Children's)

Sisterhood (follow up to The Bonds of Sisterhood)